Published by Shanghai Press and Publishing Development Co., Ltd.

Copyright © 2024 Shouhua Qi

All rights reserved. Unauthorized reproduction, in any manner, is prohibited.

Illustrations: Jin Zhanghan
Cover Design: Jin Zhanghan, Xue Wenqing
Interior Design: Xue Wenqing

Editors: Wu Yuezhou, Yang Wenjing

ISBN: 978-1-63288-051-2

Address any comments about *Becoming Monkey King: The Untold Story* to:

SCPG
401 Broadway, Ste. 1000
New York, NY 10013
USA

or

Shanghai Press and Publishing Development Co., Ltd.
Floor 5, No. 390 Fuzhou Road, Shanghai, China (200001)
Email: sppd@sppdbook.com

Printed in China by RR Donnelley Asia Printing Solutions Limited

1 3 5 7 9 10 8 6 4 2

Shouhua Qi
Illustrated by **Jin Zhanghan**

SCPG

For Emmett and Evelyn:
Voracious Readers and My Muses

Contents

Prologue 11
1 Wishful Wish 16
2 Vain Awakening 23
3 As I Will 40
4 Heaven's Equal 53
5 Party Crasher 64
6 My Waterloo 76
7 Puddle of Piss 83
8 Why Me? 95
9 Why Not Me? 109
10 Master and Disciple 119
11 Man of Cloth 135
12 Carpe Diem 146
13 Old Steady 159
14 Damned Either Way 166
15 Dream Visions 184
16 Gracious Me 201
17 Comic Relief 219
18 Seriously? 242
19 Altered Ego 262
20 Third Time's the Charm 279
21 In the Land of Nirvana 296
22 Home Free 310
Epilogue 313
Acknowledgements 316

In the beginning, the world was nothing but sheer chaos and a murky blur.

Born into this world was Pan'gu, a giant, who woke up one day and set to work with an enormous axe—to create Heaven and Earth.

He worked for eighteen thousand years growing stronger and wiser each day. When the work was finally done, Heaven formed of bright and pure yang and Earth formed of dark and misty yin, Pan'gu laid to rest, his breath becoming the wind; his voice the thunder; his eyes the sun and the moon; and his body mountains, rivers, and fertile land.

Into this world came Nüwa, a goddess, who set to work and created humans with clay.

All was good until a titanic battle broke out between Gonggong, a god of water, and Zhurong, a god of fire. In the rage of battle the two titans damaged one of the four pillars holding up Heaven, causing torrential rains, massive floods, and unspeakable human suffering.

To save humans from the catastrophe, Nüwa cut off the legs of a huge turtle and used them in place of the collapsed pillar.

She then gathered colored stones, a total of thirty-six thousand five hundred and one of them, and melted the stones together to repair the holes in Heaven and restore life on Earth.

Unbeknownst to the goddess, one of the colored stones slipped from her fingers as she busied herself with the task at hand.

Prologue

Imagine, if you can, carrying this thing on my back for more than five hundred years.

This Five-Element Mountain (*Wuxingshan*), metal (*jin*), wood (*mu*), water (*shui*), fire (*huo*), and… okay, earth (*tu*).

Anyone else would have been crushed into nothingness four hundred ninety-nine years three hundred sixty-four days twenty-three hours and fifty-nine minutes and fifty-nine seconds ago. Who wouldn't have? The mountain being taller than the tallest skyscraper in the world and one hundred times fatter, heavier, like a million super-heavy tanks welded together.

Me? I am still here, although not exactly the last one standing.

What have I not seen and weathered through all these years? Scorching heatwaves, bone-chilling winds, soaking downpours, and worst, hungry wolves, tigers, leopards, and bloodthirsty demons grumbling and wailing, their eyes like laser beams piecing through the thickest of nights.

I don't need to tell you what it feels like when a giant spider busies itself with weaving a web across my face and all I can do is to grunt menacingly and lick holes into the budding web hoping the eight-legged beast will go elsewhere to set its trap.

Oh, I've been stung by hornets quite a few times, on the forehead, right between the eyes, you name it, my face swollen for days, fat and ugly like that of a pig. I cannot even wink and blink and make some noise when the vicious, venomous jet tries to build a nest in my ears. All of me has been fair game for these creepy, flying fiends except for my butt, safely shielded by the mountain I carry on my back.

Mostly, I miss being me, the carefree me, not worrying about a thing in the world, kowtowing to this one, following the marching order of that one, serving at the pleasure of... you catch the drift of what I'm saying?

What have I done to deserve this, this ignominious punishment?

For a few longevity peaches, a few immortality beans? Who on Earth, who in Heaven doesn't want to live forever? Who doesn't want immortality? Says who that whatever elixirs of life out there should be the exclusive indulgences of those select few in Heaven, longevity peach extravaganza today, immortality beans extravaganza tomorrow? Why can't we earthlings crash the party once in a while, in a long, long while, just for curiosity's sake, if nothing else? Are we somehow created less equal?

Okay, I'd be the first to admit that I might have been just a teeny-weensy too free-spirited, too this, too that, for my own or anyone's good. After all, I've had the pleasure of reflecting, and repenting, if you will, for more than five hundred years.

An un-examined life is not worth living, some ancient sage said something like that, right? What about an over-examined life? Too much conscience makes cowards of us all, you know who said this, right? And too much thought makes us lose our resolve, our ability for action? I know that you know that I know that a little learning is a dangerous thing. Hahaha.

I've been told to wait for someone to come along and get

me out of this ignominious predicament. I don't really have a say in this matter other than waiting. In my mind, though, only me can save myself, but what do I know, really know? I thought I was indomitable and had somersaulted one hundred and eight thousand *li*, in the blink of an eye, to the edge of Earth; I'd even marked the feat with a good relief of my bladder pressure. Oh, so much for my self-confidence. Just look where I am now. Humbling enough, isn't it?

I fancy that you've heard of me in some form or shape, through the story told by Mr. Wu Cheng'en from the 16th century and retold by Mr. Waley and a whole bunch of others since. Believe me, I'm more than flattered. Who doesn't want to be the protagonist, dare I say hero, of a classic of worldwide fame, an epic, no less? Okay, one of the protagonists.

I can even see Mr. Wu a writing brush in hand laboring deep into the night, day after day after day for years, nonstop, as if possessed, sometimes pausing, eyebrows knit, sighing, coughing, then going again, his shadow thrown against the walls by the flickering oil lamp, on the ceiling where swallows coo dreamily in their nests on the beams. Every stroke, a dot, a hook, a sudden turn, a long curve, a precipitous fall, you name it, of his seven-hundred-sixty-five-thousand-one-hundred-fifty-three-character story has to come from the tip of that ink brush of his, each character a picture with a heart, a mind, and a personality of its own, yet standing next to, I mean, on top of each other, humans and demons, peaches and bees, regardless, columns upon columns of them cascading down the sheet of rice paper. If we're talking about one hundred or so such characters on a page, averaging, exactly how many pages have gushed from the tip of Mr. Wu's writing brush? Go figure. I can't even begin to name all the gods and goddesses, dragon kings, dragon queens, and baby dragons, all the spirits, monsters, giant bandits, you name it, who are named in his story. Oh, the elegance of those poems, hundreds of them, so perfectly rhymed, rhythmed, and making perfect sense. Who can top that?!

Yet, between you and me, there has been this unease gnawing at me, sometimes. I feel like, somehow, I've been made out to be this heartless, impulsive killing machine, a weapon of mass destruction of sorts. I mean that hurts. I think I know just a teeny-weensy more and better.

I know, I know, knowing oneself is the trickiest business in the world, and I may not be the most impartial, the most reliable narrator when it comes to telling a story of my own life, but who in Heaven, who on Earth, and who anywhere in between, is, eh?

"You're protesting just a teeny-weensy too much," you may be saying to yourself. "Who on earth you think you are, anyways?"

I am Monkey King.

ONE

Wishful Wish

They say be careful what you wish for.
Sometimes I do wish that I had never left my home, my birthplace.

Flower Fruit Mountain (*Huaguoshan*).

I've been to places, but have never seen anything even remotely like it, a real paradise on earth, if you ask me. A beautiful island mountain in a boundless sea, cloud-kissing cliffs, cascading waterfalls, murmuring creeks, flowering trees and mouthwatering fruits of all kinds, animals of every color, size, shape, and stripe, lions, tigers, wolves, pigs, horses, donkeys, water buffalos, unicorns, and yes, monkeys, and birds of all feathers, all getting along super-well and having a swell of time.

Into this paradise on earth I was born, not with a pitiable whimper, mind you, but with a bang of sorts. Okay, no bright star appeared, no wise men came to look for me, but two beams of dazzling light did pierce the sky and my birth, I was told later, did cause enough of a disturbance, alarm in Heaven:

An ominous sign that some troublemaker, trickster, is afoot, on its way to wreak some havoc?

A scout was dispatched to peer down and find out what was going on. The report came back fast enough:

A rock on Flower Fruit Mountain has just cracked open and given birth to a stone monkey, no more than three or four feet tall. Harmless.

Thus reassured by the intelligence, all in Heaven laughed, perhaps a teeny-weensy too heartily, and resumed whatever business or pleasure they had been busy pursuing, their daily routines, strolling in the orchards, taking long naps, holding extravagant parties, ogling fairest of fairies long-sleeve or belly dancing in grand palaces, you name it.

At first glance, this little stone monkey looked harmless, yet appearance could be deceptive, as I've learned.

Story goes that this stone monkey is born from the colored stone that slipped from Nüwa's hand when she was busy repairing the collapsed Heaven. True or not I've no way of knowing.

Some say this stone monkey embodies all five elements of the world, metal (*jin*), wood (*mu*), water (*shui*), fire (*huo*), and earth (*tu*). I wouldn't know unless you take a tissue from me and put it through some cellular imaging device. What do I know about such fancy gadgets anyway?

All I know is this monkey is blessed with a pair of eyes, a beating heart, a thinking mind, a soaring soul, like everyone else, only perhaps a teeny-weensy more so than most.

The moment I was born, I learned to crawl, kowtowed to East, West, North, and South, and then bounced onto my feet, and ran to join all the other monkeys on Flower Fruit Mountain.

Imagine the carefree fun I am having, darting wildly in rolling hills, fording into cool streams, eating whatever berries, lychees, melons, pears, peaches, apples I fancy, hungry or not, playing with my monkey buddies, chasing dragonflies and glowworms, climbing thousand-year-old trees, making sandcastles and mud towers, holding tug-of-wars, grandpas vs. grandmas, boys vs. girls, you name it, cheered on by large crowds of wolves, lions, tigers, buffalos, zebras, pigs, pheasants, eagles, sparrows, swallows, my body glowing with joy, my voice hoarse from laughing and screaming, my limbs stiff and sore, and then sleeping like a baby, star-studded Heaven as roof, moon-soaked Earth as bed, like that, day after day after day.

Until one day, fooling around and having fun, we stumble upon a creek meandering down between big rocks, jump in, and have a good time bathing and splashing water at each other.

We've never seen this creek before. It seems to be springing from nowhere.

Out of sheer curiosity, we follow it upstream until we see in front of us a humongous white curtain crashing down from a sky-kissing cliff, the air abuzz with mist and deep-throated murmur.

We look at each other, awestruck, silent, and turn our eyes to the dizzying, cascading curtain again, following its tumbling current till it pours into the shimmering blue mass edging the nebulous horizon.

This thing, whatever it is, must have been crashing down from the sky long before I was born and will be doing so nonstop long after I am gone.

"Whoever dares to go in and find out what's behind and at the bottom of this," someone not far from me says in a throaty voice, as if wondering aloud, "and report back without a single hair being ruffled, should be made our king."

It is Old Sage, the oldest, most sagacious monkey amongst us all.

"Hear! Hear!" cheer all the monkeys within earshot in unison.

"I'll do it," I blurt out before realizing what I was saying.

Old Sage looks at me and asks, without asking: "Are you sure?"

I nod. It'd be chicken-hearted of me to back out now.

I close my eyes and jump into the roaring waterfall, or the proverbial rabbit hole.

After what seems a woozy, whirling eternity, although it might've been just a few seconds, my feet hit something hard, and I open my eyes:

I am on a bridge, a very long iron bridge; underneath the bridge a swift stream rushes toward some edge where it tumbles down—hence the awestriking water curtain?

I follow the bridge wherever it leads and soon I'm in a big open space:

Bluest of sky, billowing white clouds like jade walls and stairways, tall bamboos, pines, plum trees, you name it, and stone beds, stone chairs, stone benches, stone basins, stone bowls, stone stoves underneath which charcoal still smolders, the air abuzz with mouthwatering aroma…, someone has just hosted a fun party here?

In the middle of this place stands this big stone tablet:

Flower Fruit Mountain Blessed Land
Water Curtain Cave Avalanching Sky

A stone palace in the belly of Flower Fruit Mountain.

I hurry back and report what I've seen. All the monkeys are thrilled: "Let's go check it out!"

They all follow my suit and jump into the deafening waterfall; a few, scared, screaming, have to be helped with a little push from behind.

Once inside the stone palace, everyone is ecstatic and marvels at everything they see and touch.

"What do you all think?" I ask, proudly. "How about us living here from now on so no wind, rain, frost, snow, lightning, thunder can touch us anymore?"

"I say yes!" enthuses Old Sage, beaming. "Let's make this our home and live here happily ever after."

"Hear! Hear!" cheer all the monkeys.

"I'm a monkey of his word," says Old Sage, as if making a proclamation. "I propose that we make the discoverer of this beautiful home for us our King from now into perpetuity! What say you?"

A chorus of loud cheers arise; a bunch of my buddies lead me to a big, throne-like stone chair and sits me there. They all prostrate in front of me and chant:

"Long live the King! Long live the King!"

I was crowned, without an actual crown, although I knew I would be not much more than the first among equals, serving at the pleasure of none, but for the pleasure of all: organizing parties, refereeing games, adjudicating disputes over benches, berths, you name it.

We began to live in Water Curtain Cave, this blessed new home of ours, not having to put up with the whims of the weather anymore, one day hot like a fire furnace, another day colder than the north pole, not having to mingle with all the other animals—lions, tigers, wolves, and such carnivorous beasts are fine as they are, believe me, but you don't really want to mess with them when they are hungry.

In a word, we became a world within worlds away from everyone else. We were having as much fun as before, and perhaps even more. What more would I want for myself, anyway?

Time flies, as they say, when you are busy having fun. Another three to five hundred years of carefree fun passed in a snap of fingers. We could have lived like this for hundreds of years more if I had not happened to catch my reflection one morning in the clear water of a pond.

"What a beautiful king he is," I thought to myself.

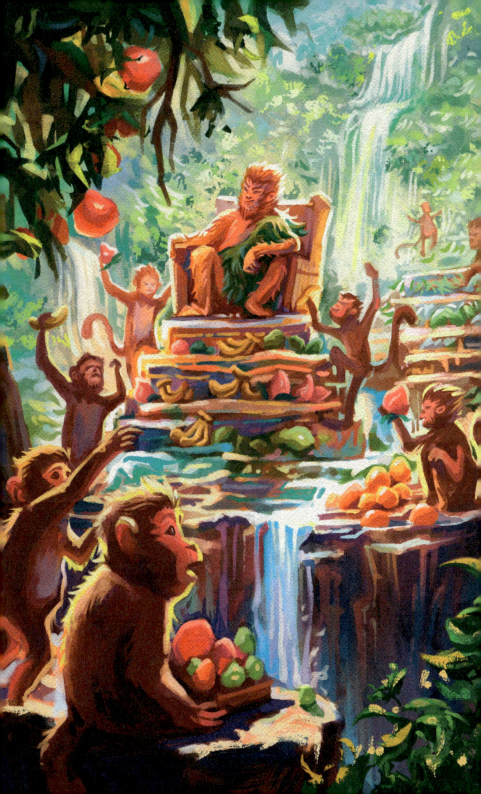

This, admiring my own reflection in the pond, happened a few more times. I don't know why.

It hit me one day that all this good time, this carnival of life, may not go on forever. One day this pond will not see the face of this beautiful king anymore. That one day can be tomorrow, right? What happens after that, then? And the day after that? Who knows. All I know is one day this party will be over. All the monkeys, Old Sage, Square Head, Little Mischief who likes to sit in my lap tickling me and playing with my ears, they will all be gone from this world one day. How I wish time would stop, I, we all, could be timeless. Where on earth can I find the secret of life, of immortality?

One morning, finding me sitting by the pond again and sighing, Old Sage asked: "What bothers you, my king, may I ask? Why aren't you as merry as before?"

I told him what had been on my mind.

"I guessed as much," Old Sage said. "As far as I know, only three kinds will live forever, gods, buddhas, and fairies. All the rest of us earthlings, we are listed in a book controlled by King Yama, God of Netherland, of Death—"

"Why?" I cut him short. "What injustice! Why gods, buddhas, and fairies can live forever, not me, not us earthlings?"

"I don't have answers for that," said Old Sage with a sigh. "However, if this really bothers you, my king, why not do something about it? As the saying goes, no pain, no gain? nothing venture, nothing—"

I nodded.

I busied myself the next few days making a raft of tree branches and bamboos. Then I bid a tearful farewell to all my folks, and set sail, so to speak, in search of the secret of life, of immortality.

I had the faintest idea what the world had in store for me. My destiny was yet to manifest itself.

TWO

Vain Awakening

Not long after I managed to get the raft to the open sea, I caught a southeast current, so I sat down and let it carry me like a leaf surfing on a breeze. A big bird, an albatross? followed me for some time and then, getting no crumbs from me and having no mask to perch on for the ride perhaps, flapped away.

Days after days I drifted on the sea and began to feel a teeny-weensy lost and lonesome.

Then, I saw seagulls, falcons, and so on, hovering in the sky and then diving, lightning speed, to snatch fish perhaps from wavelets.

I saw land in the distance.

I saw human figures along the meandering beach, fishing, picking up clams, harvesting salt, whatever.

I jumped off the raft when water was still chin deep and waded ashore.

At the sight of me, humans abandoned whatever they were doing and ran as fast as their legs could carry them, as if terrified. What? You've never seen anyone like me?

One of them tripped and fell. So, I caught up, stripped him

of his clothes, put them on, and strolled into town.

Strange that humans, hurrying hither and thither and hollering at each other along the streets, sound gibberish to my ear and do not make any sense at all. Before long, though, picking up a phrase here and an expression there, I understand enough to get the impression that they are all driven by greed and vanity than any nobler purpose. What a way to live your life, I thought.

For days and days, I searched high and low, from village to village, town to town, amongst madding crowds and multitudes, all seemingly too busy to even notice me. Those few that I managed to stop and ask would shake their heads and go on their way, befuddled by my appearance and the thick accent with which I talked, as if I were some terrestrials from another planet.

This going on for eight or nine years, I, disappointed, got back to my raft with a vague hope that the current would carry me to a more promising land.

After days and nights drifting on the sea, I saw a massive mountain in the distance, got ashore, and climbed to its summit.

The view from atop the mountain a real feast for my eyes: cliffs thrusting thousands of feet into Heaven, canyons dropping thousands of feet into Earth, tall, ageless trees wrapped in serpentine vines of hungry ivy, fruit trees flowering everywhere, and vales and hills far and near filled with birdsongs.

A blessed place this must be, I figured, what I am looking for must be stashed somewhere here waiting to be uncovered.

I heard someone singing downhill:

Gathering charcoal in the woods
Trading them for as much wine as I could
Indifferent to vanity and worldly gain
Simple life becoming fairest of fairies

....

A fairy lives here?

I followed a trail downhill and saw a grey-haired man, simply clothed, working hard to knock down a dead tree with an axe.

"Old Fairy," I called out, falling on my knees, "please accept this bow from your disciple!"

The grey-haired man turned around, axe slipping from his hand at the sight of me, and said: "Oh no, you're quite mistaken. I'm but a simple charcoal man, what on earth are you addressing me as Old Fairy for?"

"Weren't you singing, just a moment ago, sir, simple life becoming fairest of fairies, something like that?"

"Oh, that," the grey-haired man chuckled. "That's some idea I've picked up from a real fairy, who happens to be my next-door neighbor. My life may have been simple, but it is a hard life, losing my father when I was eight or nine years old, reared by my mother all by herself, growing up with no brothers, a poor, lonely only child, you know. But my mother fed and clothed me the best she could and there was no want of love. Now, it's my turn to take care of my mother in her old age, bedridden with illness. My song was not meant for anyone's ear but mine, to keep myself company and my chin up, even when the going gets tough sometimes."

What a story of hard luck, hard life. I can perhaps never imagine what it would be like losing my father at that young age, having known no father, no mother for that matter.

"That fairy neighbor of mine is the one you should visit, whatever is on your mind," the grey-haired man suggested and gave me the directions.

I thanked the kind man and followed the trail deeper into the woods, climbing up and down a few more hills, turning left here and turning right there, and then saw Tilted Moon Tristar Cave wrapped in a strange, bluish halo, camouflaged by a thousand flowering trees, serenaded by birds of colorful feathers flitting around singing their joyous songs.

Hearing a loud mumbling in my belly, I said to myself, "First thing first," bounced onto a branch of the big pine tree guarding the cave's entrance and helped myself to a few nuts.

"Who on earth dares to make a disturbance here?" a young boy's voice called out from below me.

I jumped off the tree, apologized, and explained who I was and why I was there.

"No wonder Master Bohdi told me to come and open the door. A new disciple has indeed arrived."

Master Bohdi?

How could this Master Bohdi have known I was coming? Am I part of some plan that I am not aware of, that has yet to reveal itself to me? Or I'm still home, Water Curtain Cave, Flower Fruit Mountain, and this is just a dream?

I followed the boy into the deep meandering cave, all the way to where a master sat, salt and pepper hair, dignified, embodiment of boundless wisdom, flanked by thirty or forty disciples chanting I had no idea what, but it sounded pleasing to my ear like music.

I prostrated in front of Master Bohdi and kowtowed a thousand times:

"Master, Master, I've finally found you!"

"Who are you? Why are you here?" asked Master Bohdi.

I told him my story, incoherently, without a clear arc; I was a teeny-weensy too excited and nervous.

"You, a monkey, want to learn the secret of life, of immortality?" Master Bohdi roared with a hearty laugh. "That's a first for me."

I was thunderstruck. Where else in the big wide world can I go now? This is all so hopeless, so vain of me....

"However," Master Bohdi continued, "you look sincere

enough and have come from afar, so, I might as well take you in. A big iron stick can be ground to a fine needle, you know that sagacious saying? Who knows, one day you may come to something."

I couldn't believe my luck and kowtowed a thousand times again to thank my master.

"Now that you're a disciple of mine, you should have a name."

A name? What's in a name?

"Mmm, let me see. How about Wukong, Vain Awakening, meaning you are a quick study and will soon awaken, soon be enlightened enough to know that all is vain, empty in this world and beyond unless…."

All is vain, empty? Then why bother searching and seeking?

Yet, Wukong sounds good enough for my ear. I am here to learn and see what happens, right?

There and then, the first day of my schooling began. I don't know if I was a quick study or not, but I was a diligent student for sure, always the first to get up in the morning, before the cock crows, and the last to go to bed, on the dirt ground, of course, turning the day's lessons over and again even in my dreams. Within days I can cite and recite rites and rituals, verses and chapters as good as any of my fellow disciples. You can easily tell which voice is mine when we chant our lessons in front of Master Bohdi. Burning incense at the altar, trimming bushes, hoeing weeds in the garden, gathering charcoal in the woods, whatever we had to do I threw myself in wholeheartedly.

Time flies when you're busy having fun studying. In a snap of fingers, six or seven years had passed. One day, Master Bohdi gathered all his disciples in the ravine to give another one of his important sermons. I listened, nodded, and sometimes couldn't help marveling rapturously.

"Wukong!" Master Bohdi paused and looked at me sternly.

"How dare you laugh at your master? Your bottle is not even half full yet!"

"Forgive me, Master," I hastened to explain. "I wasn't laughing at you at all. I was enjoying everything you've been teaching us, a teeny-weensy too much, perhaps?"

"Really?" said Master Bohdi incredulously. "No disciple of mine, past and present, has had an easy time understanding this sermon. You understand it, upon the first lesson?"

I nodded.

"In that case," said Master Bohdi, "Come to my chamber right before the first cock crows so I can give you a pop quiz."

A pop quiz in that ungodly hour?

I nodded and thanked the master.

I went to bed as usual, but tossed and turned and turned and tossed, too excited to have a wink of sleep. When finally I sensed it was about time, I got up and tiptoed to the master's chamber.

Quietly I knelt by the master's bedside; he seemed fast asleep on his side, his face toward the wall. After what seemed like an eternity, I heard the master's voice, as if speaking in a dream.

"Who is it, daring to disturb me in my sleep?"

"It is me, kind master, Wukong, ready to take the pop quiz."

"What pop quiz?!" mumbled Master Bohdi.

I didn't dare to remind him of what had happened during the day.

"Oh, that," said Master Bohdi, slowly sitting up in bed, and then put his hand on my head. "Wukong, of all the disciples I've had, you seem to be the smartest and you are but a monkey." He sighed.

What's wrong being a monkey?

"So, here is the pop quiz for you," Master Bohdi said with

another sigh. "Come closer."

I moved closer to the master, and he began to whisper in my ear all the secret knowledge he knew of life, of the world.

"One day you can become a buddha, too," Master Bohdi said when the pop quiz was over, "when you've mastered the true essence of what I've just taught you."

Me becoming a buddha…one day? What wouldn't I give for that?

I kowtowed a thousand times in heartfelt gratitude and left the master's chamber, elated, my mind bursting with all the new knowledge the master had just conveyed to me. I studied even harder from that day on, throwing in even more of myself into studying, heart, mind, and soul.

Before I knew it, another three years had passed. One day, I was busy cleaning incense burners in the temple when I heard Master Bohdi calling me. I hurried to where he was. The master seemed to be taking a quick shuteye in his grand chair.

"Wukong," said the master without opening his eyes. "What have you learned lately?"

"Master," I said proudly. "I've learned all there is to know in this world."

"Really?" snapped Master Bohdi, his eyes, now wide open, glistening with good-humored contempt. "Then, do you know that three big calamities are waiting for you?"

Three big calamities?!

"You are not kidding me, kind master, are you?" I asked, sheepishly.

"I kid you not!" said Master Bohdi. "Listen carefully, Wukong. You think you've learned all there's to learn already, but you have not learnt enough to avert these three calamities that will strike you in the years ahead."

That really got my attention, so I was all ears.

"The first calamity that will strike you in five hundred

years from now is thunder. You'll have to learn to duck, dart, and dodge, lightning speed, to avoid being struck dead. Can you handle that?"

I don't know, having never been struck by thunder.

"The next calamity that will strike you in another five hundred years is fire. This is not your ordinary kind of fire. It is from Netherland and can burn you to ashes before you even know what's just happened. Why aren't you laughing anymore, eh?"

This is no laughing matter anymore for sure.

"The third calamity waiting to strike you, in yet another five hundred years, is wind, not the kind of wind you know, east wind, west wind, hurricane, typhoon, what have you. This wind spears and slivers its way into you through your eyes, your ears, your nose, your mouth, and all the other holes and pores of your body and you'll be blown into a thousand itty-bitty pieces before you can even cry 'mama!'"

Oh, mama! I was terrified.

"My kind master," I kowtowed a thousand times and begged. "Please teach me how to avert these calamities. I'll repay your kindness a thousand folds!"

"Who wants any repayment from you?" Master Bohdi looked insulted. "I wouldn't even if I could, anyone but you."

"Why not me, master?" I felt hurt.

"Because you're different."

"Different what, master? I have a head, a body with limbs as strong as anyone else, and I have a heart, a mind, a soul, as big as everyone else, too."

"You are cheek-less," said the master.

Cheek-less?

I felt my face with both hands and, and…to my horror I found nothing but hollowness where cheeks were supposed to be.

I'm indeed cheek-less.

Why on earth nobody has ever told me this before? Me, cheek-less, have thought I am beautiful, a beautiful Monkey King, no less, the whole time!

But I am not ready to quit; I've come a long way after all.

"Beauty is in the eye of the beholder, if I may," I ventured. "Isn't that what you've been teaching us, my kind master? And all these material, corporal things, like our looks, are vain, transient, transitory...."

The master looked unmoved, his eyes fixed on me.

"Besides, master," I continued, holding on to the last chance to make my case for dear life. "What I lose in the cheeks I more than gain in the crop." I winked, pointing at a bulge below my throat, and rubbing it a few times. "This big crop of mine can hold a lot of food, and perhaps knowledge too. Haven't I been the quickest study you've had, kind master, if I am not mistaken?"

"You cheeky, thick-skinned, smarty-pants of a little monkey!" Master Bohdi chuckled. "Fine. Come closer to me."

I could hardly contain myself for joy when the master began to whisper in my ear more secret of life.

What on Earth, in Heaven, and anywhere in-between will I be afraid of, thunder, fire, wind, whatever, when I can morph into just about anything I want to under the sun? This cheek-less monkey will soon be match-less!

Once again, I threw myself, my heart, my mind, and my soul, into learning and practicing until I thought I had mastered all the seventy-two ways to transfigure, to metamorphosize, to change into anything I wish.

One day, when I was hoeing weeds in the garden, Master Bohdi happened to stroll by.

"So, Wukong, any progress since the last pop quiz?"

"Yes, master!" I said proudly. "I've learned and perfected them all!"

Master Bohdi mumbled something I didn't quite catch, his eyebrows knit.

"For one, I can now do cloud flying."

"Really? Show me."

So, I took a deep breath, did a few jumping jacks and cartwheels as warmup, and then bounced twenty feet high into the air. I flew, like a cloud, for about thirty minutes, the time it would take one to finish a meal, made a big circle, and landed back in front of Master Bohdi.

"You call that cloud flying?" My master burst out laughing. "That is cloud crawling, cloud clawing, at the best!"

I was dumbfounded.

"Those who have really mastered cloud flying, they can leave North Sea in the morning, make a tour of East Sea, West Sea, South Sea, and then return to North Sea for supper all in a single day!"

"Really?!"

Master Bohdi nodded.

I was crestfallen.

"I wish I could do that too," I said, unsure of myself for the first time. "It seems so hard, probably too hard for me to learn."

"Don't shortchange yourself, Wukong," said Master Bohdi in a kinder voice. "Where there's a will there's a way. You've heard me saying that a few times before, right?"

I nodded. There is no shortage of will in me, that I know for sure.

"Let me teach you how to do this cloud flying properly then," the master said.

I kowtowed a thousand times in heartfelt gratitude.

"You murmur this spell," he whispered something in my ear, "then tighten your fists, shake your body once, and jump! A single somersault can take you to one hundred and eight thousand *li* away!"

My fellow disciples, who happened to have gathered around, laughed. "If Wukong can learn this, he'd make a good messenger boy, faster than a pigeon, and make a pretty good living doing this."

Me, anyone's messenger boy?!

I didn't say anything, though. Words are cheap. I put my mind, heart, and soul into to learning this and other new secret of life again.

Spring came and went and then summer came along on schedule. One mid-summer day, we were all relaxing and bantering under a big pine tree when one of the fellow disciples said:

"Wukong, favorite of the master. He has taught you so much more on the side. Why not show us a trick or two, like changing yourself into something?"

"Easy thing," I said offhandedly. "What do you guys like me to change to?"

"How about a pine tree?" another disciple suggested.

I murmured a spell, gave my body a quick shake, and voila, I became a pine tree, a tall, majestic one for that, its branches loaded with blossoms of white snow glittering under the sun, even though it was summer.

"Amazing! Amazing!"

"If I hadn't seen it with my own eyes!"

"Damn! That's diabolical!"

They all cheered, and I was so pleased with myself.

"Who is making this disturbance at such a sacred place?" demanded a sonorous voice we all knew so well. I saw from my high vantage point Master Bohdi strolling toward us.

Oh boy, I'm in trouble, big, deep trouble.

I barely had time to change back to my real self when Master Bohdi's towering figure stood in front of me, visibly upset.

I threw myself on the ground and tried to explain that I was just showing what I'd learned.

Master Bohdi cut me short.

"You showy, vainglorious little monkey! Today you're showing off what you've learnt, tomorrow you can make so much trouble only God knows where! Oh, this is on me, I should have known better."

I begged the kind master for forgiveness and promised I would never do it again.

"What's there to forgive?" Master Bohdi muttered between his teeth. "You're but a little monkey and don't know any better. Monkey or not, you can't stay here anymore. Pack up and go back to where you came from. Wherever you go and whatever you do, do not ever mention that you were once a disciple of mine. I wash my hands off you. If you dare even mention half a word about me, I'll catch you, skin you alive, and send your soul to the lowest circle of Netherland so you'll never see the light of day again, and… and you'll regret the day you were born!"

With that, Master Bohdi turned and marched back into Tilted Moon Tristar Cave.

I was frozen there. Speechless. What a dumb, idiotic ass I've been!

Yet…, yet somewhere deep in me there has been this feeling, a faint, vague, hard to describe undercurrent of sorts. I've ignored it for so long, and it now somehow, suddenly, for no reason at all, bubbles to the surface, and now I know what it is.

I'm homesick.

I have been away from home for more than twenty years and it's high time to go home, pay my folks a visit, and see how they've been, what they're up to, and so on.

Teary-eyed, I kowtowed in heartfelt gratitude toward Tilted Moon Tristar Cave, knowing for certain that I would never see Master Bohdi again, then I murmured the spell my kind master had taught me, somersaulted into the cloud, and rode it back to Flower Fruit Mountain.

I left home a mere, ignorant earthling, and now I'm back a thousand times wiser, loaded with all the knowledge of Heaven, Earth, and anywhere in-between, its secret ways, and ways to avert even the worst of calamities.

A thousand monkeys jumped out of the bushes when I landed near the entrance of Water Curtain Cave, not with joyous hurrahs of seeing me again, but with heartrending cries of pain and misery.

"What's going on?" I asked. "What's happened?"

"My king," Old Sage came forward, bowed, and spoke. "You Majesty must have forgotten about us, being away for so long. We've been plagued by monsters nonstop since the day you left. They came, ransacked our home, and took everything they could lay their hands on, and even kidnapped many of our children."

I took a quick glance at the crowds around me and didn't find the familiar face of Little Mischief.

What has the world come to, in the short span of time I was away?

I was enraged.

"Who're these monsters? I'm going to show them who they're dealing with!"

"My king," said Square Head, the husky young fellow now quite a middle-ager, "the king of these monsters is no joking matter. He is big and tall, like a giant, and even the strongest among us is no match for him. He comes as cloud, goes as fog; he is now wind, and then rain; he strikes like thunder or lightning—"

"Don't you worry," I said confidently. "This monster king has now found more than his match."

I somersaulted into the cloud, looked down, and saw a tall

mountain in the not far distance, its summit piercing through thick, eerie nebula, canyons on the left heaving like dragons and on the right like tigers, donkeys plowing the fields here and there.

I spotted a few little monsters fooling around near the entrance of a big cave covered with serpentine vines.

I landed where these little monsters were, like an eagle, and at the sight of me they ran screaming inside.

The ground shook and a giant of a monster marched outside the cave, a fierce and imposing sight, crowned with a glittering helmet and armed with a humongous knife twice as big as me.

"You pitiable midget of a monkey thing," the giant monster burst out laughing contemptuously. "Your head can barely reach my belly button, you're bare-handed, not even armed with a stone slinger. How dare you come and make a disturbance here?"

"You addle-brained, empty-headed fool," I said as calmly as I could although I was mad as hell and a teeny-weensy nervous, too. "Never heard of your granddaddy, Monkey King? You think size's the only thing that matters? Let your granddaddy teach you a lesson today so you'll regret having ever been born and lived this long!"

The giant grunted, bared his fang-like teeth, and took a few menacing steps toward me.

"Watch out!" I warned. "Take this from me!"

I jumped and threw the giant a punch on the chin; he ducked, and my fist landed on his big ear; he winced and then laughed:

"You foul-mouthed little monkey. It'd be beneath me to fight you with this big knife of mine."

He tossed the knife on the ground and threw me a hard punch. I ducted and felt a chilling gust sweeping over my head.

All right. Here we go!

We went at each other like crazy. I jumped, dived, flew in from left, faded away on the right, landing a few jabs on his ribcages and even a straight one on his chin, and he barely touched a single hair of mine, all his punches landing on thin air.

A teeny-weensy unnerved, perhaps, after a few rounds like this, the giant monster picked up the big knife from the ground and came wielding it madly at me. As I ducted, I could hear the glittering knife whistling from my left and right and all around me.

I have to try something different.

I leaped into the air as the giant monster charged at me with the big knife again, pulled a hair from my body, put it in my mouth and chewed it a few times, and spat it out:

"Change!"

A few hundred itsy-bitsy monkeys, each the size of a baby chick, appeared from nowhere and landed on the giant monster, laying their hands on the monster's hair, nose, ears, arms, legs, crotch, you name it, pinching, punching, pulling, kicking; they were all over him, from head to toe, and were having so much fun hitting him as if it were some game.

Imagine being attacked like that by an army of little monkeys and couldn't even move, let alone fight back.

I ripped the superheavy knife from the monster's hand, called back all the little monkeys, and cut him into halves.

Blood spouted and splashed every which way, a few big drops falling on my cheek-less face and streaking into my mouth.

My first taste of blood.

It would hardly be my last, as I would find out soon.

It was an out-of-body experience. I can see it playing in my mind's eye even today, slo-mo, frame by frame, like it happened yesterday.

Riding on the dizzying euphoria of having beaten a giant monster several times my size, I rushed into the cave to finish off all the other monsters daring to put up a fight and freed Little Mischief and all the little ones who had been languishing in bondage.

I returned triumphantly, all my people so overjoyed seeing me and the freshly liberated little monkeys back home; they all jumped, danced, and chanted:

"Long Live the King! Long Live the King!"

I was on cloud nine.

THREE

As I Will

Triumphing over that giant monster was gratifying, but it was also a wake-up call.

The world is not what it used to be anymore; the good ol' days of peace, harmony, everyone, monkeys, wolves, tigers, foxes, you name it, all getting along super well are gone. There's evil out there and we've got to be prepared for the unexpected. Besides, once the word gets out, kings of humans, animals, fairies, demons, you name it, will be alarmed and think we are rebels, revolutionaries, or simply, troublemakers, and post a threat to them.

So, I led my people, all able-bodied ones, old and young, in drills every day. It was quite a sight to see them all, thousands of them, armed with wood swords, bamboo spears, what have you, practicing advance and retreat, attack tactics, frontal, from both flanks, from the rear, and defense, setting up camps and decamping, parading in neat formations, chanting and singing to the beat of drums, like any army boot camps you've probably seen.

Morale was high.

I was feeling good.

Until one day it occurred to me that all such drills were nothing but child's play and this feel-good show of bravado would do us no good. Why? 'Cause I am the only one armed with the real thing, that big iron knife courtesy of the giant monster I've slayed. This sea of monkeys, wielding all these wood swords and bamboo spears, toys for little boys, will be snubbed out like flies in real battlefields.

I confided this unease of mine to Old Sage.

"That's what's been bothering my king lately?" he said. "I've a remedy for that. Easy."

Easy? Easier said than done. This know-it-all old monkey seems to have an answer for just about anything. Wisdom comes with old age, as they say?

"If you go east from here for about two hundred *li*," Old Sage said, as if having read my mind, "you'll probably find a kingdom underneath water there. I've heard that it is quite a big kingdom, so it must have its share of goldsmiths, silversmiths, ironsmiths, bronzesmiths, what have you, who can make weapons of all kinds. My king can perhaps go and buy or ask them to custom-make some for us?"

"Only two hundred *li* away?" I marveled, "I'll be back in a sec."

I somersaulted into the cloud, rode it east for two hundred *li*, and looked down.

Underneath the water looms a big city, streets, markets, people busy going hither and tither... They must have tons of ready-made weapons, I figured, yet buying weapons from them would be a cumbersome business transaction, bargaining back and forth, paying, money I have not, or bartering, but with what? Why shouldn't I simply go down and help myself to whatever I want and need?

Hahaha, I know what you're going to say now: The way you think, justify what you're going to do, is not much different from that of a thief, or worse, robber. Well, what can I say in my own defense? Nothing perhaps. Guilty as charged, probably, but fair or foul, what choices do I have? It's a brave new world out there and I've got to do all I can to protect my people. Anything wrong in that picture?

I murmured a spell, took a deep breath, held it, and then blew it all out.

My breath became a humongous sandstorm that roared and fell on the city like a tsunami. Terrified, townspeople scurried home and shut their doors; guards abandoned their posts and ran for cover wherever they could find; tigers and lions and wolves bolted back to their caves; and even carps, crabs, eels, thinking perhaps the end of the world must be coming, reeling and scuttering every which way.

I landed in the city, found its arsenal, and was delighted by what I saw: knives, spears, swords, daggers, scissors, halberds, axes, cymbals, scythes, whips, palladiums, crossbows and arrows, forks, you name it, all made of iron, the real deal.

I pulled a tiny hair from my body, chew it, murmured the spell, and blew it out:

"Change!"

Hundreds of little monkeys appeared from thin air; they grabbed whatever they fancied, stronger ones each taking five or six weapons and weaker ones two or three. In the blink of an eye, we were done and took off, like a humongous flock of birds, and I somersaulted into the cloud and rode it back home.

"Come and see what I've got for you," I called out, after landing and after all my capable little helpers putting the new weaponry on the ground and vaporizing into thin air.

All my people, old and young, rushed out of Water Curtain Cave, each picking up whatever they liked, knives, swords, spears, axes, daggers, you name it. That very day, we drilled not with toys, but with the real thing that could go in white and come out bloody red.

Imagine an army of forty-seven thousand strong, now armed to the teeth, so to speak? Who and what on earth are we afraid of from now on?

Our loud marching and drilling must have awakened all the animals on Flower Fruit Mountain, wolves, tigers, leopards, deer, foxes, raccoons, elephants, scorpions, orangutans, bears, wild hogs, you name it; their kings hurried to Water Curtain Cave and paid tribute to me with gifts of all kinds. A new system, a treaty of sorts, unsigned but understood, came into practice: They pay an annual tribute to me in gold, silver, grains, whatever they have. Some even sent their best to join us in drills.

Flower Fruit Mountain has become a golden, shiny city on the sea.

I've become king of kings.

There was just this one little thing not to my satisfaction yet. This iron knife of mine, gift from the giant monster, feels a teeny-weensy too cumbersome to use effectively in real combat.

"Easy, my king," Old Sage suggested again, "if you can go deep underwater."

"Absolutely," I said. "I can go anywhere I want to. If I want to go up in the sky, a pathway unfolds itself right away. If I want to go deep into the earth, a door opens wide for my passage. I can follow the sun or the moon without leaving behind a shadow and walk through gold and stonewalls like it is air. Water can't drown me. Fire can't burn me, either. So, going deep underwater is like taking a stroll in the park!"

That sounds just a teeny-weensy too boastful, right? But I was only telling the truth, as I knew it.

"My king's power is boundless!" said Old Sage. "I've heard that there is a waterway underneath Iron Bridge right outside our home. It can take you to the palace of Dragon King of East Sea. There you may find something you'd really like, I think."

"All right, will be back in a sec!"

I came to Iron Bridge, murmured a spell, and jumped into the water, like a scuba diver. The waterway soon led me to the bottom of East Sea, to the gate of a magnificent palace. I was stopped by a patrol.

"Who goes there? Your name or else!"

"What?" I cried out incredulously. "You've never heard of me, king of Flower Fruit Mountain, your next-door neighbor?"

The patrol looked puzzled, shook his head, and went in to report.

The gate of the palace opened wide, and Dragon King himself, wrapped in glorious regalia—golden crown, fancy silk gown, accompanied by his queen, princes and princesses, baby dragons, grandbaby dragons, crab generals, shrimp soldiers, you name it, all came out to greet me.

That's more like it.

Once I was seated in a grand chair and served tea, Dragon King asked: "May we ask what pleasure we at East Sea have that brings our famed neighbor to come and visit us today?"

"Oh, pleasure is all mine," I replied pleasantly. I told him a quick story of me, my knowledge of the secret of life and the world, my prowess, and feats, you name it.

"I'd be indebted to Your Majesty," I said in conclusion, "if you could spare me a weapon from your massive arsenal I've heard so much about."

"That," Dragon King said, visibly relieved, "that can be arranged although I may not have exactly what you have in mind."

A gang of perches carried out a big iron knife for me to see.

"Knives are not exactly my cup of tea, you know what I mean?" I said, unimpressed.

A gang of eels carried out a humongous pitchfork, with nine long, sharp, and shiny hooks. That caught my eye, so I jumped off my seat and took it in my hand.

"Light as a feather! No good in real combat."

"Oh my!" Dragon King exclaimed. "That pitchfork weighs three thousand and six hundred *jin*. Too light for you?"

A gang of carps carried out a humongous halberd for me to see.

This thing, with a spike at one end and a hooked ax at the other, looked promising, but still felt too light in my hand.

"That thing weighs seven thousand and two hundred *jin*. Still too light?" Dragon King was now visibly annoyed. "Then, we can't help you, our famed neighbor."

"Try harder then," I suggested. I am not one easily dismissed.

Dragon King sat there, without another word, as if he hadn't heard me.

An impasse ensued. Expecting me to blink first? Hell no!

The magnificent palace was dangerously quiet. I could hear the heartbeats of Dragon King and all those around him like a hundred out of whack church bells striking at the same time.

Dragon Queen walked a few tiny steps closer to her darling husband and whispered in his ear. I pretended not to listen but heard every word she said:

"Your Majesty, looks like we cannot get rid of this uninvited guest today unless he gets what he wants. We do have something extraordinary in our palace treasure collections, a magnificent pole. This pole has been behaving strange lately, beaming in dazzling brilliance day and night. Perhaps that would—"

"You mean that pole?" Dragon King shook his head. "The one used by Yu the Great, Da Yu, to gauge the depth of waters and tame the Big Flood in ancient times? What could this monkey use it for?"

"Worth a try, my king," Dragon Queen said, "since nothing else has worked."

"Agreed," said I, nodding, as if I was thinking aloud.

Dragon King and Dragon Queen were both taken aback that I had heard them.

"Why not give this thing a try?" I suggested helpfully. "Please bring it here so I can take a look."

"That thing is way too heavy to bring over here," Dragon King said, his patience running thin.

Graciously I offered to go and take a peek myself.

Deep in the palace I saw this storied pole from the legendary Yu the Great:

Twenty feet tall, five feet thick, cool to the touch and solid like iron, shining in all its marvelous glory.

This would be perfect for me, except—

"Wish it were just a teeny-weensy smaller—"

As if on a cue, the pole became ten feet shorter and two feet thinner.

"Wonderful!" I exclaimed. "A teeny-weensy smaller again?"

The magic pole became even smaller, until it was like a carrying pole in length and rice bowl in thickness. I picked it up. It felt just right in my hand; the gold bands at both ends pleased my eye, too. Then I saw these words carved in its midsection:

As-I-Will Gold-Banded Cudgel (Ruyi Jin'gu Bang)

"It weighs thirteen thousand and five hundred *jin*," Dragon King said.

This might be it. I can use it as I will in fighting just about anyone.

I wielded it a few times and did a few moves, giving an imaginary adversary a hail of blows from left and right and head to toe... Dragon King, his queen, all his courtiers and attendants, watching, their mouths agape in both wonder and terror.

"Found what you wanted?" Dragon King asked when I finally sat down again.

"Yes," I enthused, quite pleased. "but I need some clothing, some regalia, to go with this Gold-Banded Cudgel."

"What?" Dragon King could hardly hold back his anger now. "You're insatiable in your demands!"

I know as a guest I am being just a teeny-weensy too much, but I can't help it. Since I've already come this far, I might as well go all the way, so I'll be armed, armored, and dressed like a real king of kings to face and take on the brave new world.

"You've been a gracious host," I said, to placate Dragon King. "I personally would be perfectly fine with what you've already gifted me, but this Gold-Banded Cudgel, you see, would not take no for an answer."

I tightened my grip on the new weapon in my hand.

"Okay, okay, my famed neighbor," said Dragon King, "I'll do what I can, with the help of my younger brothers, all dragon kings of other seas."

At the sounding of an iron drum and a gold bell, Dragon King of South Sea, Dragon King of North Sea, and Dragon King of West Sea all appeared in front of us.

When my host, Dragon King of East Sea, told them what was going on, this band of dragon king brothers was visibly upset, spoiling for a fight. My host, their elder brother, shook his head, pointing at the Gold-Banded Cudgel in my hand.

So, grudgingly, they each presented me a gift: a pair of lotus silk shoes, a set of golden armor, a phenix feather crown, what have you.

As I was leaving, quite pleased, I heard them talking about lodging a complaint to Jade Emperor of Heaven (*Yuhuangdadi*).

What Jade Emperor? Never heard of him. What can he do to me anyway?

When I resurfaced near Iron Bridge and appeared in front of my people, armed with the new Gold-Banded Cudgel and clothed in the new glorious regalia, they all hurrahed and jumped for joy. Square Head and a few other big, strong guys tried to lift my new weapon—all had to give up after trying so hard their eyeballs were ready to bulge out.

"Heavy as a mountain!"

I told them about this magic Gold-Banded Cudgel and showed them a few moves.

"Smaller. Smaller," I said, until the Cudgel became the size of an embroidery needle, and I put it in my ear.

"Bigger. Bigger," I said, until the Cudgel became twenty feet tall again, like a young pine tree.

"Bigger. Bigger!" I continued, until the Cudgel grew to ten thousand feet tall, like the peak of a mountain.

The Cudgel's power is boundless! Highest heaven and deepest hell, whatever, this Cudgel can reach and do whatever, as I will it.

Unbeknownst to me, as I was showing off the magic Gold-Banded Cudgel to my people, the whole world was shaking as if a major volcanic, a seismic event was about to happen. Frightened, all the animals, tigers, wolves, hyenas, and even all the monsters and demons, came kowtowing, congratulating me, and pledging their homage yet again.

From that day on, I was on cloud nine, literally, every day: riding the cloud to go and roam the four seas and indulge in the sights and sounds of a thousand mountains, meeting old friends, making new ones, showing off my Cudgel and what I could do with it, chatting about magic, philosophy, meaning of life, you name it, over the best of wine and tea. I was living the life of king of kings, and it couldn't get any better.

Until one day, after a big feast and an award ceremony, I, a teeny-weensy tired, dosed off under a pine tree near Iron Bridge.

Two armed commandos, dark-cloaked, appear from nowhere, wake me up, show me an official paper bearing my name, tie me up and drag me to the gate of a city. I struggle to open my eyes and see an iron tablet:

Netherland (Youmingjie)

Netherland? That's Hell, where King Yama (*Yanluowang*) lives, right? Why bring me here?

"Your life on earth is about to expire, in case you wonder why we bring you here," says one of the Hell Commandos.

"I am Wukong, Monkey King, and I've learned and mastered all the secret of life and I'm above and beyond any laws! Don't try to pull a fast one on me!"

Ignoring my protests, the two Hell Commandos keep dragging, pushing, trying to get me inside the gate.

Infuriated, I pull out the Gold-Banded Cudgel from my ear and give it a shake: It grows as big as a carrying pole and thick like a rice bowl. With one blow, I smash the two commandos into a meat pie, and then fight my way into the palace of Netherland, legions of Hell Commandos, ghosts, demons, monsters, all running for cover, till I am in the presence of King Yama.

"Who on earth are you?" King Yama asks nervously in his scratchy voice, shifting uncomfortably in the grand throne.

"Why on earth have me dragged over here if you don't even know my name?" I cry out at the top of my lungs.

"Must be a mistake, that can be easily corrected."

King Yama accompanies me to an archive place where floor-to-ceiling shelves are loaded with volumes upon volumes of Book of Life and Death for just about any and every living thing, tigers, lions, wolves, birds, fish, insects, you name it.

Amongst this sea of volumes I finally find one on monkeys. I turn the pages and find my name, with this notation:

Born A Stone Monkey
Life To Be Lived:
Three Hundred Forty-Two Years

Three hundred forty-two years? How big is that number? Regardless, it is not immortality, right?

Besides, I don't even know how many years I have already lived.

That won't matter anyway if I just blot out my name?

"Get me ink and a writing brush!"

A bookkeeper hands me a big wet writing brush nervously.

With one angry stroke, I blot out my name from the Book of Life and Death.

Since I'm at it now, why not do so for all my people?

"There you have it," I throw down the writing brush when finally done, my wrists a teeny-weensy stiffened from so much brushwork.

Then I fight my way out as I did coming in. None dares to even try to stop me.

"You can't get away with this!" I hear King Yama shouting in his scratchy voice as I exit the palace of Netherland. "I'll lodge a complaint to Jade Emperor now!"

Here you go again, Jade Emperor! Who cares? What can you do to me anyways?

In the wink of an eye, I was back on Flower Fruit Mountain; I strode past the pine tree near Iron Bridge and found myself inside Water Curtain Cave, elated.

Did it really happen? Was it just a dream? Who knows, really, and who cares anyways.

When I pronounced to all my people that we are immortal now, they all jumped in raptures. Who wouldn't?!

While our hurrahs were still resounding over the hills and valleys, it was announced that we had a visitor. Some neighborly king to come and pay tribute again?

"Who on earth are you?" I demanded to know at the sight of the silver-haired, long-bearded visitor with enormous wings. "To what do I owe the pleasure?"

"I am Goldstar," the visitor said, "a messenger for Jade Emperor, with an invitation for you to visit Heaven and be bestowed an official title there."

An invitation from Jade Emperor of Heaven himself?

To be bestowed some official title up there?

Ode to joy! Joy to the world!

Unbeknownst to me at the time, Dragon King of East Sea, along with his brothers, and King Yama of Netherland had already had audiences with Jade Emperor of Heaven complaining about what I had done.

How could a harmless little stone monkey, born three hundred years ago, have acquired such power? How dare this monkey thing defy the laws for all mortals and take himself out of the cycle of birth, life, and death?

A special emergency council was held on how to deal with this rebel. Jade Emperor would have been happy to send down some Heaven Commandos to take care of business, but Goldstar, a sagacious and trusted courtier, advised that this Monkey, now armed with not only secret knowledge of life, but also a matchless Gold-Banded Cudgel, is no easy thing to annihilate or apprehend, and that it would be far less troublesome to neutralize this troublemaker by bestowing on him some official title in Heaven, blah-blah-blah.

What can that title be?

The suspense was killing me as I somersaulted into the cloud and rode it toward Heaven.

FOUR
Heaven's Equal

I was going so fast that I soon left Goldstar breathlessly behind.

Upon reaching the gate of Heaven, I was blocked by guards armed with iron knives, spears, swords, you name it.

"I'm a guest of Jade Emperor!" I shouted at them. "Why am I being treated like some obnoxious party crasher?"

"You little monkey, guest of Jade Emperor, His Majesty?" They laughed in my face. "Why don't you take a pee and have a good look at yourself in it, that face of yours?"

I was mad as hell and was ready to fight my way in when Goldstar caught up. He apologized to me profusely and then told the guards to step aside and open the gate wide for a distinguished guest of Jade Emperor.

Imagine how my eyes were dazzled by the magnificent splendor of Heaven: mountains of emeralds, sapphires, pearls, diamonds, you name it, glittering whichever way I turn; long meandering covered walkways ornamented with pictures of mythological figures and stories, leading to thirty-three palaces and seventy-two treasure repositories; a hundred longevity altars surrounded by flowers that will not fade for thousands upon thousands of years; alchemist stoves for refining immortality beans girthed by trees, flowers, and grasses that will remain green for tens of thousands of years; an armed, smartly dressed guard every step of the way, standing at attention, statuesque, you wouldn't know they are living things if not for an occasional blinking of their eyes; dragons, pheasants, peacocks, unicorns, and beautiful singsong girls dancing and laughing in some deep courtyards; the very air buzzing in a thousand purple hazes, ten thousand golden beams, and gazillions of dizzying aromas.

I was finally led to the presence of Jade Emperor, seated in the grand throne glistering with gemstones, his head enveloped with so much dazzling halo that I could barely make out what this King of Heaven looked like: young or old, handsome or plain looking, oh yes, his cheeks, full or somehow hollow like mine?

"So, this is that troublemaking little monkey I've heard about lately?" boomed an imposing voice that sent a thousand echoes down the deep corridors of Heaven.

"That's yours truly," I said, stiffening my back and holding my head high. "Wukong, Monkey King, not guilty as charged!"

"This impertinent monkey!"

"What an egomaniac!"

"Having the balls to speak to King of Heaven like this!"

"Let's drag him out and behead him!"

Courtiers flanking Jade Emperor were flabbergasted by my not so pietistic attitude and were ready to jump on me.

"First offence of an ignorant earthling who doesn't know any better," Jade Emperor chuckled charitably. "I'll let it go this time."

I hastened to bow, with a slight drop of my knee.

There and then, Jade Emperor bestowed on me the official title of Imperial Stables Assistant Steward (*Bimawen*).

I didn't know what that title meant but it sounded grand

enough to my ear. So, I thanked Jade Emperor profusely, this time with both of my knees on the ground, my heart swelling with pride and joy.

Once at the Imperial Stables, I called together all the staff, supervisors, record-keepers, attendants, you name it, and listened to their reports attentively:

Imperial Stables in charge of a thousand heavenly horses, each famed and having an honorable title: Faster Than Light, Purple Swallow, Galloping Cloud, Red Lightning, Thousand *Li*, so on and so forth.

Imagine being entrusted with the wellbeing of this big legion of imperial horses!

I rolled up my sleeves and got to work right away, cutting grasses, washing horses, combing their manes, putting sweetest of straws into their troughs, supervising everyone in the meantime, giving them a harsh dressing down if I catch anyone slacking, working tirelessly and joyously, being *bimawen* is oxygen to me.

Time flies when you're busy having fun working. Half a month passed before I knew it. All the imperial horses would neigh happily at the sight of me first thing in the morning. They have fattened visibly in that short span of time, quivering with bulging muscles and explosive power whether you inspect them from front, rear, or sideways.

One day, during another one of our many boisterous feasts, I asked, out of sheer curiosity: "What's the rank of my official title *Bimawen*?"

After a few seconds of awkward silence, one of my assistants said, "It's an official title, that's all." He then tried to steer our attention to a different direction. "The wine today tastes just an itsy-bitsy fruitier, don't you think?"

"But what exactly is the rank of this title?" I insisted. "How high is it? I demand to know!"

"Well, it is rank-less," suggested an assistant recordkeeper sheepishly.

"Rank-less? Too high to be ranked, you mean?"

"Too low," mumbled a horse whisperer, a few seats away, trying to avoid eye contact with me. "Below even the lowest, 'cause what glory is there in attending to horses? We're nothing but stable boys, a thankless job, and we'd thank God if we don't get blamed for anything."

"What?!" I was beside myself in fury. "Me, Wukong, king of kings where I come from, being lured here to be a lowly stable boy and nothing more?"

No one dared to answer or look at me. They kept their half-drunken gaze elsewhere, expressionless.

Having the balls to pull a fast one over on me? Go take a pee and see what you look like in it!

I took out the Gold-Banded Cudgel from my ear and knocked all the plates and bowls and delicacies off the big dining table: "Sorry, fellows, no more party here!"

I fought my way out of the gate of Heaven back to where I was king.

Oh, the kind of welcome back I received from my own people! It was so gratifying and heartwarming.

"We all miss you so much, my king," said Little Mischief, now a husky youngster.

I laughed heartily. "I've been away for barely half a month, and you all talk about missing me already? You've got a flatterer's tongue!"

"My king," said Old Sage. "You've never heard of the saying that one day in Heaven is one year here on earth? You must have been really enjoying yourself up there. So, what grand title has Jade Emperor given you that you don't want to come home anymore?"

"Grand title, my butt?!" I said, burning with shame and

outrage again. "That Jade Emperor, not knowing better than judging a book by its cover, gave me this title, *bimawen*. Turns out, nothing but a lowly stable boy, lower than the lowest of anything. Can you imagine me, Monkey King, being treated so shabbily?"

They all booed, catcalled, and Square Head led a chant about going to Heaven and raising hell there.

Is that what it'd take to set things right? I wondered myself too although I tried my best to calm them down.

Upon the news of my return, all the kings far and near came to congratulate and pay homage again. When I told them the story of my short, not so glorious stint in Heaven, told without much embellishment, one of the kings said:

"Your Majesty, king of kings, with boundless magic and power, a lowly stable boy in Heaven? That's injustice, pure and simple!"

He paused and then said:

"In our eyes, you're Great Sage Heaven's Equal (*Qitiandasheng*), your grandeur's second to none!"

"*Qitiandasheng*?" I rolled it over in my tongue a few times. "I like how that sounds to my ear!"

There arose an earth-shattering chant:

"Hurrah!"

"Long Live the King!"

"Glory to Great Sage Heaven's Equal!"

It resounded over mountains and vales, from sea to sea, between Heaven and Earth. Imagine how elated I was, having been crowned a truly grand title, Great Sage Heaven's Equal, second to none!

A huge standard with these very words on it was made that very day. It would follow me wherever I would go and fight battles against all evils in the world. It was Heaven on Earth indeed.

Midmorning the next day, I was half asleep, benefit of a hangover when I was awakened by loud cacophony outside Water Curtain Cave. I got up, hastily put on my full regalia and went outside to see what was going on.

A legion of Heaven Commandos has set up camp outside, cavaliers, foot soldiers, you name it, bugle blaring, drumbeating, battle cries, deafening enough to awaken homeless souls in the deepest circles of Netherland and scare the living light of the boldest, bravest amongst earthlings.

Not me.

This legion of Heaven Commandos was commanded by a boyish looking warrior, fully armed and gloriously armored, but looked barely pubescent, as far as I could see, not a hint of moustache around the lips, no Adam's apple yet, and a few inches shorter than me.

"Who on earth are you?" I asked dismissively. "I can smell your mama's milk from a *li* away! You have the balls to come and disturb me?"

"You little rascal of a monkey," the boy warrior said. "You've never heard of me, the third prince of a heavenly king, Nezha!? I'm here with an arrest warrant signed by Jade Emperor himself!"

"Nezha who? Arrest warrant from Jade Emperor? For what?"

Nezha pointed to the standard flapping in the wind featuring the grandest of title I've crowned on myself:

Great Sage Heaven's Equal (Qitiandasheng)

"A little ignoramus of monkey daring to claim grandeur equal to Heaven! Have you eaten leopards' gallbladders? Now, let this sword of mine be our introduction!"

With that, the boy warrior, Prince Nezha, began to attack me.

"Bring it on, you pitiable mama's boy!" I laughed. "I won't

even bother to lift a finger to fight you."

Fuming with fury, Prince Nezha murmured some spell and shouted,

"Change!"

Boy, standing before me now is a Nezha with three heads and six arms, armed with a sword, a knife, a noose, a fork, a stick, and a fire wheel, all coming to me at the same time from all directions.

Recovering from shock and realizing that I'd be underestimating this boy warrior at my own peril, I murmured a spell of mine and shouted,

"Change!"

A three-headed me with six arms wielding three of my Gold-Banded Cudgel now taking on Prince Nezha measure for measure, blow for blow.

Shocked because he had not seen that coming, but recovering fast, Nezha changed into a hundred heads, then a thousand heads, and then a million heads with millions of arms brandishing millions of swords, knives, nooses, forks, sticks, and fire wheels, all coming to me at the same time, only to be matched by a million heads of me going after him with millions of Gold-Banded Cudgels.

Have to be honest: it was a worthy fight cause we were well matched. We fought a thousand rounds, a sea of swords, knives, nooses, forks, sticks, fire wheels, Gold-Banded Cudgels all fighting one another from all imaginable angles and directions, like a million spasms of lightning striking at the same time, all the stars in the galaxies caught in some mad, maddening cosmic dance, a dazzling feast for the eye of any bystander for sure, but for me and for him, if we miss by a thousandth of a second, a ten thousandth of a hair of mine, we'd be done. It was quite a show, an out of body experience; I could see it all playing, slow-mo, in my mind's eye even as I was caught in the thick of it, as I speak now.

This going on for a while, an idea came to me. I pulled out a hair from my body and blew it into air:

"Change!"

An exact copy of Nezha, from head to toe to the smell of his mama's breast milk, appeared between me and the real Nezha I had been fighting.

As the real Nezha blinked, puzzled by the apparition of another self, I went for his head; he darted, the Gold-Banded Cudgel hitting his left arm instead. Nezha winced in pain and cried, "Mama!"

"Hahaha," I said to him triumphantly. "Now that I've taught you a lesson, go back and tell that Jade Emperor of yours that I will not cause him any more trouble if he does what I ask, granting me the title of Great Sage Heaven's Equal, 'cause I am second to none! I will not take no for an answer. Otherwise, more trouble to come!"

Prince Nezha fled in shame, casting backward glances now and then.

I was overjoyed although I'd never had to fight this hard, notwithstanding my transmute tricks and matchless Gold-Banded Cudgel. A victory is a victory is a victory, though, and I'll take it any day.

Good news travels fast! Before I had time to change back into more casual attire and relax, kings far and near came in troves to congratulate me. An earthling beating a heavenly prince and a legion of Heaven Commandos? That's a first, ever.

Midmorning the next day, as I emerged from Water Curtain Cave to command another round of drills and parade of our legions, tens of thousands of monkeys, other animals, ghosts and demons, I saw a silver-haired old man descending from the cloud.

That sagacious Goldstar, messenger of Jade Emperor,

paying me another visit, on the heels of my victory over Nezha? Just in time, I thought. Although it didn't quite work out the way we all wanted the last time he came with an invitation from Jade Emperor, I can't chalk it up to him. Of all courtiers in Heaven, Goldstar seems the only one who sees that I have it in me to do some real good or trouble.

I called out my honor guards and, with the "Great Sage Heaven's Equal" standard flapping the wind, gave the old man the welcome he deserved.

I invited Goldstar to sit next to me, but he preferred to be standing while addressing me.

The sagacious old man said that upon hearing Prince Nezha's report yesterday all of Jade Emperor's courtiers urged him to send a bigger legion of more fierce Heaven Commandos to subdue this rebellious little monkey; he, Goldstar, was the only one who advised against more war: if Prince Nezha, a young warrior with unmatched fighting power in Heaven, could not defeat this monkey, who else can? Also, since all this monkey wants is this new title, Great Sage Heaven's Equal, why not grant him that? A title is just a title and nothing more; it will not cause anybody anything, not even a hair, yet there will be peace in Heaven and life will return to normal. Isn't that a good deal? When all the other courtiers still spoiled for war, Goldstar bet with his honor to Jade Emperor that this time it would work.

"Your Majesty," Goldstar said to me. "It's such a good deal for you too, getting the grand title without having to lift even a finger. I guarantee you, upon my honor, and my wings, that it'll work this time."

Convinced and elated, I somersaulted into the cloud and travelled heavenward again, taking care not to leave the sagacious old man too far behind.

I was warmly received at the gate of Heaven this time, all

guards, warriors, and courtiers raising their hats as I marched past them.

I was in the presence of Jade Emperor again and bowed deeply in heartfelt gratitude when he bestowed on me the new title, Great Sage Heaven's Equal.

"This is the highest rank in Heaven," Jade Emperor said in his imposing voice. "So, I hope you'll be happy this time and will not cause any more trouble in Heaven."

What more trouble would I make now that I am Great Sage Heaven's Equal, second to none?

What more perks would I want now that I can help myself to the sweetest, preciousest nectar and wine wherever and whenever I fancy, partying all night, sleep in, and don't have to get up even when sunshine is full blast on my butt, whatever?

I am in Heaven, literally.

FIVE

Party Crasher

By now you should know me well enough to know how much I would enjoy my grand new title. It is what I wanted, what I deserve, and I got my wish, fair and square.

I was thrilled the moment I entered Mansion of Great Sage Heaven's Equal, quite a regal place, the real deal, like having my own palace in Heaven: I have my own crew of personal aids serving every need, desire, want, and whim of mine, breakfast, lunch, dinner, afternoon teas, midnight snacks, free of any responsibility, and free to roam any palaces, make new bosom friends and sworn brothers, bowing to kings, warriors, elders, and being bowed back. Says who that there is no such thing as free lunch? I'm enjoying room and board and everything else free of charge, not just that I don't have to pay, but also that I don't have to do anything, to lift a finger, and I'm being pampered like a king, and I am a king anyways!

One day, I was called to the presence of Jade Emperor.

"Any newer, higher title for me, Your Majesty?" I bowed and asked, expectantly.

"Your title is already Heaven's equal; how can it go any higher?" Jade Emperor chuckled. "I hear that you're having a swell of time here, but I'm concerned that you'll soon be bored with having too much leisure on hand. How about a new title for you, Imperial Longevity Peach Orchard Inspector?"

Great minds think alike! Just when I am beginning to feel a teeny-weensy bored and worried that being too idle for too long I may lose my mojo.

Longevity. Immortality. Elixirs of life.

Isn't that what I've been looking for?

And another grand title, a bonus, right?

I thanked Jade Emperor profusely and hurried to Imperial Longevity Peach Orchard.

I was warmly received by Head Keeper who called together all the workers to welcome the new Imperial Inspector from Jade Emperor, each of them a samson in his own right, specialized in weeding, watering, trimming, cleaning, picking, you name it.

I took my first inspection tour right away, guided by a teeny-weensy obsequious Head Keeper. What I saw was nothing short of a spectacular mouthwatering feast for my eyes:

A sea of the precious peach trees, some budding, some full flowering, some loaded with fruits, tender green, pink, rouge, milky, all planted by Queen of Heaven (*Yaochiwangmu*) herself! Is she Jade Emperor's mama or bedmate? I don't know even to this day, but what does it matter?

Three thousand and six hundred peach trees altogether!

One thousand two hundred of the trees, on the front rows, bear relatively small fruits; they ripen every three thousand years; whoever eats such fruits will enjoy good health.

One thousand and two hundred are in the middle rows, their fruits ripening every six thousand years; whoever eats them fruits will feel like on cloud nine and having had a glassful from Fountain of Youth.

The most precious are the one thousand two hundred

peach trees in the back row, their fruits ripening every nine thousand years; whoever eats these fruits will live as long as Heaven and Earth.

I was so overjoyed. What I've been wishing for ever since I became Monkey King presents itself right here, out of the blue, without me even looking for it! Isn't that amazing? Aren't I the most blessed in the whole world?

From that day on, roaming the palaces and chatting with the kings and warriors interested me no more. Taking an inspecting tour of Imperial Longevity Peach Orchard every three or five days was all the joy I needed.

One day, while inspecting the Orchard, I saw a big tree loaded with ripening fruits and couldn't help salivating: What does it taste like? But I couldn't just pick one, what with Head Keeper and the entourage accompanying me during such inspecting tours.

"I'm going to take a nap in this pavilion here," I said to them, feigning a delicious yawn. "Why don't you all continue without me?"

Once they were gone, I removed my regalia, crown, robe, tassels, what have you, jumped onto the big peach tree, and reached for the ripest fruit. Oh, boy, the moment I sank my teeth into the juiciest, sweetest fruit between Heaven and Earth, I had my first bite of longevity peach, I couldn't stop. Who could? I ate until I was so full that my belly was ready to burst. My taste buds delighted, and heart contented, I jumped off the tree, put on my regalia, and returned to Mansion of Great Sage Heaven's Equal.

This I would do every two or three days, coming up with all kinds of tricks to divert Head Keeper and the entourage and then have my heart's desire.

One day, after another feast in Imperial Longevity Peach Orchard, I felt a teeny-weensy drowsy, so I took a nap.

I see, like in a dream, seven fairest, princess-like girls coming to the orchard's gate, robed in silky red, green, purple, yellow, creamy, you name it, each carrying a daintiest of baskets.

"Mama has sent us here to pick the ripest peaches for her annual Longevity Peach Extravaganza," one of them says to Head Keeper.

Longevity Peach Extravaganza? All right!

"Absolutely!" Head Keeper bows obsequiously, a big smile on his face. "This year we're doing things slightly different. I'll have to report to Great Sage Heaven's Equal first 'cause Jade Emperor His Majesty has put him in charge here."

"Where is this Great Sage Heaven's Equal?" asks another princess in her sweetest of voice.

"Must be taking a nap in the pavilion. One of his routines these days."

Head Keeper comes to the pavilion, sees my regalia on the floor, but cannot find me.

"Why don't you go ahead, and I'll report to him afterwards," he tells the princesses, perhaps not wanting to be blamed for any further delay.

I see the princesses going into the orchard and looking for ripe peaches to pick, but they are far and few between. You know the reason why. They manage to get only two half baskets of half ripe peaches from the front rows, another three half baskets of half ripe peaches from the middle rows but cannot find even one ripe peach in the back rows: the few peaches still hanging on trees are small and green.

One of the princesses cries out rapturously upon seeing a big peach showing a hint of tender red and reaches to pick it, with her long, softest of fingers.

That ripening peach is none other than yours truly.

I've changed to the size of a peach so I could nap comfortably perched on a twig in the gentle breeze.

Thus awakened, I changed back to my Great Sage Heaven's Equal self.

The seven princesses screamed at the sight of me.

Half annoyed and half out of habit, I pulled out my Gold-Banded Cudgel and demanded to know why they were stealing my peaches.

They curtsied, begged His Highness, me, for forgiveness, explained that their mama, Queen of Heaven, had sent them here to gather peaches for the annual extravaganza.

"No worries, Your Highnesses, please rise," I said gently. "Do you happen to know who are on the list of guests invited by your mama, I mean, Her Majesty?"

"The usual, you know, Your Highness," said one of the princesses, "all the kings, queens, buddhas, fairies, from East, West, South, and North, ten continents, five constellations, three islands, palaces big and small, high in the sky and deep in the ocean, the who's who of the whole world."

"Am I invited?" I said casually, although I already knew the answer.

"Mmmm," replied another princess hesitantly. "Don't recall your name ever being mentioned,"

"What?!" I was shocked. "Me, Great Sage Heaven's Equal, should be seated amongst the most distinguished of the guests. Not being invited?!"

"Well, we don't really know for sure."

"All right, why don't you all go home now. I'll find out soon enough myself."

I somersaulted into the cloud and sailed in the direction of Empyrean Pond (*Yaochi*) abode of Queen of Heaven where she will host the annual extravaganza.

On my way, I saw an old man, Barefoot Fairy, hurrying in the same direction. He must be one of the invited guests. An idea came to me, so I landed in front of him.

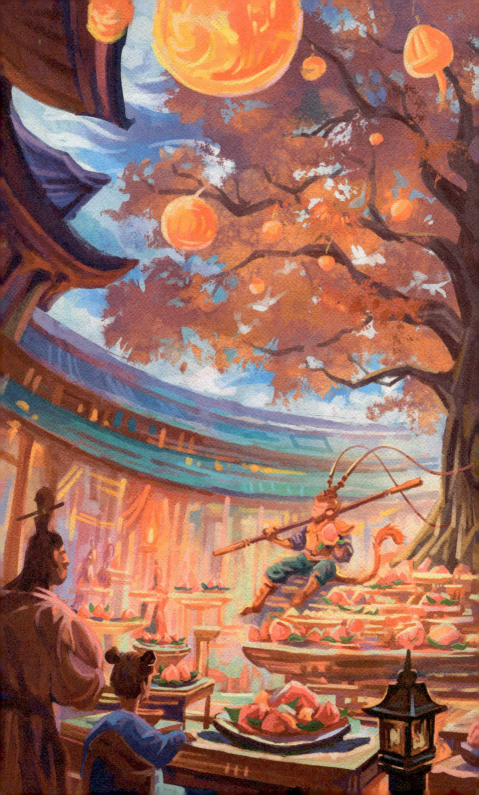

"Jade Emperor has sent me to notify all the guests, a last-minute change of the protocols this year," I said to Barefoot Fairy after we exchanged some silly pleasantries. "Unlike the past years, all guests this year gather in Palace of Illuminati first to socialize and then go to Empyrean Pond for the extravaganza."

"Hosting the same party at two places? That's new. A bit more footwork for me and a giant leap for appetite, hahaha!" Barefoot Fairy tried a lame joke and hurried toward Palace of Illuminati.

Me? You guessed right: with the murmur of a spell, I am now Barefoot Fairy, an honorable guest of the extravaganza, hurrying toward Empyrean Pond.

What a feast for my eyes when I step into this storied place:

Dreamy fragrance, pearl lanterns, jade windows, pheasant themed powder rooms, a thousand emerald flower vases, long gold buffet tables loaded with delicacies of dragon livers, unicorn bone marrows, bear paws, orangutan lips, body parts from rarest of rare things that fly in the sky, walk on earth, and swim underneath water, you name it.

A waft of sweetest aroma drifts into my nostrils. It comes from a long walkway leading to a winery where casks of nectars and wines lined up neatly and fresh ones are being made.

Let me have a taste of that first. I pull out a hair and murmur a spell:

"Change!"

A swoon of sleep-bugs flies to those busy winemakers, and with just one sting on their faces, they are knocked out, yawning, and falling into a slumber.

I grab some delicacies from the gold buffet tables, hasten to the winery, pick up the first cask I see, and drink until I can't drink anymore.

Then, a sliver of lucidity cuts through my foggy mind: Boy,

when all the guests arrive and see the mess I've made here, I'll be cooked. Better return to my mansion and sleep it off.

With buzzing in my head, I stagger my way not home, Mansion of Great Sage Heaven's Equal, but into the palace of Laozi, Father Daoist (*Taishanglaojun*), located in the stratosphere above thirty-three skies.

You must've heard of this truly sagacious old man, author of *The Book of the Dao and Its Virtue* (*Daodejing*). Pretty deep stuff. This is someone you wouldn't want to mess with on any day. I can hear the muffled sound of Laozi giving one of his sermons somewhere deep in the palace. Once in a lifetime opportunity presenting itself to me today!

I go straight to the main theme, *Bagua* Stove.

Okay, okay, just a quick crash course. *Bagua* means Eight-Trigram, each trigram consisting of three lines, each line either "broken" or "unbroken," representing *yin* or *yang*, you know, forming a labyrinth of patterns supposed to foretell one's fortune. Hard for me to explain. How about me showing you an illustration?

There you are. Better? Truth be told, I can never make sense of it and between you and me, I suspect many of those who claim to have read that classic, *The Book of Changes* (*Yijing*), whatever, and really understand it are either faking it for vanity or con artists of sorts.

Okay, I digress and let me get back to the business at hand.

Charcoal fire underneath *Bagua* Stove is still alive and well. I look around and find a jade gourd nearby, open it with trembling fingers, and see a bunch of pearly beans inside. Immortality Beans!

I dump them all in my mouth and gobble them down, without giving them a good chew to see what they taste like.

Heart contended, overcome by drowsiness, I fell into another nap not far from *Bagua* Stove. When I woke up finally and saw what I'd done, cold sweat trickled down my spines:

Boy, I'm really cooked this time. Better get out of here now before anyone sees me!"

With a murmur of spell, I became invisible, found my way to the western gate of Heaven, and rode a cloud back to Earth.

When I landed on top of Flower Fruit Mountain, I shouted triumphantly:

"I'm back!"

All my people rushed out, overjoyed to see their king, king of kings, home again.

When the excitement subsided somewhat and I was back in Water Curtain Cave, my stone palace, Square Head, having grayed somewhat around the temples, ventured to say,

"Your Majesty, if I may, how could you have the heart to leave us for so long?"

"Yeah, for so long!"

"Thought we'd never see Your Majesty again."

Others mumbled something like that in discordant chorus.

"Get hold of yourselves," I said, laughing, "I've been away for only a few days and you're all complaining again?"

"You've been away for a hundred years, Your Majesty," Old Sage said; he looked quite frail and ancient; his eyes though glistened with wisdom as ever before. "Remember one day in Heaven is a year here on earth?"

"Hahaha, I know," said I. "I've indeed had a swell of time in Heaven this time, being Heaven's equal and all. For you guys' ears only: I've just helped myself to a whole bunch of longevity peaches in Queen of Heaven's Empyrean Pond and immortality beans in the palace of Laozi, Father Daoist. I am not sure what Jade Emperor will say when he finds out, so I'm back for a short visit, to wait out the storm, you see what I mean?"

When we finally sat down for the welcome feast, I sipped our home-made wine in a big stone bowl.

"Not good, not good," I couldn't help saying it, shaking my head.

"Your Majesty," Square Head said. "Your tastebuds must have been spoiled by the nectars and wines in Heaven so now you don't want to bother with food and drinks of your own folks?"

This kiddo is as brash as ever, I thought, not a bit wiser although much older.

"I didn't mean to hurt your feelings. I was only telling the truth. Okay, let me go back and get some for you all to taste so you all know what I mean."

I somersaulted into the cloud and rode it directly to Empyrean Pond where all the servants were yet to wake up from their slumber, benefit of my sleep-bugs, grabbed a few casks of heavenly nectars and wines, returned to Water Curtain Cave, all in the wink of an eye, and held my own Longevity Extravaganza. It was nothing short of Heaven on Earth.

One day, when I was relishing whatever was still left of the heavenly nectars and wines with a bunch of kings and warriors, a sentinel came reporting breathlessly:

"Trouble befalling us, Your Majesty. A legion of Heaven Commandos is here to take you into custody!"

"What are you talking about, scaredy-cat," I brushed it off. "I'm enjoying myself with my guests here, don't you see?"

"They've already advanced outside Water Curtain Cave. We can't hold them off anymore!"

What balls! Taking me for some nameless nobody?

I put on my regalia and led my kings and warriors out of Water Curtain Cave to fight this legion of Heaven Commandos.

This time, the heavenly army was led by Navagraha (*Jiuyaoxing*), a star in charge of human life on earth, flanked by Prince Nezha and other fierce warriors.

"You little lowly *bimawen*, stable boy, looking for death?"

Navagraha shouted. "Having the balls to steal Queen of Heaven's longevity peaches, Laozi's immortality beans, and spoil Her Majesty's annual extravaganza! That's trampling Heaven kind of capital crime, punishable by death, you know that?"

"Great Sage Heaven's Equal not being invited to the extravaganza, that's capital injustice in my dictionary!" I said defiantly. "So, I crashed the party and had some fun. What crime is that, eh?"

"You cheeky party crasher!" Navagraha said. "It'll save you and me a lot of trouble if you simply surrender yourself. Otherwise, we'll flatten this molehill you call home and turn this pitiable cave of yours upside down and inside out!"

"Don't talk big, you foul-mouthed rascal," I shouted, enraged. "Here's my answer to the charge!"

I charged toward Navagraha and his warriors, wielding my Gold-Banded Cudgel left and right. It was quite a show of all kinds of imaginable weapons all around me, dragon-shaped knives, cloud piercing spears, tiger-eye whips, long, twisty hooks, lightning bows and arrows, you name it, dust of battle overcasting the sky.

Navagraha, like Nezha before him, proved no match to me and fled into the woods in defeat.

What were they expecting, me, Monkey King, Great Sage Heaven's Equal, surrendering myself with hands tied behind my back?

When I returned triumphantly and landed on Iron Bridge, I was surprised to see my kings and warriors laughing and howling at the same time and asked them why.

"We're laughing to celebrate Your Majesty's victory over Heaven Commandos again and crying 'cause they've taken quite a few of our warriors."

"Oh, that?" said I said, with a wave of my hand. "That

should be expected if you've read Sunzi's Art of War. If you lose three thousands of your own but kill ten thousand enemies, that's still a victory. And a victory is a victory is a victory, right?"

We had a big feast to celebrate the victory and then rested to ready ourselves for tomorrow.

A bigger, more fierce battle afoot?

SIX

My Waterloo

The next morning, as we were repositioning ourselves on Iron Bridge, the legion of Heaven Commandos came out of the woods and charged at us again, the very air quivering with bone-chilling drumbeating and battle cries.

"Where's Great Sage Heaven's Equal?" shouted a tall, princely looking young warrior when they reached our end of the bridge and stopped.

"Here I'm," I said proudly. "Who on earth are you?"

"I'm Mucha, elder brother of Nezha, disciple of Guanyin."

"Guanyin who?"

"You ignoramus of a little monkey, never heard of Guanyin, the kindest of Bodhisattvas?"

"I may have or have not, so what? To what do I owe the pleasure, anyways?"

"Guanyin is one of the most distinguished guests of the annual Longevity Peach Extravaganza in Heaven, a regular, you know. She was there at this year's when Barefoot Fairy, Queen of Heaven, Laozi, and everyone and his brother complained to Jade Emperor how you spoiled everything and what a troublemaker you've been. Goddess of Mercy, out of her boundless kindness, sent me here to see what's going on."

"Oh, I know that Guanyin, Goddess of Mercy! She resides in South Sea, right? If you are her disciple, why don't you stay there and continue your studies?"

"You're indeed as brazen as everyone has said. I'm here to take you in custody. Now surrender yourself to me!"

"No way is the answer from my Gold-Banded Cudgel!"

His big iron club and my magic Cudgel went after each other, at lightning speed, hitting from left, right, top down, bottom up, blocking, darting, dancing, as if we were putting on a show for the world to see. We fought for fifty, sixty rounds with no clear victory for either when I scored a big one on Prince Mucha's right arm, he flinched and fled in defeat too.

I thought I'd taught them all a lesson, so they knew who they were dealing with. End of the story. But no, more was afoot.

The next morning, the legion of Heaven Commandos launched another attack, this time led by another boyish looking warrior, good-looking, almost girlish. Why can't Jade Emperor send some grownups to fight me, men with moustache who have seen real battles? What an insult!

This boy warrior does look different though: eyes glistening, long earlobes touching the shoulders, crown featuring three pheasant feathers, donning a light-yellow robe, bow and arrows hanging on his waist belt, a pair of three-pointed and double-edged knives in hand.

"Boy," I shouted when the boy warrior and Heaven Commandos advanced to where I stood on Iron Bridge. "Who the deuce are you, having the balls to come and challenge me?!"

"You insolent monkey, don't know me, Erlangshen, Second-Born Fairy, nephew of Jade Emperor?! Think you can get away with the big mess you've made in Heaven? In your dreams, stable boy!"

"Oh, you're that bastard son of Jade Emperor's sister and a lowly earthling," I said contemptuously. "I've heard something about it from the grapevine; it turns out to be true? You're nothing but a boy, imperial nephew or not, so go back home to your mama before I crush you to meat pie with this Cudgel of mine!"

"You foul-mouthed monkey!" Erlangshen said, fuming. "You don't really know who you're dealing with! You know who recommended me to Jade Emperor, my uncle? None other than Guanyin, Goddess of Mercy, cause she knows that I'm the only one who can subdue you!"

That Guanyin again. Looks like I'm destined to hear more about her in the days ahead.

"Have a taste of my knives then, stable boy!" shouted Erlangshen in his pubescent voice.

I heard a whistle near my ear, darted in time to avoid being hurt, and lifted my Gold-Banged Cudgel to meet his strangely shaped knives blow for blow. It was a well-matched fight, wielding our weapons at lightning speed, going after each other from every imaginable angle, like a thousand meteors shooting across the sky at the same time, cheered on by deafening drumbeating and battle chants from both sides.

We fought for more than three hundred rounds with no clear victory for either. With a quick shake Erlangshen grew to thirty-thousand feet tall, and then came down at me with his knives like Mount Hua was crashing over my head. With murmur of a spell, I morphed into an exact copy of Erlangshen, tall and massive as Mount Kunlun, and blocked his knives with my Gold-Banded Cudgel. The two Erlangshens fought like Siamese twins, couldn't tear away from each other, and couldn't win either.

In the thick of this dirty fight, I heard my people screaming in fright and turned to see what was going on. They were fleeing.

MY WATERLOO

That was the fatal mistake I'd regret forever: I changed back to my real self and hurried to protect them.

"You've got no place to run or hide," Erlangshen shrilled right on my heels. "Surrender now so I can spare your life!"

Chased by Erlangshen from behind and blocked by Heaven Commandos in front, I put my Gold-Banded Cudgel into my ear, morphed into a sparrow, and flew onto a tree.

"Where's the damned monkey now?" shouted the Commandos, shocked that I'd vanished right before their eyes.

Erlangshen took a quick look around and said, "There, that sparrow's the sneaky monkey!" He morphed into a sparrowhawk and charged toward me. I morphed into a big cormorant and sailed higher into the sky. Erlangshen morphed into a big seabird, coming at me fast. I dived into the water and became a small fish, followed by Erlangshen as a falcon, its fierce eyes searching; the moment I surfaced to see if the coast was clear, the falcon flit over and tried to snatch me. I changed into a water snake and crept into the grass. Just when I thought I was safe this time, I saw a red-crested crane coming down fast.

This day will end differently, I thought vaguely, but I'm not a rolling over and crying uncle sort.

I tumbled downhill and changed into a temple, my mouth, still gasping for air, wide open as its entrance, my tail, nowhere to hide, its flagpole in the back.

Erlangshen came downhill too and saw this temple.

"This must be that monkey, trying to lure me in and bite and chew me for lunch? No way! Let me punch the windows, kick the front doors, and see what happens."

Front doors are my teeth, windows my eyes, can't let him do that!

I somersaulted into the cloud and disappeared.

Erlangshen somersaulted into the cloud too and searched for me. "Where's the damned monkey now?"

One of his Commandos, manning a powerful Demon-Detecting Mirror I'd heard of, turned it every which way, Heaven, Earth, you name it, and exclaimed:

"Hurry, Your Highness, that damned monkey is now going to your temple!"

Yes, that Erlangshen at the door of his temple is me. Where else can I go?

It was the first time in my life I was in a desperate run, sort of.

Inside the temple, many pilgrims were burning incense and asking for blessings. As abbot of the place, I patiently listened to reports, turned the pages of record books, and thanked patrons for their generous donations.

"Strange," I heard one young monk marveling. "Our kind master has just returned and is checking things inside. How come here comes our master again?"

"What master?!" I heard Erlanshen yelling. "It must be an imposter!"

He marched to where I was to confront me, so I changed back to my real self and laughed: "This temple is mine now, so get out!"

An infuriated Erlangshen charged at me with his three-pointed, double-edged knives, which I blocked with my Gold-Banded Cudgel. Thus began another round of fight between me and this bastard imperial nephew, from inside the temple to outside, all the way to Flower Fruit Mountain. This time, for the first time ever, I was not fighting to win, but to get away so I could be with my folks. Somehow, I couldn't.

I am besieged watertight, a blinding glare shines in my eyes—must be that damned Demon-Detecting Mirror, eighteen sky nets fall on me and thirty-six earth meshes catch me from ground up, tightening. I am still trying to break out, wielding my Cudgel, when some sharp, heavy metal hits my temple.

Fuck!

This Erlangshen, bastard nephew of Jade Emperor, is being helped not only by that damned Demon-Detecting Mirror, but also by another secret weapon I've never heard of. It is an unfair fight, but a win is a win is a win, no matter how it is won, didn't I say this before? Didn't I get myself into this massive mess myself?

As I think such vague thoughts, I trip, fall, and recoil when Erlangshen grabs my right leg and takes a big bite.

I kick and scream and curse as they bind me up hand and feet.

I black out.

SEVEN
Puddle of Piss

Upon coming to, after an eternity, I found myself tied to a pole on an execution scaffold.

Samson like executioners took turns trying to kill me with big iron knives, spears, swords, but I took them all like nothing was happening to me, and laughed contemptuously, to the shock and fury of the executioners and mobs of spectators; they all cried for blood.

"Let's burn the bastard then!" shouted one executioner in a scratchy voice.

They put a mountain of dry bushes and tree branches underneath me and lit it up. Seething fire roared underneath me like I'm being grilled alive and I could use a bucket of ice water to cool me off. Otherwise, I felt fine.

"Let's strike the bastard with thunder and lightning, then!" shouted another executioner hoarsely.

Earsplitting thunders and dazzling lightning hit me left and right. The mobs of spectators, terrified, covered their eyes and ears. Me? It was like having a good full-body massage to loosen my nerves and bones at the end of a long hardworking day, or battle.

It was then that I thought of my first teacher, Master Bohdi, who had told me that I would meet three deadly calamities, thunder, fire, wind, each in five hundred years and taught me how to avert them. Although his prophecy seemed a teeny-weensy off, 'cause these calamities were befalling me now not exactly in that neat order without five hundred years in between, my heart swelled with gratitude. I wish I had listened to Master Bohdi and been a worthier disciple. There is no what if in life, only what to do now, why, and how.

They untied me from the execution pole and dragged me to the palace of Laozi, a familiar place of sorts. What are they up to now? By now they should know I've eaten more than my share of Queen of Heaven's longevity peaches, drunk casks of Her Majesty's nectars and wines, and gulped down quite a few of Father Daoist's immortality beans, more than many of the distinguished guests could have dreamed of, put together. I am death free!

At the sight of that giant *Bagua* Stove, heated by red hot charcoal underneath, I knew what they were going to do to me.

A roasted pig, especially when it is done right, golden brown, crispy outside and mouthwateringly tender underneath, is a must-have for just about any party, but a roasted monkey, a small, skinny monkey?

Laozi, long-haired, long beard hanging on his chest, came up to me with a dry smile around his lips, and untied the ropes with his bony hands.

"Hahaha, you smarty-pants of a monkey," Father Daoist said, winking. "Heard of the Law of Conservation of Mass? So, those precious immortality beans you've stolen from me may have been transmuted into different forms in your body, but they have not disappeared, right? Dust to dust, ashes to ashes, as they say, hahaha!"

A few big, thick-armed monks grabbed my arms and legs

and dumped me inside that *Bagua* Stove,

Remember the Eight-Trigram picture I showed you earlier? Each trigram has a name, sky (*qian*), earth (*kun*), quake (*zhen*), wind (*xun*), field (*kan*), fire (*li*), mountain (*gen*), pond (*dui*)?

You guessed right: I quickly found the wind *xun* corner of the *Bagua* Stove and stayed put there. I am being cooled off by wind and no fire can hurt me, but smoke can, endless puffs of thick smoke, so I have to rub my eyes all the time, 'cause they hurt so badly. That's how I earned me the fame of being "Fire Gold Eyes" (*Huoyanjinjing*). From that day on, I could see more and farther than anyone, as good as that damned Demon-Detecting Mirror they used to capture me. More on this soon.

A watched pot never boils, as they say. It's a thousand times worse if you're being boiled inside that pot. They kept me in this Bagua Stove for seven times seven forty-nine days! When the heavy lid above me was finally lifted, I jumped out, knocked off the *Bagua* Stove, and kicked the charcoal guys on the shins; they all crumbled on the ground and howled in pain.

Poor Laozi, Father Daoist, jumped on me from behind; with one slight shake of my body I sent him crashing to the ground. I had to go easy on him though on account of his old age.

I pulled out my Gold-Banded Cudgel and brushed aside anyone, warrior, fairy, no matter, who dared to stand in my way. Mad as hell, I fought my way to Palace of Illuminati and was stopped by a fierce looking commander of Heaven Guards.

"You egomaniac!" the commander shouted. "Where do you think you are going? Have you eaten leopard's gallbladders?!"

Yes, perhaps. And it'll be beneath me to argue with such lowly warriors.

I kept wielding my Cudgel and fighting my way in as warriors of thunder, lightning, wind, all came to stop me. Countless more piled on, tightening the nets they cast on me. I changed to a three-headed, six-armed me, fighting with three Gold-Banded Cudgels. This was the dirtiest of battles I had ever had to fight; they couldn't get to me, but I couldn't break out either.

"Stop the fight!" I heard a deep voice calling, an out-of-the world voice, so close yet so far away.

We, me and all the warriors of Heaven, stopped, as if hypnotized.

"Who on earth are you, daring to stop me?" I demanded to know, having barely recovered from the shock.

"I am Rulai," replied the deep voice, "Father Buddha, from West Land. I wouldn't expect you of all earthlings to have heard of me. All you need to know is Jade Emperor has asked me to come and subdue you because of the disturbances you've made in Heaven, defying all the rules, rituals, and rites of passage."

Rulai now appeared in front of me, tall, regal, wide shoulders, long arms, huge palms, beaming with kindness, dazzling in all his glory.

I was stunned, not knowing what to say, tongue-tied for the first time.

"Tell me your story then," Rulai said, kindly. "Who exactly are you and what are you up to?"

I quickly recovered myself.

I am not one easily fooled by appearance, though. He may look and sound teeny-weensy kinder than all I've had the pleasure to deal with, yet he is here to subdue me on behalf of Jade Emperor, to keep the status quo, because whatever is right, right? The most powerful in Heaven and on Earth breathe through the same nose and wear the same pants conspiring to rule us all?

I gave Rulai a thumbnail version of my story: my birth as a stone monkey, Flower Fruit Mountain, Water Curtain Cave, pilgrimages I've made to learn the ways of the world, all the knowledge I've learned about life, and why I am Heaven's Equal, second to none, and so on.

"What mandate, manifest destiny does Jade Emperor have to sit in his throne forever? Hereditary entitlement? If I'm just as powerful, if not more, he should vacate the throne for me! Only the best, the bravest, deserves it. Fair is fair is fair."

"You ignominious little monkey," Rulai said contemptuously. "Having studied for barely a few days and thinking you now know more than enough to replace Jade Emperor in Heaven's throne? He began the studies when still a child, having stood one thousand seven hundred and fifty tests, each test lasting one hundred twenty-nine thousand six hundred years! Go figure, if you know enough arithmetic to do so, how old is he now, how long has he sat in that seat of supreme power? You're nothing but a newborn baby, daring to set your sight on Heaven's throne? What a shame. What a shame."

What a poor apology on behalf of Jade Emperor, but I don't have a rejoinder yet.

"My advice for you," Rulai continued. "Forget about all that nonsense of yours, give up the fight, surrender, and begin all over again. Otherwise, you'll pay a dear, really dear price."

"Okay," I finally found my tongue again. "He might be a few years older than I am and have studied a teeny-weensy longer, but to have occupied the throne for so long? Have you heard this saying, it goes like this: Emperor's throne revolves like a wheel and who knows next year it will be my turn?"

Rulai knit his eyebrows.

"I'll end the fight here and now," I offered, "if he graciously yields the throne, and Palace of Illuminati; otherwise, there will never be peace in Heaven again."

"What can you do," asked Rulai, his piercing eyes looking me upon and down, "other than changing into different forms, daring to issue such crazy ultimatum?"

Here's the opportunity I've been dying for.

"All right, you want to know my power? Where should I begin to count? I can change into seventy-two forms! I can stand ten thousand tests yet do not become one day older. With one somersault into the cloud, I can travel for one hundred and eight thousand li! Isn't that proof enough that I deserve the throne as much as anyone?"

"Mmm," said Rulai pleasantly. "Let's have a bet then. If you can jump out of my right palm with a somersault, you win and can have the throne and Palace of Illuminati, no question asked, and I'll invite Jade Emperor to go and live with me in West Land."

That's easy! I thought, grinning. Rulai, grandaddy of all buddhas in the world, seems such a fool! I, Monkey King, can go one hundred and eight thousand *li* with a single somersault. That palm of his is big, but not bigger than a banana tree or lotus leaf, so me jumping out of it is nothing!

"If you fail to jump out of my right palm, however," Rulai added, like an afterthought, "you'll be sent to the bottom of Netherland, Hell, to study there and be tested for a few more rounds. Only after that, perhaps, you can reemerge, and we can talk again."

"You promise, Father Buddha?" I asked, just to make sure. "You're fully authorized to honor this bet, right?"

"Absolutely!" Rulai said, beaming, and opened his right palm.

Beside myself in excitement, I put my Gold-Banded Cudgel into my ear, jumped onto Rulai's palm, murmured a spell, lifted off with a somersault, and sailed toward horizons at lightning speed, enjoying the vistas along the way.

Something far away, where Earth and Sky meet, catches my eye:

A tall mountain with five peaks.

Can just call it Five-Fingered Mountain, if you will.

That must be the edge of the world. I've gone so far away from Rulai's right palm, a thousand times than needed. Jade Emperor's throne and Palace of Illuminati are mine for sure.

In the blink of an eye, I land at foot of the tall mountain.

Just to be on the safe side, I should leave some mark here as proof that I have indeed been here, I thought. So, I pull out a hair, blow some magic breath into it, and murmur,

"Change!"

A huge writing brush appears in my hand. I put these words proudly on the middle one of the five peaks:

These Words Herewith Bear Witness:

Great Sage Heaven's Equal Has Been Here

Not the best penmanship, I'd be the first to admit, the strokes are a teeny-weensy childish, but confident, evidential enough in any court of law.

Then I thought it'd be a good idea to take a pee here, to put some icing on the cake, if you will. As it happens, bladder pressure has been mounting in me and oh, I don't need to tell you how good it feels to open the valve and let it all go.

It is a teeny-weensy lighter me that somersaults back to where I started:

Rulai's right palm.

"I'm back," I announced triumphantly. "Time for you to deliver the promise."

"You stinky leaky bladder of a monkey!" Rulai roared with laughter. "You've never left my palm!"

"How can you say that?" I was taken aback. "I've gone as far as the edge of the world and even seen a tall mountain there, with five peaks."

Rulai stared at me mirthfully, waiting for me to continue.

"I've even put a mark on the mountain, just in case. You want to come with me and see for yourself there?"

"Don't bother. Just bend your head and tell me what you see!"

Imagine how shocked I was when I saw these very words on his middle finger:

These Words Herewith Bear Witness:
Great Sage Heaven's Equal Has Been Here

Then I saw a puddle of stinky piss at foot of his big thumb.

I was reddening in both shame and anger.

How come?! Never heard and seen anything like it my entire life! I wrote those very words onto a cloud-kissing peak of that mountain, and it turns out to be his middle finger? I pissed at the foot of another peak, just to make it an ironclad case, and that peak is his thumb? So, this guy, Rulai, is a thousand times more powerful and knows a thousand times more? How come?! Shouldn't I go back and double check, so nobody pulls a fast one on me?

I gave my body a quick shake and was ready to jump and somersault into the cloud again when I felt a crushing, stupefying blow.

My body, my being, my entire world, is smashed onto the ground.

On my back now sits something humongous, oppressive, and suffocating as hell.

I struggle to breathe, stretch my neck out as far as I can, and look around frantically.

That damned five-peaked mountain, magnificent in all its sickening glory, now sits snugly on my back, or rather, I'm vised, ironclad, underneath it.

What good does it do me with all this knowledge bursting in me, all the transfigurations I've mastered, oh, yes, that Gold-Banded Cudgel still in my ear, if I'm buried under this monstrosity, when I cannot even move a toe or lift a finger, when all I can do is to breathe, a stone monkey, literally, and nothing more?

This is the beginning of the end for me. Damn!

I hear stomach-churning chants of "Hallelujah!" "Glory to God!" "Bless the Lord" resounding everywhere between Heaven and Earth.

I see Rulai, without another word, turn his back on me, and sail to Palace of Illuminati.

He is wined and dined by Jade Emperor himself, with who's who in Heaven attending, Queen of Heaven, Laozi, you name it. Remember that Barefoot Fairy? He kowtows to Jade Emperor a thousand times and presents Rulai with two peaches, I don't know what kind, and a few fresh nuts to show his gratitude.

A grant feast, no, an extravaganza, of dragon livers, pheasant bone marrows, nectars, and wines, oh yes, longevity peaches and immortality beans, the prettiest of girls singing and dancing long sleeve dance, fan dance, belly dance, what have you.

My eyes, I'm Fire Gold Eyes, remember? burn with anger. What injustice! They did this to me, imprisoning me in this hell of a jammed lock, just so they can enjoy such extravaganzas themselves, not caring a fart about earthlings like me, not tolerating even an occasional party crashing?

I see Jade Emperor awarding grand titles and handsome prizes to all who have lifted a finger in putting me, this audacious party crasher, troublemaker, self-styled Great Sage Heaven's Equal, in my place. But what is my place, anyways? Underneath this damned mountain?

"Your Majesty, my noblest, boundlessly merciful friend," Jade Emperor, a tall, diamond-studded wineglass in hand, addresses Rulai, guest of honor seated next to him. "We'd never have been able to restore law and order, peace and prosperity here in Heaven if you had not most graciously come and helped us."

He pauses and looks around, a seasoned public speaker for sure.

A sea of heads nods gratefully.

He turns to Rulai again.

"So, I'm going to impose on you again, Your Majesty, my noblest, boundlessly merciful friend."

Rulai beams, not knowing what to expect, perhaps.

"Can Your Majesty do me the honor of giving today's celebration a proper name so it can go into our annals, so we can memorialize and mark this day in the future?"

"Of course, Your Majesty," Rulai says, looking much relieved. "How about Heaven Restoration Day?"

"Fantastic! Let's all drink to Heaven Restoration Day!" Jade Emperor raises his diamond-studded glass and dumps whatever nectar, wine in it into his mouth.

"Glory to God!"

"Bottoms up!"

"Bless the Lord!"

"Every last drop!

Disgusting cheers resound from Palace of Illuminati to the five-peaked mountain.

Under normal circumstances I'd be salivating for all the nectars, wines, longevity peaches and immortality beans, what have you, 'cause I know exactly what they taste like; I know what they taste like not because Jade Emperor has been a teeny-weensy charitable to me, but because I've had the guts to force the question, and squeeze the universe a few times. We all want the same, just that some, like those reveling at the extravaganza in Heaven now, are created more equal than others is all. That really disgusts me, so the sight of this extravaganza, all that fancy stuff being relished by all at the party, is vulgar in my eyes and leaves a revolting taste in my mouth.

Sour grapes? Maybe, but I've been there and done that. No

big deal—now.

I stretch my neck a teeny-weensy further out to see what happens next.

Rulai and his encourage bag all the gifts, thank Jade Emperor again, and get ready to take their leave.

"That monkey is sticking out his head again!" screams a Heaven Guard.

"Don't worry," says Rulai. He takes out a scroll from his sleeve, on which are written these words:

唵 ōng 嘛 mā 呢 nī 叭 bēi 咪 mēi 吽 hòng

All nonsense words I cannot make any sense of at all.

One of Rulai's aids takes the scroll, sails to where I am, and sticks it onto a big square rock on my back.

"Father Buddha says you should keep an eye on that monkey," I hear this aid saying to some fairy on the mountain. "Feed him iron beans when he is hungry, give him melted copper to drink when he is thirsty. When he's reflected and repented enough, someone will come and save him."

Someone will come and save me?

Who?

When?

How long do I have to wait?

EIGHT
Why Me?

I have been wondering about this ever since I embarked on the journey.

It all happened like a dream that would keep replaying in my mind's eye.

I am giving one of my sermons in front of thousands of pilgrims, regulars, walk-ins, what have you. I am talking about prohibitions of the five offenses, killing your father, killing your mother, shedding the blood of a buddha, spreading heresies, and so on, and the four noble truths about suffering being an innate condition of human existence, arising from insatiable desire, the hope of cessation of suffering by letting go of desire, and so on, you may have heard some of these being mentioned here and there, I assume, when I see someone from amongst the multitudes down there coming up to my podium.

A monk, barefooted, wrapped in rags, head and face covered by scabies rash.

"Master, what you are teaching is Hinayana (*Xiaochengfojiao*), the smaller and inferior vehicle of Buddhism. Do you know how to preach Mahāyāna (*Dachengfojiao*), the greater and superior vehicle of Buddhism?"

Being thus questioned in front of everyone is a bit off-putting, but I am a Buddhist monk and know how to control my feelings. I bow slightly and answer the question put to me.

"Hinayana is all I've learned from my masters. I've heard of Mahāyāna, but don't really know the difference, let alone preach it."

"This Hinayana you're preaching cannot lead you to true salvation, nirvana," explains the scabies-headed monk, or rather, lectures, like he has taken over my podium. "It offers only alleviation for your worldly existence and nothing more. It is also too narrow, focusing only on your own personal perfection, enlightenment, and salvation."

If we each person, every one of us, achieve perfection, enlightenment, and salvation, doesn't that mean we all...?

"Mahāyāna, on the other hand, is a much greater and superior vehicle of Buddhism. Studying Tripitaka, Triple Basket, ancient collections of Buddhist sacred scriptures, can lead not only you, but also your fellow beings, the masses, the multitudes, to journey from the delusional shore, where there is so much suffering, to the enlightenment shore, to salvation, to nirvana, that freest, truly blessed, and blissful state of being."

This is really preaching to the choir! Isn't this why I have studied Buddhism all my life and become a Buddhist monk in the first place? Not just to save myself from suffering, which I know so well, but also to save my fellow beings from greed and such insatiable desires that cause so much suffering.

My life, from birth, is a story of humans led astray by insatiable desire.

Where should I begin? Begin from the beginning?

Chen Guangrui, a young man from a small village, took the imperial examination in response to Emperor Xuanzong's call to select the best and brightest to serve the Tang Dynasty,

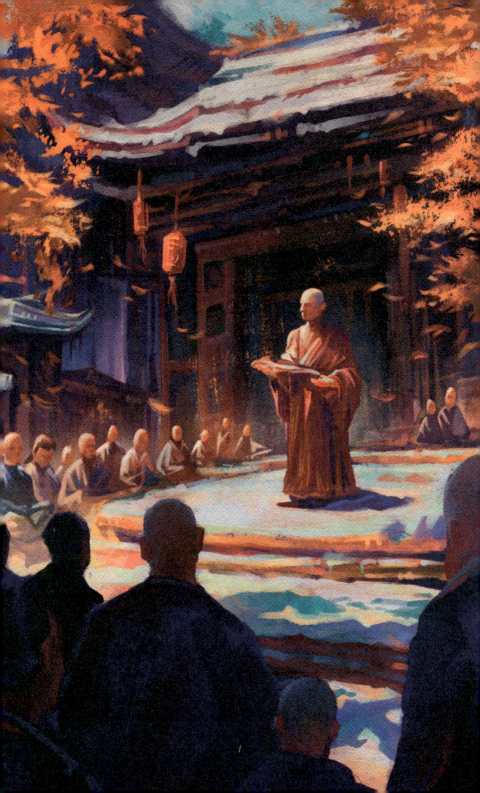

received the highest score *zhuangyuan*, optimus, and was appointed governor of Jiangzhou.

A three-day celebratory parade followed. When Wen Jiao, daughter of a grand chancellor, saw from the window of her maiden chamber the young *zhuangyuan* atop a beautiful horse, in full regalia, handsome, full of promise, she tossed her silk flower ball (*Xiuqiu*), and it hit Chen's black gauze cap (*Wushamao*). That's how my father and mother met and got married. You can say that's love at first sight.

After a grand wedding, the newly-weds bid farewell to my *nainai* (Paternal grandma), and my *waigong waipo* (Maternal grandparents), and got on their way to Jiangzhou to assume the office of governorship there.

While crossing a river, the two ferrymen, a Liu Hong and a Li Biao, tempted by the beauty of the young bride, murdered the groom and his personal aids under the cover of night, pushed their bodies into the river, and then forced the bride, pregnant at the time, to go along with Liu who would travel to Jiangzhou impersonating the newly appointed governor.

I didn't know all this until many years later, when I was about eighteen years old, a young monk at a monastery. I only knew that I was an orphan adopted by the kind abbot who had been like a father to me.

One day, I was bantering with a few fellow young monks at the monastery about Buddhist scriptures and somehow, they were put off by what I was saying, perhaps my tone.

"You little smarty pants," one of them said. "So arrogant, like you're somebody! You don't even know who your parents are and what your family name is!"

I was shocked and went, sobbing, to ask the venerable abbot: "Who am I?"

"If you really want to know who your parents are, here's something you should see," the abbot said kindly. He took out a faded cloth from the bottom of a wooden box and showed it to me.

On this cloth were words written in blood.

"One morning about eighteen years ago," the abbot said, "when I was deep in meditation, I was startled by a baby's cry. So, I followed it and found a baby boy on a piece of wood drifting to our monastery; the baby was wrapped in this piece of cloth with the names of his parents and an account of what had happened to them. I took pity on the baby, took him in, named him Xuanzang, meaning erudite and strong, and taught him all I knew about Buddhism."

I'm Xuanzang, that poor baby boy.

Tears gushed up in my eyes.

"If you really want to find your parents, you should go to Jiangzhou with this blood shirt as proof."

You can imagine how we, my mother and I, cried when I found her in the grand governor's residence of Jiangzhou. I removed my shoes to show her my left foot missing the little toe. I showed her the cloth with words she had written by biting her own fingers before putting her baby son on that piece of wood, out of despair, and hope.

Then, I went in search of my father's mother *nainai*, and found her living in a broken kiln; she couldn't pay for the place my father had rented for her so she could recover from illness and rejoin him in Jiangzhou. *Nainai* was so overjoyed upon seeing me and for a moment thought her son had finally come to get her. "You look and sound just like him! An exact copy. Where're your father and mother now?" It was the first time that *nainai* knew what had happened to her son and daughter-in-law.

The next stop I made was at the residence of the grand chancellor, my mother's parents. The grand chancellor, now white-haired, burst into tears upon reading the letter their long-lost daughter had written for me to give to them. He petitioned Emperor Xuanzong right away so the two murderers would be brought to justice. The very next day, the residence of the governor of Jiangzhou was surrounded by Imperial Commandos and Liu Hong, the imposter governor, was arrested. His accomplice, Li Biao, was apprehended, too. They both confessed to the crimes they had committed.

Imagine the tearful reunion of my mother and her parents. My mother begged for forgiveness for having stayed with Liu for so many years; she did so to save the baby she was carrying inside her with the hope that one day she would see him again and have revenge for her husband's death. What torture, excruciating pain, like daggers stabbing at her heart every day for so many years, for my mother to be living with that murderer of her husband, sharing the bed with the man who was so repulsive in every possible way. It breaks my heart to just think of it.

For their heinous crimes, Li and Liu were each flogged a hundred times first; then, Li, the accomplice, was given the death by a thousand cuts on the public square; Liu, the imposter governor, was taken to the riverside, his heart and liver were cut out (I had to cover my eyes and tried my best to hold back sickening convulsions in my belly ready to erupt and throw out the little food I had eaten that morning; but revenge is revenge is revenge and we were all so happy justice was finally served) and tossed into the muddy currents as atonement for the murder.

When this was finally over and we all cried again, we saw a corps drifting toward us from afar. When it got closer, my mother gave out a heart-piercing cry: "That's my husband!"

When we got the corps ashore, it sat up, looked at everyone, a bit perplexed, and said: "Why are you all crying here?"

Between tearful sobs, my mother told him what had happened.

"Now I remember," said Chen Guangrui, my father, looking barely a few years older than I, color beginning to return to his cheeks, "it's all coming back now: that violent push from behind on that boat eighteen years ago, how I choked and drowned to the bottom of the river, and, and how I was saved by a dragon king because I had once saved him. Mother, still remember that golden carp I bought from the market to cook some soup for your recovery? I took pity on the fish because it was still alive, so I released it back into the river? That golden carp turned out to be a dragon king. Isn't that amazing? He's kept my body and soul in a safe place in his palace. Never did I ever dream that one day I would see you all alive again!"

It was a perfect family reunion, so much joy after so much bitter suffering: father and mother, husband and wife, grandparents, sons, and grandson.

Remember I was interrupted during a sermon by a scabies-headed monk? That monk turned out to be none other than Guanyin, Goddess of Mercy herself!

Guanyin came to East Land on a mission from Rulai, Father Buddha.

After subduing a rebellious monkey who had wreaked havoc in Heaven, Rulai thought that East Land, our great Tang Dynasty, is in dire need of true scriptures of Buddhism, Tripitaka, because it is plagued by greed, corruption, sensual indulgences, murder, and is a sea of bitter misery. Tripitaka, covering truths and teachings about Heaven, Earth, and Netherland, has thirty-five books, fifteen thousand one hundred and forty-four volumes.

Guanyin's mission was to find someone in East Land to go on a pilgrimage to West Land, where Rulai resides, and obtain those true scriptures.

It was around this time that Emperor Xuanzong had a few ominous dreams.

In one dream, Xuanzong is taking a leisurely stroll in a moon-lit garden outside the imperial palace when someone kneels in front of him:

"Save me, Your Majesty! Save me!"

Xuanzong is startled and does not know what to make of it.

"I'm a dragon king taking the form of a human and I am scheduled to be executed by a minister serving Your Majesty, Wei Zheng. Please save me!"

Xuanzong's heart is moved by the plea. "I'll see to it that your life will be spared."

The next morning, Xuanzong told his dream to his ministers and courtiers and was surprised to see that Wei Zheng was not in court. When the minister was called to court, Xuanzong played a chess game with him. Somehow the minister dozed off during the chess game and upon waking up, he prostrated and begged Xuanzong for mercy.

"What crimes have you committed, begging for mercy?"

"I've had the dragon king executed in my dream while dozing off."

"How could that have happened?" Xuanzong was shocked. "You have been playing chess with me the whole time?"

"I may have been playing chess with you physically, Your Majesty, but my soul wandered off to the place where the dragon king was tied to an execution pole by Heaven Commandos. I pronounced the death sentence from Heaven and had the dragon king beheaded despite his tearful begging for mercy."

Emperor Xuanzong was saddened by what had happened, his mind troubled by pictures of the dragon king begging for mercy and his bloody head rolling from the executioner's big knife.

Midnight that same day, Xuanzong had another dream.

In this dream he hears the dragon king, his bloody head in

hand, howling heartrendingly outside the imperial palace gate:

"Your Majesty promised that you'd save me, how come you have me executed? Let's go to King Yama and see what he has to say about this breach of promise!"

The dead, headless dragon king grabs Xuanzong's arms and tries to drag him down to Netherland.

As the dragon king and a terrified Xuanzong wrestle, Guanyin, Goddess of Mercy, already in the capital of Tang Dynasty at the time on a mission from Rulai, comes to the emperor's rescue. Unplacated by comforting words from Guanyin, the dragon king goes on to Netherland and lodges a complaint against Xuanzong there.

When he woke up from this ominous dream, soaked in cold sweat, Emperor Xuanzong screamed: "Ghosts! Ghosts!"

The Queen and all the ministers and courtiers were so worried. They had the imperial doctor prescribe medications upon medications, but nothing helped and within seven days, Emperor Xuanzong died.

As the long procession of mourners bowed and bid tearful farewell to their deceased emperor lying in state in the imperial palace, the soul of Xuanzong already found its way into Netherland.

King Yama invites Xuanzong to sit next to him as an honored guest, an emperor from sun-lit Earth.

"I'm a sinner, Your Majesty, having committed a crime against ways of Heaven, so I am not worthy of that chair."

"I've indeed received a complaint against you," says King Yama. "I'd like to hear your side of the story though."

"In a dream of mine," begins Xuanzong, a bit perplexed, "I did promise to save the dragon king, but Wei Zheng, a minister of mine, had him beheaded in his dream. That was beyond my control. Besides, that dragon king did commit a capital offence in Heaven, so it was justice served."

"I understand, Your Majesty, that's why I've sent him to the purgatory to prepare himself for reincarnation." King Yama pauses and then continues:

"Now that I have you here, perhaps we should take a look at the Book of Life and Death to see how much life you still have on the sun-lit Earth."

It takes King Yama's bookkeepers a bit of time to find the right volume of Book of Life and Death and then the right page. On it are written these words:

Emperor Xuanzong Scheduled to Die Upon Thirteenth Anniversary of Ascending to Throne

"How many years have you been on the throne, Your Majesty?" asks King Yama.

"This is exactly my thirteenth year," answers Xuanzong.

"Now I know why you're here," says King Yama. He reaches for a writing brush, replaces *een* with a *y*, so thirteen becomes thirty.

Emperor Xuanzong bows in boundless gratitude to King Yama and takes leave of Netherland a much happier man.

On his way back to the sun-lit world, he passes a tall mountain of monstrous rocks enveloped in a thick pall of dark haze, heartrending cries of misery everywhere.

"What's this place?" Xuanzong asks the Netherland official escorting him. "It sounds so awful!"

"Here are the eighteen levels of Hell," the official says. "At each level a different kind of punishment is being dealt out to the wretched souls you hear howling so miserably."

"Eighteen levels of Hell? What are they? What kind of punishments?"

"Well, where should I start? There are levels of punishment by having them grilled on firepits, having their tendons, teeth, intestines, tongues, what have you, yanked out, frying them in hot oil, forcing them to walk on the 'grass' of sharp knives, having them pulled by horses in all directions, whipping them until their skins crack and flesh... Should I go on?"

Xuanzong cringes and shakes his head.

"It's called karma," the Netherland official continues. "Virtue rewarded and vice punished. These wretched souls are suffering because of what they've done in the sun-lit world, telling lies, murdering innocents, stealing, robbing, having adultery, being unfilial to parents—"

"Justice, of course," murmurs Xuanzong. "But such horrific punishments they have to bear."

After crossing a river, they pass through a city filled with ghosts, some headless, some without arms or legs, many having no eyeballs, noses, or ears. They all come rushing toward Xuanzong, wailing:

"Give back my life! Give back my life!"

Emperor Xuanzong is taken aback.

"Why do they blame me for their deaths and suffering?"

"They were all your subjects," his escort says. "They all suffered wrongs while alive, their lives taken away from them wrongfully, murdered or wrongfully executed. These are homeless, hungry ghosts because they do not have the money to pay for their passage to the shore of salvation. Your Majesty can help them in this regard."

Xuanzong nods solemnly.

A bit further on their way is another city, basking in a glorious halo, the very air buzzing with quiet, joyous chants.

"What's this now?" asks Xuanzong.

"Six lanes of reincarnation. All those who've been kind, merciful, loyal, filial and pious, fair and just, are readying themselves for being born again, for another round of happy, healthy, and prosperous life."

Xuanzong nods again solemnly.

"Where do we go next?" Xuanzong wonders when he feels

a push from behind and falls into turbulent waters.

He re-emerged in the glorious sun-lit world, riding a grand horse. When he charged into the imperial palace, the Queen and all the ministers and courtiers were busy preparing for the ascension of the young prince to the throne. They were all terrified at the sight.

"It's our emperor, His Majesty!" someone shouted. "He's resurrected, returned from death!"

Imagine how overjoyed were the Queen and the entire court. They called in the imperial doctor right away. Many a nourishment concoction was prescribed to help Emperor Xuanzong recover his health.

The next day, barely able to sit up on the throne, Emperor Xuanzong launched an investigation of all felony cases to see if anyone had been wrongfully committed.

He also issued a general amnesty to pardon all criminals in the world. Even those who had committed capital crimes and scheduled to be executed were allowed to go home and say final goodbye to their elderly parents and make arrangements for their young children.

Then, Emperor Xuanzong arranged to have hundreds of ounces of gold and silver paid on behalf of those wretched souls in Netherland so they could hope to be born again for a better life.

Emperor Xuanzong went even further: He put out a public notice to recruit the best Buddhist monk to lead a grand Buddhist revitalization project and a ceremony for the lonely souls in Netherland.

This decree caused a spirited debate among his ministers and courtiers. One of them, a rather erudite official, Fu Yi, argued vehemently against it:

"This religion from West Land does not follow our ways defining the relations between king and minister, father and son, and husband and wife. It is a sophistry, loaded with mysticisms, its scriptures written in Sanskrit, a strange language no one understands. Besides, life and death is all part of Nature, why misleading and fooling the masses with the phantom, fantastical idea of reincarnations? Our civilization, from time immemorial, has been thriving without the invasion of this foreign religion, why should we do it now?"

Xiao Yu, the prime minister, however, argued in favor of the emperor's decree:

"Buddhism was introduced a long time ago and has been thriving during many dynasties. It promotes kindness and mercy, restrains evil, and serves the best interest of our great Tang Dynasty. There is no reason why we should ban Buddhism now. Defying the saintly and sagacious Rulai is the same as defying our glorious Emperor Xuanzong His Majesty, and anyone who dares to do so should be punished accordingly!"

"The foundation of our rituals and laws," Fu Yi retorted, "is to take care of the parents and serve the Emperor. Buddhist monks, however, abandon their family in pursuit of their personal faith. That is pursuing personal interest in defiance of the Emperor, Son of Heaven, and adopting a foreign faith at the cost of blood kinship. It is a faith for those who disrespect their father. Such unfilial people should have no place in the world."

"Well, Hell is designed for those who are unfilial," said another minister in support of Fu Yi.

"Buddhism is about cleansing people of worldly desires," said Xiao Yu, the prime minister, heartfeltly, "and promoting kindness and mercy. The three great religions, Confucianism, Daoism, and Buddhism, have coexisted harmoniously since Emperor Wu of Northern Zhou, from time immemorial, have been given highest veneration. Therefore, to ban and abandon Buddhism now would ill-serve out great Tang Dynasty."

At that, Emperor Xuanzong stopped the debates and issued another decree:

Anyone Daring to Speak Ill of Buddhism
Will Have His Arms Cut Off

Of course, I did not know all this, including the ominous dreams Emperor Xuanzong had and the impassioned debates about the future of Buddhism in our great Tang until I was chosen, on account of me being the best and the brightest, the most promising of all Buddhist monks, to preside over the service for the lost souls and lead the dynasty-wide Buddhist revitalization project. Under my supervision, we built and rebuilt many Buddhist monasteries to educate a new generation of monks, thousands of them. We also delivered countless sermons on Buddhist scriptures for pilgrims and laypeople far and near.

It was during one of the sermons I gave, as I alluded to earlier, that I was challenged by a shabbily dressed monk about the kind of Buddhist scriptures I was preaching.

Around noon the next day, I was called to the court of Emperor Xuanzong:

I have been chosen to travel to West Land, where Rulai resides, to obtain the scriptures of Mahāyāna so the great masses of our great Tang Dynasty can learn and journey from the shore of greed, desire, and misery to the shore of nirvana.

NINE
Why Not Me?

Emperor Xuanzong knew my story, what happened to my father and mother, the misery we suffered in the hands of people consumed by greed, how a mere act of kindness, letting go a golden carp, was rewarded with another shot at life, how Guanyin had guided me, a newborn baby, drifting on a piece of wood, to the venerable abbot who had brought me up like a son and taught me all there was to learn about Buddhism.

Looks like I was born and preordained for this grand mission to West Land, tens of thousands of *li* away, to obtain the scriptures of Mahāyāna for the spiritual wellbeing of our great Tang Dynasty.

Emperor Xuanzong was delighted to see me in his magnificent palace before I embarked on the journey. After some pleasantries and small talk about Buddhism, His Majesty presented me with three treasures he had received as priceless gifts from Rulai, Father Buddha, hand-delivered by Guanyin herself:

A Kāṣāya Robe.

A Nine-Ring Khakkhara Staff.

A Gold Headband.

Having on this Kāṣāya robe, woven of the finest silk by

fairies and goddesses in Heaven, will protect me from elements, rain, frost, snow, wind.

That nine-ring khakkhara staff will aid me when climbing tall mountains, navigating steep downhills, and crossing turbulent rivers.

That gold headband with a spell to tighten it? Its magic power I won't find out until I have acquired three new disciples to escort me in my journey to West Land.

Three new disciples?

Who are they?

Will they listen to me?

Emperor Xuanzong His Majesty walked me out of the gate of the imperial palace to see me off.

"I know I can trust you with this grand mission," said Emperor Xuanzong when we had walked one more li after another. "So much depends on it, the future of our great Tang Dynasty and happiness of my people. You're my sworn brother from now on."

"I'll give my uttermost to live up to your kindness and trust, Your Majesty," I promised solemnly, bowing again in boundless gratitude. "I'd deserve to be condemned to the bottom of Hell if I do not succeed in reaching West Land and returning with all the true scriptures!"

Emperor Xuanzong then gave me a purple gold bowl and poured some rice wine in it.

"Your Majesty," I said, bowing, "as a Buddhist monk I have sworn never to touch wine, meat, and—"

"This one is an exception," said Emperor Xuanzong. He picked up a piece of earth and dropped it in the gold bowl.

I knew what His Majesty meant, tossed the wine into my mouth, and coughed because it was my first taste of wine ever; it turned my tongue and my throat and rolled into stomach like a ball of fire.

Emperor Xuanzong smiled.

When I handed the gold bowl back to Emperor Xuanzong, His Majesty shook his head. "Keep it, a gift from your sworn brother."

I bowed again in boundless gratitude.

"When do you think you can return and set foot on the soil of your motherland again?"

"Three years."

Emperor Xuanzong, His Majesty, my sworn brother, if I dare to call him thus as he told me to, did not turn to return to the imperial palace until we had walked together another *li* farther away outside the capital.

"I've heard that the way to West Land is endlessly long," one of the young disciples seeing me off said when the magnificent imperial capital became but a blur behind us, "and plagued with countless tigers, leopards, demons, and monsters. I'm a bit worried, forgive me for saying this, my kind master, whether you can keep the promise to His Majesty."

"I've given my pledge," I said solemnly, as if to reconfirm, rededicate myself. "I'll honor it with my life. I said three years, it may take longer. Who knows. See that tall pine on that mountain gate? If one day, say in three, five, or seven years, you see it turn east, it is a sign that I'm back. If not, you know—"

I didn't want to finish that thought.

Can I get it done?

Am I up to the job?

What if we get our wish, get the scriptures, but fail to live by them?

What does it really take to journey from misery to the other side, to salvation?

What's the secret?

Some mindboggling texts written in a language only a few understand, who hold all the power of interpreting and preaching them? I'm one of those privileged, powerful few, right?

I quickly dismissed all these troubling thoughts. Mine from here onwards not to reason why, mine but to do and hopefully not die.

The autumnal sky was high, the air pristine, tree leaves beginning to fall, villages becoming far and few between, stillness punctuated by an occasional cry of some unknown beast, a lone wild goose flapping away silhouetted against the setting sun.

We, me and two of my disciples selected for their intelligence, stamina, trustworthiness, kept going for days on end and then one day, when we had traveled for about ten *li*, we were faced with a hill covered with thick bushes.

Barely a few minutes after we followed a small trail into the thicket when all three of us, including the horse, fell into a ditch.

Stunned and dizzy, I looked up from the bottom of the pit and saw a monstrous face looking down.

"I've got you! I've got you!" the face screamed gleefully.

A bunch of big-muscled monsters jumped into the pit, tied us up, and hoisted us above.

We were dragged in front of a giant monster, green-faced, sharp-pointed teeth, eyes glittering with bone-chilling light.

Nearby were a big firepit and several long stone tables.

The giant monster laughed heartily welcoming his guests arriving in troves.

They were all excited at the sight of us, salivating, baring their jagged fangs.

I was terrified. I've barely begun my pilgrimage and it'll now be cut short, and I'll end up in the mouths of these hideous monsters.

Butcher monsters sharpened their knives on stones and

then came to us. They grabbed the two young disciples of mine first. They howled "Master, help me!" "Save me, Master!" heartrendingly and their master, me, couldn't lift a finger to save them. They howled to Heaven for mercy, but Heaven did not respond. Knives went into their chests, blood spurting into the sky, their hearts, livers, and whole bodies cut to bloody pieces and served to the giant monster and his guests.

I swooned as a fierce-looking butcher monster came to me with a knife.

"Why not save him for tomorrow?" I vaguely heard one of the monsters saying this and blacked out.

When I came to, an eternity later, I felt a gentle breath in my face.

I struggled to open my eyes and saw a silver-haired old man looking down at me concernedly.

"Save me," I begged weakly.

"Who are you, young man? What happened to you?" the old man asked in the kindest voice I'd heard since I began the journey.

I looked around. All the monsters were fast asleep, some snoring, some mumbling and licking their lips in their dreams.

In a tearful voice, I told the kind old man why I was going to West Land and what had happened to my two disciples.

"This place is plagued with monsters and demons," the old man said. "The sooner you get out of here the better."

"Save me," I begged again, sobbing.

"Follow me!"

The old man helped me on my feet, led me to my horse tethered to a tree nearby, and then through a trail of twists and turns to an open space with a road cutting through it. As I turned to thank the old man again, he soared into the sky like a breath of clean air, unfolding a banner on which was written this message:

> *Goldstar of Heaven on Errant for Rulai Father Buddha*
> *Disciples Await to Escort You Henceforth So Fear Not*

Tears of gratitude welling in my eyes, I pressed onward, alone on a thin horse.

I found myself in the midst of grotesque rocks, dog tired, hunger pangs roiling in my belly, with no signs of human habitat in sight.

Two ferocious tigers blocked my way, grunting hungrily; behind me were long snakes, their tongues spitting out fiery venoms; on both sides of me were gigantic insects with a thousand legs coming toward me menacingly, their beady eyes shining with bloody thirst. Even my horse was terrified and refused to go one step forward.

I rolled off the horse, prostrated and prayed, leaving my life and death in the hands of Heaven.

A man, a big man, donning animal fur hat, coat, belt, and boots, a three-headed iron fork in hand, came charging at the tigers, snakes, and other ferocious beasts.

"Save me!" I cried at the top of my lungs.

"You're safe now," said the big man when he had driven away my attackers. "I'm a hunter. Who are you? Where are you going?"

I struggled on my feet again and began to tell the hunter my story when a ferocious lion lurched to us from nowhere, roaring thunderously. My legs gave way, and I flumped on the ground again.

The hunter turned around swiftly and met the ferocious lion head-on.

It is a worthy fight between man and beast, full of power and fury. The lion jumps onto the hunter, bloody mouth the size of a water basin wide open; its front paws can knock out a buffalo with just one blow; its tail, long, thick, as if electrified, can sweep an elephant off its feet.

The hunter stops the lion inches away from his face with his iron fork, man and beast staring at each other so close, as if to see who blinks first.

Suddenly, the hunter lets go the fork, jumps on the lion's back as it falls on its paws, grabs its mane, and punches its ears, temples, and eyes with his big fists.

The lion, infuriated, tries to bounce and shake the hunter off its back, but the hunter hangs on tight, like a rodeo man, and keeps punching.

As the lion moans and loses its strength, the hunter rolls off its back, picks up the fork, and pierces it into its heart, blood sprouting into the sky and every which way.

When the fight was all over, I got on my feet again and thanked the hunter profusely for saving my life by killing this lion, acutely aware of me being morally compromised forever as a Buddhist monk. But it's a life and death situation and what choices do I have? Kindness to one can mean unkindness, even cruelty, to another, right?

Oh, this is no time to be pedantic, to be fastidious.

Mine not to reason why, mine but to do and not die.

I was welcomed by the hunter's family: his wife, young sons, and his elderly mother.

As the lion was being skinned and cut up from under a tree, I sat down nearby and began to pray.

The hunter's mother brought out incense sticks, handed them to me, and said kindly: "Please include my husband in your prayer. Today happens to be the anniversary of his passing."

I nodded and kept praying.

Truth be told, it was not easy to stay focused with all the hustle and bustle around me, aroma of meat cooking thick in the air and sneaking into my nostrils, a mishmash of hunger and sickness churning inside me.

Supper was finally served. We all sat down around the

wood table loaded with steamy lion meat cooked with ginger, onion, red pepper.

The hunter picked up a big chunk and was about to place it in my wooden bowl when I hurried to cover it with both hands.

"Thank you, my kind benefactor," I said apologetically. "I'm a Buddhist monk and have never touched one morsel of meat since I was born."

The big man burst into a hearty laugh. "You monks are an itsy-bitsy too fussy, too finicky for your own good. As you can see, we're a hunter's family. Other than animal meat and some bamboo shoots and mushrooms, we don't have much to prepare you a vegetarian meal. You don't want to sleep on an empty stomach tonight, do you?"

The big man's mother gave her son a reproachful look. "Our distinguished guest is a man of faith, so cut you irreverent prattle. Let me see what I can do."

She got up and went inside the kitchen again. Before long, she came back with a bowl of millet and corn and a bowl of dried vegetables. It smelled so delicious.

"I have saved these for rare occasions," the kind woman said.

I was ready to cry. She so reminds me of my own mother. I haven't seen her since I left soon after our family reunion. How've you been, mother? And father, *nainai*, *waigong* and *waipo*? I know I'm an unfilial son, not following Confucius' teaching that when your parents are alive, do not travel far, but the Great Sage also says, if you have to travel, be sure to have a specific destination, right? Don't you worry about your son, mother, because he's being well taken care of by kind strangers and knows how to take care of himself too!

After supper, I washed myself clean, sat down in front of the family altar, lit the incense sticks, and prayed again, this time, particularly for the soul and spirit of the dear departed; I prayed well past the midnight.

At the breakfast table the next morning, the hunter's mother said to her son, her face lit up with joy: "I had a dream last night. You dear father came back home and said thanks to this kind monk's pray he has been forgiven for his worldly sins and will soon be reincarnated into a rich family for a good life!"

"Really, Mother?" exclaimed the hunter. "I was just about to tell you. I had the same dream last night!"

"Oh, I dreamed of father-in-law too!" exclaimed his young wife, usually quiet, who hadn't said as much a word since I came. "He looked so happy and said he came to say goodbye before going to a rich family to be born again, all because of the kind monk's pray!"

All three bowed and thanked me profusely.

This was the first time I saw the power of my pray. Like a miracle.

That's perhaps why I've been chosen, born and preordained for this, for the grand mission to West Land.

I bowed back deeply, my heart filled with boundless, joyous gratitude too.

Packed with dry food the kind family prepared for me, I got on the way again.

Westward.

I knew that henceforth on my way to West Land I'd have to depend on the kindness of so many strangers.

After days of traveling alone, often lost in deep thoughts, I came in sight of a big mountain, with five tall peaks.

"Master, what took you so long?" I heard someone shouting to me, half complaining, half overjoyed.

TEN
Master and Disciple

I was so excited at the sight of a monk atop a horse wobbling along a rugged trail up to where I was.

A mirage?

Workings of an overwrought mind?

Or the one Guanyin told me about, coming at long last?

When Guanyin, Goddess of Mercy, passed by, escorted by her disciple Mucha, remember him? I've been bearing this humongous thing, Five-Element Mountain, on my back for more than five hundred years.

I don't need to take another look at myself in a pond or anything to know what I look like, having been exposed to the elements for that many years.

Yeah, I remember what Old Sage has said, one happy day in Heaven is one full year on Earth. What about one miserable day like this on Earth? It's like a full year of nightmare in Hell from which I struggle to wake up but can't.

Lush moss has grown on my head like ridiculous tall hats; I can feel it although I can't see. Moss also hangs around my eyebrows like eaves above windows; this I can see partially. Oh, yes, thickets of grass grow out of my ears and nose like goose feathers, this I just know.

My head is so buried underneath this bushy, untamed camouflage that only when my eyeballs move, thank God I can still move them and see, that I know I'm still a breathing, living thing. It seems that the whole world has forgotten about me, like I've never existed.

I haven't forgotten about myself, though. I hang on to the happy memories of me being Monkey King of Flower Fruit Mountain, replaying them in my mind super slow-mo, frame by frame, relishing each memory so much that I'm all but transported back to there and then, all but oblivious to the revolting humiliation I'm breathing every second of my being.

I was trying to doze off, to have a quick shuteye so I didn't have to face the shame I'm living all the time when I heard someone saying something not far off, a limerick of sorts written by some bad poet:

A little monkey so full of himself when
his bottle not even half full,
Gulping down longevity peaches immortality beans
like his own food;
Self-styled Great Sage Heaven's Equal when
only a rank-less stable boy,
Wielding a Gold-Banded Cudgel
like somebody invincible not anyone's toy,
Nothing but a teeny-weensy nobody pissing
in Rulai's palm a stinky pool.

That insult woke me up real fast.

I saw Mucha, that son of a heavenly king and brother of Nezha that I had fought when he was doing an errant for Jade Emperor, trying to subdue me, and failed, of course. Who in Heaven or on Earth could if it had been a fair fight? Excepting Rulai, perhaps.

Mucha was winking and beaming broadly at my expense.

"Hey, how dare you rub salt into a wound still raw just because I've defeated you before?!"

I saw the person standing next to him and squinted to look harder.

The kindest face, like that of my mother I've never met, her whole being exuding an awestriking yet tranquil, comforting halo.

"Guanyin, Goddess of Mercy?!" I exclaimed.

She nodded and smiled, the beautifulest smile in the whole world.

"Please set me free," I beseeched. "I don't think I can last here another day, another second. It's been too long."

"I know," said Guanyin. "But you know why you've been put here—to help you repent what you did. If I free you prematurely, who knows what you'll be up to again."

"I swear in the name of my father and my mother—"

Guanyin put a finger on her lips.

"I promise I'm ready to turn a new page."

Guanyin kept her eyes on me, as if to fathom the depth of my soul.

"I believe you," she said at last. "Listen, in perhaps just a few days someone, a Buddhist monk, will come along, set you free, take you in as his disciple, and you'll escort him on a mission to West Land, that's thousands upon thousands of *li* away."

Each second since Guanyin left has dragged on like a long day. A watched pot never boils when you're dying for a cup of oolong tea?

That's why I couldn't believe my eyes when I saw this young monk atop a skinny horse meandering into my vision.

"What took you so long?" I called out when he finally came close. "Please set me free now, master!"

The young monk was startled by this outburst from me. He stared at me, perplexed, his eyes wandering between my hollow cheeks and pointed chin. I began to doubt whether he was the one Guanyin had said would come and save me.

"Me your master?" The young monk found his tongue, finally.

"Yes, if you're a Buddhist monk on a journey to West Land."

"I am he. What happened to you?"

I told him my story, a quick version, without any embellishment.

The young monk knitted his eyebrows when I finished.

"Set me free from this," I said, rolling my eyes upward to indicate the mountain on my back. "I can be your disciple and protect you all the way to West Land."

"How?" the monk lifted his head high to see the tall mountain, so high he almost fell off from the horse.

"Easy. Guanyin, Goddess of Mercy, told me that on the top of the mountain there is a big square rock with a scroll stuck on it. You take off that scroll and I'll be free."

The young monk got off the horse reluctantly and worked his way up the mountain, breathing hard. This young man is not much of a traveler, I thought. He'll be a handful and needs lots of help. Lots.

"What's this?" I heard the monk reading aloud some words:

唵 ōng 嘛 mā 呢 nī 叭 bēi 咪 mēi 吽 hòng

I saw these words more than five hundred years ago and they still don't make any sense to me.

The moment the monk took the scroll of the big rock, whatever that had been sitting on my back began to feel a thousand times lighter, and lighter, until I succeeded in wiggling myself out of its hell-like chokehold.

When the young monk finally wobbled his way down the mountain, I was already standing by his horse, ready, willing, and able. He looked pleased.

The horse, however, seemed a teeny-weensy shy of me. Perhaps I still have the vibe of Imperial Stables Assistant Steward, okay, nothing but a lowly stable boy, but a horse whisperer no less, knowing how to speak to the wildest of them.

Thus began a long, tortuous relationship of master and disciple as I escorted Xuanzang, Tripitaka, Tang Monk, whichever name you prefer, I call him Master (*Shifu*), he calls me Wukong, Monkey, whatever, on his journey to West Land, me leading the way with his luggage on my back, him atop the horse close behind.

Before we had gone far, a fierce tiger came charging at us, roaring, its tail stirring up a cloud of dust.

Master almost fell off the horse for fright.

Me? I was delighted, a godsent opportunity to show to my new master what I can do.

"Don't be afraid, Master!" I said reassuringly. "This tiger is here to deliver my new clothes."

I pull out the needle from my ear and give it a quick shake in the breeze; it grows to ten feet long and rice bowl thick. Oh, how I've missed doing this, haven't done it for more than five hundred years.

I rush to the tiger, wielding the Gold-Banded Cudgel at lightning speed. The beast, shocked by this dazzling outburst, freezes in midair. I let the Cudgel land on the beast's head, its skull cracking into a thousand pieces, blood spurting every which way.

What's happening to my new master?

He all but swooned atop the horse, and then steadied himself.

"My goodness," Master said in a tremulous voice. "That hunter the other day had to fight that lion for hours and you did this thing in with just one hit!"

I still have the mojo, master, and you haven't seen anything yet.

"Oh, that's nothing, Master!" I said, helping my master off the horse. "You sit here and take a breather. Let me undress this tiger so I can put its clothing on myself."

"What clothing does this tiger have on?" asked Master incredulously. "I don't see anything."

"Just you see!" I said, pulled out a hair, and gave it a gentle blow.

"Change!"

A sharp knife appeared in my hand. Those of you who are a teeny-weensy squeamish, do me a favor, please: cover your eyes for a few seconds.

I slid open the tiger's belly, remove its beautiful all-season coat in one piece, trim off some loose ends, turn it into a nice jacket and put it on myself, belt it up with the beast's tail, a nice accessory, right?

"What do you think, Master?" I asked, turning around for Master to see. "It's still a teeny-weensy rough. I can borrow some needle and strings later to sow it up for better fit."

Master just stared at me and didn't say a word. His mind seemed elsewhere.

"Where's that big Cudgel you used to kill the tiger?" Master asked, hours after we got back on the road.

"Oh, that's what's been on your mind, Master? It's now as small as a needle, hidden in my ear."

I should have left it at that, but I know you know me well enough to know that once I've opened my mouth, I just can't shut it.

I told my new master what happened in Heaven, how I used the Cudgel to fight and defeat even the best of them, Prince Nazha, Prince Muzha, you name it, and if Rulai had not intervened....

Master listened pensively without saying a word.

I had a vague feeling that this oversharing might not do me any good but could not unsay what I've already said.

We pressed onward for hours without saying much to each other, each nursing our own private thoughts.

The sun, a fiery ball, sank onto the horizon in the west and soon below. The sky was a bloody red.

We stopped at a village home, and I knocked on the door. An old man opened it.

"Ghost! Ghost!" the old man screamed, trying to shut the door.

"Don't be afraid, my kind benefactor," said Master, bowing, as I held the door open. "He is a disciple of mine."

"You look like a kind Buddhist monk," the old man said. "But how can you bring such a thing to my home?"

I could have taught the old man a lesson about who I am right there but for the lesson, or lessons I've learned. Besides, I do look a teeny-weensy weird, a monkey wrapped in a piece of tiger skin.

"Hey," I said. "I am not a thing. I was once, in my former incarnations, Great Sage Hea—"

Master frowned and I zipped my lip.

Reluctantly the old man and his family took us in. They prepared some warm water for us to bathe in. Other than my face being soaked in downpours now and then, I haven't had a bath for more than five hundred years. Imagine how I felt afterwards, clean and fresh like a baby.

I borrowed a needle and some strings from our host and sewed up my new tiger-skin jacket, so it'd look more presentable on me. The old man's wife beamed as she watched me doing some needlework like womenfolk. I chuckle to think about that even now.

Early morning the next day, we bid farewell to our kind,

albeit unenthusiastic, benefactor and resumed our journey, loaded with dry food they had prepared for us the night before.

It was early winter, the whole world, every tree limb and twig and every grass blade, was blanked with a thin layer of frost. I could see my breath tumbling into the air like a jet of warm steam. Where will we put up for the night today?

Mid-afternoon, we stopped for a quick rest and lunch and barely after we got on the way again, a gang of bandits, six of them, jumped out from the thicket of bushes.

"That monk, your horse and luggage, or your life!" They shrilled, wielding their weapons.

Master fell off the horse for fright.

"Master!" I hurried to help him on his feet. "They're here to deliver some more clothes is all!"

"Are you deaf?" Master said angrily. "They'll kill me if we don't give them everything they want!"

"Don't you worry," I tried to calm him down. "I'm going to reason with them and see what happens."

"How? You are one little monkey, and they are … six big men?"

I walked up to the bandits and bowed slightly.

"Why on earth are you stopping us?" I asked. "We don't owe you anything, do we?"

"You've never heard of us?" the biggest, fiercest of the bandits said. "Our fame travels far and wide! Say no to our demand and you'll be crushed to a thousand pieces!"

"Oh, yeah, you puny highway robbers," I laughed. "Never heard of your granddaddy, me, Monkey King?!"

"No!" their ringleader said. "Now hear our thunderous names: Eye Candy, Ear Fury, Nose Delight, Tongue Craving, Heart Desire, Body Worry, go piss in your pants!"

"You puny, pitiable bandits!" I laughed. "Get out of our way or you'll regret you've ever met your granddaddy today!"

The six bandits jumped on me all at once, screaming.

I stood there and let their blows fall on me, left and right, and every which way, but not a hair of me was hurt. I let them have their fun for a minute or two and then pulled out the needle from my ear.

"You bastards tired and bored?" I asked good-humoredly. "Now it's your granddaddy's turn."

"Hehehe, what's that for?" their ringleader shrieked "We are not here for some acupuncture treatment from a weirdo quack!"

"It'll cure you all for good!"

In the blink of an eye, my needle grew to ten feet tall and rice bowl thick. Eyes popping out in shock and fright, the bandits ran for their lives, crying "mama!"

With one small jump, I caught them up, knocked them down like grasshoppers, and returned to where my master was with a bundle of new clothes. I was thrilled and couldn't wait to be commended for the impressive feat.

"You troublemaker!" Master sounded quite upset. "These highway robbers, even when tried in the court law, would not be sentenced to death. You may know some tricks, but that doesn't give you the right to kill people. How can you be a Buddhist monk? We're supposed to be extra careful even when sweeping the courtyard, so we won't hurt any ants."

I was incredulous and just stood there, letting myself be lectured.

"There's not an inkling of kindness in that heart of yours," Master continued. "Good thing is this is wilderness, and no one will find out. What if you kill like this again in a town or city? You'll tarnish my impeccable reputation beyond repair!"

Your impeccable reputation. The real reason why you're so mad at me now?

"Master," I said in my own defense. "If I hadn't killed

them, they'd have killed you."

"Well, as a Buddhist monk," said Master proudly. "I'd rather be killed than killing. And even if I had been killed, that would be only one life, but you've killed six lives! If this were to be tried in court, you wouldn't be able to get away with it even if your father were a sworn brother of the Emperor His Majesty."

What fool wants to be a sworn brother of any Emperor His Majesty?

"Guilty as charged, master. I don't know how many lives I've killed since I became Monkey King more than five hundred years ago, but all for justice, or self-defense. If that's wrong, why haven't I faced any lawsuits?"

"You little forgetful monkey!" Master said furiously. "How did you end up under that big mountain? Isn't that the biggest trial for all the crimes you've committed and the biggest punishment?"

Rubbing salt into a wound that's still raw. That's low, real low.

"If you carry on like this," Master said, "I won't keep you and would rather continue the journey alone."

"No use talking anymore," I said, unable to contain myself anymore. "If that's how you think of me, I'll leave then, now!"

Master looked stunned and sad, but how could I stay when he thought so ill of me? I somersaulted into the sky and sailed in the direction of home, Flower Fruit Mountain.

On the way, I made a stop to visit an old friend of mine. Remember him, Dragon King, who graciously gifted me this Gold-Banded Cudgel of mine?

"I'm so happy that your ordeal under that mountain is finally over!" Dragon King said, beaming. "You must be eager to return to Flower Fruit Mountain and enjoy life again in Water Curtain Cave!"

"I'd love to do that," I said modestly. "However, I've converted to Buddhism and am actually traveling with a monk of the great Tang Dynasty, per recommendation of none other than Guanyin, Goddess of Mercy, on a historical mission to West Land to obtain true scriptures of Buddhism."

"That's so amazing!" enthused Dragon King. "You sound like a true born-again Buddhist!" He paused, and then said, hesitantly. "Why are you here, then? Not that I don't enjoy the visit of an old friend."

"Well, well, a long story," I struggled for words. "That monk, Xuanzang is his name, let's just say, is a teeny-weensy too fastidious, squeamish. I killed a few highway robbers to protect him, vicious robbers who'd have killed him in a heartbeat, but he kept reprimanding me to no end, 'cause he believes killing is an unforgivable sin, justified or not. You know my nature well enough to know that I can't put up with such nonsense. So, I left and am stopping here to see an old friend on my way home."

Dragon King pulled his long beard and sighed profusely.

"Here's what I think, as an old friend," Dragon King said finally. "If a simple life on Flower Fruit Mountain is what you really want, that's fine. If you really want to accomplish something with your life, however, to be worthy of Guanyin's trust, then, you should return to Xuanzang and use all your prowess to help him succeed in this grand historical mission. Otherwise, forgive me for speaking frankly, you'd be no better than any other commoner, knowing a few tricks and nothing more. Your decision, of course, but I hope you'll think twice before...."

Truthful advice from a true friend indeed although it sounds irksome for my ear.

I thanked Dragon King and somersaulted into the cloud again, going in the opposite direction of home.

In the blink of an eye, I saw the tiny figure of Master where

I had left him, sitting on the ground by the wayside, having not moved an inch.

I landed right in front of him.

"My master! Why're you still sitting here?"

"Where've you been?" Master looked me up and down and said. "Leaving me here by myself, not daring to continue on my own, or even to look around. The only thing I can do is to sit here and wait for you."

This Buddhist monk, my master, cannot go anywhere or do anything without me.

I began to feel sorry for him, and for having left him like that.

"Oh, I went to Dragon King of East Sea to have a sip of tea, is all. Now I'm back."

"You liar," Master said, "and not a good one! How can you go all the way to Dragon King, have tea there, and be back in such a short time?"

"Oh, that? I should have told you that with one cloud-somersault I can go one hundred eight thousand *li*, all in the blink of an eye, hehehe!"

"So," Master said, begrudgingly. "A word or two from me and you get upset, go and have tea somewhere, leaving me here at the mercy of hunger. How can you be so heartless?"

I am a pushover when the right button is pushed. All that anger and resentment melted into something squishy I don't have words to describe.

"Let me go find some kind benefactor and get some food for supper, then," I offered.

"No need. I still have some in the bag from that hunter's mother. All I need is some water so I can eat and then go on our way again."

I did as told, opened the bag to get the wheat bread for my master. Something new in the bag caught my eye:

A shiny gold-embroidered headband.

"What's that headband for?" I asked as I handed the bread to my master. "I've never seen it before."

"Oh, that," my master said innocuously. "Something I wore when I was still a child. With that headband on, I could know any new scriptures by heart without even having to learn."

"Really? That's amazing! Can I try it on and see if it works?"

Master nodded.

I put it on. A perfect fit.

Master nodded again, approvingly, stopped eating, and began to pray, murmuring something like a spell.

The band on my head began to tighten and kept tightening.

"My head hurts! My head hurts!" I cried.

Master ignored me and continued to pray.

It hurt so bad that I rolled on the ground and tried to tear off the headband, but it would not relent its ironclad grip, as if having been etched into my skull.

When Master stopped murmuring the spell, the headband would stop hurting me.

Damn the master. I never thought he had this trick up his sleeve and could be this heartless too.

I pulled out the needle from my ear and tried to probe and chip away that damned band on my head.

Seeing this, Master prayed that spell again, more urgently this time.

The headache was back on instantaneously; it hurt so bad that I rolled on the ground again, my hands wrapped around that damned band; no matter what I did, rolling, somersaulting, pulling, screaming, my eyes, my ears, my entire being hurt so bad, ready to pop, like Hell had laid its hands on me and wanted to squeeze the living light out of poor me.

Perhaps feeling that I'd been tortured enough, Master stopped murmuring that spell after I had been rolling on the ground for an eternity.

My head kept spinning, though, chasing some earsplitting whistle, some blinding light for a while before it all stopped.

Dead, deafening silence in my head.

"So, this is how you, Master," I said when I found my voice again, "teach me how to be kind, right?"

"I was only praying some new scripture," Master said, the same blank look on his face. "Not putting some spell on you at all."

"You're not a good liar either," I could hardly contain myself. "Why don't you pray that new scripture of yours again and see what happens."

The moment my master prayed that "scripture" again, my head began to churn and hurt so bad, my brains were being turned into mashed doufu.

"Okay, okay, please stop, master!" I begged, trying to hold my head together with both hands. "How do you explain this, ah?"

"Now you know I have a trick or two up my sleeve too," Master said, keeping a straight face. "Don't you dare to disobey me again."

"Never, never," I said, but not ready to submit yet.

I pulled out that needle from my ear, gave it a quick shake; it grew to ten feet long and rice bowl thick, and I lifted it above Master's head.

Imagine the shock and terror in his eyes.

Covering his head with trembling hands, my master prayed that damned spell so fast and furious like his very life hanged in the balance.

As you'd expect, my head began to churn and hurt so bad again, ready to burst in a thousand squishy pieces.

"Mercy, master, mercy!" I begged. "I'll never ever dare to disobey you again. Never!"

Master stopped, looking relieved, a faint smile playing around his lips.

"I wasn't going to hit you, master," I said. "Just wanted to scare you is all. Who taught you this trick, if I may ask?"

"Who else if not Guanyin, Goddess of Mercy, herself?"

What? Guanyin, the kindest, beautifulest in the whole world, and mother-like? How can she do this to me if she wants me to escort this monk on the long journey to West Land?

"Wait till I fight my way to South Sea and teach her a lesson or two," I mumbled, feeling so hurt inside me even though Master was not praying that spell.

"Guanyin is the one who has taught me this," Master said. "You'd be looking for death if you go and threaten her, get it, you blockheaded little monkey?"

That shut me up real quick.

Guanyin, Rulai, Jade Emperor, and this Buddhist monk, they breathe through the same nose and wear the same pants, so there is nothing I can do but to submit, Monkey King that I am, oh, no, don't you dare to bring up that Great Sage Heaven's Equal nonsense.

I threw myself on the ground and begged:

"Oh, kind master, I didn't mean to go and challenge Guanyin. I'll stay and protect you all the way to West Land if you don't pray that spell too often, like it's an afternoon tea or snack. That'll be the death of me, and you won't make it to West Land either."

Master kept his eyes on me, deciding.

"All right," he said finally. "Deal."

Crestfallen, despite, or rather, because of, that shiny gold-embroidered band on my head, yet buoyant in spirit, with renewed hope and resolve, I packed up things, helped my master back on the horse, and we got on the road again.

ELEVEN

Man of Cloth

Knowing only too well what excruciating pain it can inflict on me, and knowing that Master will not hesitate to pray that spell the moment he sees any sign of disobedience, despite him being a Buddhist monk, all the professed piousness and kindness, walking cautiously not to step on even an ant and all, I've developed a healthy respect for the headband, and tried hard to curb my enthusiasm, rein in my righteous instincts whenever my hands are itching for action.

We've been journeying forward uneventfully for a few days.

On a bone-chilling winter morning, we came to a valley and heard loud noise of water splashing. There was no river far and near.

A dragon appeared from nowhere and charged toward us, riding some phantom-like waves.

I jumped and grabbed Master off the horseback to protect him.

The dragon disappeared as fast as it came.

"Where's my horse?" Master asked when we recovered and looked.

The horse had vanished into thin air, too.

Something weird was afoot. I somersaulted into the cloud, looked far and near, and saw nothing.

"Master," I said when I landed, "your horse must have been eaten by the dragon."

"What? How can I continue the journey without my horse, still tens of thousands of *li* away?" Tears welled up in his eyes and he began to sob.

I sometimes wonder why this tear-jerking weakling of a monk has been chosen for this grand mission of the great Tang Dynasty. Wouldn't it be a thousand times easier if I were the one chosen, one cloud-somersault and it would be done? Perhaps the journey is more important than the destination? What do I know, anyways?

"Don't be a crybaby, master," I said. "Let me go and take a look again."

Without waiting to hear another tearful lament from my master, I somersaulted into the cloud, hovered over the shimmering, mirage-like river, searching, and shouting:

"Give back our horse, you little snail!"

The dragon surfaced from deep in the phantom river and shrilled angrily upon seeing me hovering overhead, "Who the devil are you, daring to insult me like that? I've eaten a horse, so?"

"So you'll have to spit it out and return it to us," I said and pulled out my Gold-Banded Cudgel, "or you'll have to eat this too!"

A fierce fight ensued.

Turns out, this dragon is quite a fierce warrior too and after a few rounds of fighting in midair, like two birds of prey, he dives underneath water and disappears into a stone cave. No matter how hard I pound on the door and shout insults at him, the dragon refuses to come out and fight me again.

When Master saw me return without the horse, he was

rather disappointed.

"How could you have beaten that tiger to death with one hit," he said, "and now you can't subdue the dragon? You are not that good, after all."

You know how I hate it when people, themselves weaklings and crybabies, whine about others not being good enough.

"Say no more, master. I'll get the horse back or will not come back to you at all. Mark my words!"

I somersaulted into the cloud again. It would be useless to try and fight someone who refuses to come out and fight. So, I sailed in the direction of South Sea.

"Why are you here," Guanyin asked, displeased at the sight of me. "Leaving your master all by himself?"

I have a bone to pick with Guanyin first before getting to the business of my visit.

"You call yourself Goddess of Mercy, yet give that crybaby of a monk that curse to hurt me so badly?"

"You little thick-faced monkey!" said Guanyin, that kindest face in the world looking a teeny-weensy harsh. "It's out of sheer kindness that I've told Xuanzang to save you from underneath that mountain and you're here to accuse me of cruelty?"

"Why did you give him that cursed headband then?" I said, like a wronged child. "If you really want to save me, why not simply set me free? Hurting me in the name of salvation, that in my dictionary is called cruelty! I don't want any bondage to anyone, not that monk, not even you!"

"Looks like that little monkey hasn't learned anything yet!" muttered Guanyin when my rant was over.

I mumbled something incoherent, hung my head, and dared not say another word in my defense.

"If I don't put a leash on you," said Guanyin in a softer tone, "you'll almost certainly cause big trouble again and be punished even more severely. Don't you know that?"

"All right," I said, defeated. "Can you help me subdue that dragon who has eaten my master's horse? If I don't return with his horse, that monk of yours will certainly pray that curse on me again and it'll kill me."

Guanyin listened quietly, as if waiting for me to continue.

"Without me protecting him, you know," I said, seeing an opportunity to put in a good word for myself. "That monk of yours will be eaten up by the first monster that'll appear down the road. You know I'm good at this and can be trusted, and that's why you've entrusted me with—"

"Okay, you smarty-pants of a monkey!" Guanyin said, beaming. "That dragon was a prince in Heaven and was condemned down here for a big fire he caused by accident. I've asked Jade Emperor to give him a second chance. Your master will surely be pleased with the new dragon horse you'll bring back to him, ten times stronger."

As if on cue, that dragon appeared in front of us, morphed into a big, beautiful white horse, and bowed to Guanyin.

"Bow to each other," Guanyin said to me and the white horse. "You're now both disciples of Xuanzang and are charged with the task of protecting him on his journey to West Land for the true scriptures."

The dragon horse and I eyed each other distrustfully and bowed as told.

As it turns out, the dragon horse and I get along super well, me still exuding that stable boy vibe, or authority, if you will, and him, a draft horse hauling the heaviest of burden, including the person of the monk himself.

Master will soon acquire two more disciples. They probably want to tell their own stories and I respect that. All I can say about these two is that they are as different as can be. Pigsy, what should I say, being Pigsy, is a lot of fun. He and I get along super well, too although we do get on each other's nerves now and then, call each other names, play practical jokes on each other, even get each other into trouble—big trouble sometimes, when we go a teeny-weensy too far. However, this trip, without Pigsy, would have been impossibly boring. Xuanzang, our master, has no sense, not even an iota, of humor, no jokes to tell, a bookworm through and through, and nothing more. As to Sandy, he is as steady as anyone can hope for, honest, reliable, dependable. He and I never had even an unpleasant word exchanged between us.

I don't need to tell you how overjoyed my master was when I returned with this big, beautiful white horse for him. I remained in his good books for days afterwards.

I got into trouble again, though, soon enough, and had to remedy the situation the best I could. And I'd be the first to admit up front that it was that teeny-weensy vain streak in my nature that got me, us, in trouble. I can't in my conscience chalk it to anyone else, can I?

After another long day of traveling, we put up for the night at a place called Guanyin Temple. It looked like such a heavenly place enveloped in some unspeakably holy aura. That abbot and his disciples were exceptionally kind, treating us like the most distinguished guests they'd ever seen. Can't do any better than this just about anywhere, right?

After supper, the venerable abbot, grizzly, a teeny-weensy hard of hearing, served us tea himself with tremulous hands.

"I am two hundred and seventy years old," the abbot said when my master thanked him for the hospitality and the tea, "and still feel like a spring chicken."

"True, kind benefactor," I said, half-jokingly. "You are just a baby, the age of my great-great-great-great-great-grandson, at the best!"

The kind abbot looked perplexed, perhaps not sure if he had heard me correctly.

Master gave me a harsh look and apologized on my behalf. What's there to apologize for if what I'm saying is god-knows-what?

As the evening progressed and the conversation drifted from one topic to the next, scriptures about desire, greed, salvation, nirvana, you name it, I'd doze off now and then, benefit of fatigue and boredom combined.

I was about to be washed over by another wave of drowsiness when I heard them talking about *jiasha*s, patchwork-like robes worn by Buddhist monks. You've seen those, haven't you? Draped over the left shoulder, a hook to fasten it around the torso, all kinds of color patterns, from simplest cloth to finest silk, what have you.

"Hahaha, speaking of *jiasha*s," said the venerable abbot, "I'm an avid collector. As a matter of fact, I've more than seven hundred of them. I guess I haven't served as abbot of this grand temple for two hundred and fifty-six years for nothing, after all."

He told his young disciples to carry out twelve heavy mahogany boxes and open each of them up. All of his *jiasha*s were made of finest cloth and shiniest embroidery and as the show was going on, the old abbot's eyes glittered, not unlike that of a miser counting his gold coins.

"Oh, yeah, that's nothing," I heard myself saying half drowsily. "You haven't seen anything yet if you haven't seen my master's *jiasha*."

Master gave me another harsh look of the evening, but that didn't stop me from going to get one of the bags that he'd instructed me to take special care of, bringing it to the table, taking out a small bundle, unwrapping layers of cloth until the treasure finally revealed itself.

The whole place was lit up with rainbow-like aura of glory.

"Oh My!"

"What a masterpiece!"

"Miracle from Heaven!"

Everyone, except for my master, cried out, wonderstruck.

The old abbot, dim-eyed that he is, picked up my master's *jiasha* to take a closer look. As his tremulous hands caressed it left and right, front and back, his body stiffened as if electrified, and then, like a dog whose back has been broken, slumped in his chair.

"How come I've never seen anything this splendid?!" the old abbot cried in a whiny voice.

He carried on like that for a minute or two, as we all looked on, and then said to my master:

"Can I borrow this *jiasha* for the night so I can take it to my chamber and indulge in its glory as much as I can, so I will not have lived my two hundred and seventy years of life for nothing, so I can die tomorrow heart content, a happy man?"

My master frowned and gave me another look. He was not pleased with this new development at all. I returned his look with a slight nod that said, without saying the words: "Don't you worry. It's all on me." Besides, how could my master refuse such a simple request from our kind host, benefactor?

We watched the old abbot retreat into his chamber with my master's *jiasha* in hands, his gait that of a bridegroom entering the bridal chamber for the first time. Hahaha, what do I know about such things anyway?

"If you don't get my *jiasha* back tomorrow morning," Master said to me as we finally settled down for the night in the altar room, "you know what I'll do."

I nodded, thinking to myself that my master was being a teeny-weensy too miserly, unwilling to share the joy of his *jiasha* with even a Buddhist monk and our kind benefactor. With another delicious yawn I fell asleep and drifted into a dream.

I hear muffled voices talking about something.

"Really easy, master, if you want to keep the *jiasha* for a few more days," someone says. "All you need to do is to keep our guests here for a few more days."

"Why not try keeping it for yourself forever, master?" another voice says. "All you need to do is to kill them and bury their bodies in our backyard so no one will ever find out."

"Easy said than done," says a third voice, sounding like a smarty-pants that he must be. "Didn't you see that monkey disciple of his? Not someone to mess with, I think. So, the easiest, safest way to do this is to set that alter room on fire, burn them to death. A credible story we can tell in case anyone asks, see what I mean?"

I can't believe this!

I rubbed my eyes open in the darkness and heard the old abbot saying:

"All right, Burn Your Enemy to Death While They Sleep, better stratagem than Sunzi could have dreamed of in his Art of War...."

These monks! For all their talk of purgation of desire and pilgrimage to nirvana, they are plotting a murder! Can't let it happen.

I got up quietly so as not to disturb my master in his sleep, changed into a honeybee, and went to check it out.

A bunch of monks are busy putting piles of drywood around the altar room. Oh, how I regret having not listened to Master. That vain streak in my nature, when can I pin you down and kick your ass out for good? How can you, Monkey King, be so gullible, judging these monks by their looks only, the robes they wear, when you, of all people, should have known better?

I had to act fast. Those piles of drywood were already in flames.

I put an invisible fireproof dome around my master, the

dragon horse, and our luggage.

I blew at the fire and fanned it in the direction of the old abbot's chamber after putting a small fireproof dome around my master's *jiasha* so it wouldn't get burned.

Fire roared furiously like a vicious beast and soon gulped down the whole place.

All the monks ran out, many of them half naked, holding on to their untied pants, and tried to put down the fire with buckets of water, screaming, crying; all they could save were crumpled roofs and fallen walls.

When east was dawning, I went inside the fireproof dome and woke up my master. He rubbed his eyes open, sniffed, and looked around.

"What's going on? What's happened?" He asked, perplexed.

"A lot and nothing," I said mysteriously.

"That doesn't make any sense!"

"Well, a lot did happen. That old abbot, our kind benefactor, became greedy and wanted to keep that *jiasha* of yours forever. So, they set fire to the altar room, but nothing—"

"What?" cried my master, flying into a fury. "All your fault! Told you not to show off and tempt people. Where's my *jiasha*? If you don't get it back to me now, I'll pray that spell until you're dead!"

"Please don't, master!" I begged. "I'll go and get it now!"

I went straight to the old abbot's chamber; toppled down statues of Rulai, Guanyin, you name it, were sprawling here and there, the whole place still smoldering.

I found the old man in a crumbled bed, fetal position, facing a broken wall, the robe on his back half burnt.

"Give back our *jiasha*!" I shouted.

No response.

I turned him over.

The old man was a goner, still hugging my master's *jiasha*

in his bosom. He got what he wished for, but did he die a happy man?

It took me a teeny-weensy of trouble to yank the *jiasha* out of the old man's stiffened arms and fingers. It was intact, like the fire had not happened.

I don't need to tell you how relieved I was when I put the *jiasha* back in the hands of my master.

TWELVE

Carpe Diem

Still remember me, one of those once met never forgotten type?

Okay, I am not much of a looker; I'd be the first to admit.

I am not one who loves to gaze at my own shadow in a pond and then sigh and be sad, you know what I mean?

I wouldn't mind having a nose job done so it looks an itsy-bitsy shorter and shapelier, an ear job done so they wouldn't be hanging like a pair of palm leaves brushing my shoulders all the time, and trimming an itsy-bitsy off of my love handles so my waistline an itsy-bitsy slimmer.

But you've got to play the best you can with the cards you've been dealt with, right? Being a crybaby will not get you anywhere if you ask me.

Besides, I'm more than compensated with a real healthy appetite for everything. I mean I have a big heart that beats robustly, I eat with gusto whatever is on the table, I throw myself into whatever work I have to do, like a donkey, you get my drift.

My philosophy for life? Life is short, so have fun! Eat like there's no tomorrow! Play like there's tomorrow! Let tomorrow take care of tomorrow!

Oh, a fun fact about me, in case you've forgotten:

I was once a better looker, so much better looker, in my former incarnation. You should have seen me then in my full regalia as a gloriously decorated marshal, Heaven Canopy Marshal (*Tianpengyuanshuai*). Mind you that a marshal is no small potato even in Heaven where anywhere you throw a stone it'll fall on the head of a god, a goddess, a king, a queen, what have you. Those days, I turned heads, princesses, fairies, old mamas, them all.

What did I do to deserve being punished like this?

It all happened at one of those annual longevity peach extravaganzas hosted by Queen of Heaven. There is so much drinking, dancing, and flirting going on. A carnival for who's who in Heaven who's invited. I still remember that belly dancer, a real hot chic, scantly covered in silk, maddening curves, swinging her hips, and thrusting her crotch in your face, oh, I'm getting excited just to think of it now. I feel her eyes, her warm gaze on me, as if saying "come on and get me." My whole body is on fire and something hot and squishy washes all over me. My furtive glances tell me that all the revelers around me, I mean all the men, are just as bewitched as I am. That evening could have ended like that, period, full stop, but no.

I get up and go to the outhouse to take a pee; I always drink an itsy-bitsy more than my share of the nectars and wines, you know. I see someone standing under a chrysanthemums tree gazing toward the star-lit sky where hangs a golden full moon. She looks like in a trance, in a dream. She looks so alone, and lonely, so in need of comforting and companionship, being heartachingly beautiful, and all. Perhaps she is being lovesick like me?

I walk to her and put my arm around her willowy waist; I tell myself to wait, to relish this moment for a few seconds before trying to turn her around and print a kiss on her forehead first, and then perhaps her lips? Who knows what this will lead to? My lucky day?

She remains oblivious, her heart and soul and whole being seem elsewhere, not present where she's at all.

Then she slowly turns to me, shakes her head, and tries to push me away with her soft hand. I know she is playing hard to get, her "no" is prelude to "yes," you know, the usual staff. So, I pull her to me an itsy-bitsy more forcefully. This seems to wake her up completely. Oh, the terror and anger in her eyes, and the scream that's heard all around Heaven.

I didn't know until later that this beauty is none other than the famed Chang'er, Goddess of the Moon, wife of Houyi, you remember that story? This guy, Houyi, shot down nine of the ten suns that suddenly appeared in the sky and scorched the earth. For this feat, he was rewarded two elixirs of immortality. Being a good husband, Houyi handed the two elixirs to his young and beautiful wife Chang'er so one day, when he was not too busy working the fields, they could enjoy the elixirs together.

As it happens, one day a thief broke into the house and tried to steal the elixirs. In a moment of panic, Chang'er swallowed the elixirs, and out of shame for having broken the promise with her husband, although in a moment of panic, she fled to the Moon.

That's how this Chang'er and Houyi, they end up being able to see each other again only once a year, one on the Moon and one on Earth.

I've inadvertently crashed the party, the once-a-year reunion, of the two ill-starred lovers. She'd have just told me what was going on and I'd have left her alone, but no, she screams like she is being murdered and keeps screaming even when I beg her to be quiet.

I was arrested by Heaven Guards, tied up, and dragged in front of Jade Emperor. His Majesty flew into a rage; good for him, full of so much righteous fury when he has three palaces and six courtyards of hot chicks selected from all over the world at his service at a moment's notice.

"Take him out and behead him!" ordered Jade Emperor.

I wouldn't be here telling you the story today if that silver-haired Goldstar hadn't put in a kind word for me. He asked for clemency on account of me being a decorated marshal and this being my first offense. I was flogged two thousand times instead, my skin cracked, my flesh splashed every which way, and then kicked out of Heaven.

This is the long and short of how I end up looking like this when I was reborn here on earth, hideous, branded by shame into perpetuality for one itsy-bitsy youthful indiscretion, a spur-of-the-moment misjudgment. More on this shortly.

I'm a hopeless romantic, you see what I mean? and being condemned to Earth is not the end of the world for me. I have to live and enjoy life wherever I find myself as much as I can. I, I mean my new reincarnation, began as a migrant worker, going from village to village doing seasonable work on farms. I was as good a farmhand as you could find just about anywhere.

Then, I came to this Gao Village and was hired by this Gao family. I worked particularly hard. I don't know why, perhaps to impress the elderly Gao, or his third and youngest daughter who was yet to be married off. She is no Chang'er on earth for sure, but oh, she is so sweet and pretty. My heart beats faster, that warm squishy feeling washes all over me when she, along with her mama, serves us supper at the end of a long day of hard work. Oh, believe me, I'm as upright and respectful as can be, never letting my eyes linger a second longer on her face or anywhere. I know what kind of trouble a simplest mistake can get me into.

As it turns out, Old Gao does not have a son, so he is looking for a good young man to marry into the family (*Daochamen*), you've heard of that, right? reverse marriage, to take care of the farm and him and his wife in their old age. When I overheard this from the other farmhands, I went to Old Gao and recommended myself. I told him that I am an orphan with no kins and any other attachments in the world. If he accepts me, this will be my home and I'll be as good a son to him as I were his very own. As it turns out, Old Gao has had his eye on me for some time and just didn't know how to approach me about it.

Imagine how ecstatic I was when Old Gao said yes, and how in cloud nine, dizzyingly happy, I was on my wedding night, how the third daughter and I became man and wife, such passionate lovers we are, shy as she is. Enough said, hehehe.

I work even harder because the farm, this whole place, is mine now. Okay, will be soon.

The only complaint they have, a good-natured one, of course, is that I'm such a big eater. Didn't I tell you I always eat with gusto? I mean, I eat ten times more than the next farmhand. I can see my in-laws watching me during supper, shaking their heads, smiling, you know. But they know I'm worth ten times more, I bring in good harvest, barns filled to the ceiling with bags of grains, pigs fattening faster, hens laying more eggs than they can collect and sell in the market.

After a while, though, I notice some change in how they look at me, like the sight of me not that pleasing to them anymore. When I come back from work and kiss my young wife at the end of a day, she turns her head away sometimes, and submits herself to me with her eyes shut. I thought she was just being playful, or bored and wanted novelty to spice up things in the bedroom, see what I mean?

As days went by, I began to notice changes in myself too,

like my mouth, my nose, my ears becoming an itsy-bitsy longer, a mane of rough hair growing in the back of my neck, my skin getting coarser, what have you. I chalked it up to me working too long, too hard under the baking sun and didn't let it bother me much.

Until one day, carrying water from the family pond, I happen to catch a glimpse of myself and it is like being hit in the head by a brick. So, my reincarnation as an earthling is finally shaping up? I'm now a pig, an ugly pig, of all things and possibilities? Just my luck!

But I recover fast. People don't judge a book by its cover, and they know this book, me, has lots of good staff to offer, right?

Evening that very day, when we finally retreat into our bedroom, I try to gather my young wife into my arms and give her a thousand hot kisses on her lips again, something I've been waiting to do for a whole long day, but she dodges, and I fall on the ground. When I pick myself up and chase after her again, she pushes me back.

"Are you upset I came back an itsy-bitsy late today?" I ask, perplexed.

"No, I'm just a bit under the weather today," says she in her usual sweet voice. "Why don't you undress and get some rest?"

I've got to respect that although I'm disappointed, like a pit of fire being doused with a basin of ice water.

When I'm already in bed, under the lovebirds themed comforter, she is still sitting in the chair before her dresser, lips pursed.

"Sweetie," I try to make peace. "Why aren't you coming to bed? It's late. Still mad at me?"

"Coming to bed with you?" she snaps contemptuously. "Look at yourself! An ugly toad wanting to eat a beautiful swan? In your dreams! Never again!"

What? I am dumbfounded and sit up.

Sitting in that chair is not the young, beautiful wife of mine, but a monkey.

"You ugly pig," laughs the monkey. "Think you can get away with forcing yourself on a beautiful young woman of a good family? No way!"

"Who on earth are you," I roll out of bed, ready to confront this cheek-less thing. "Think you can get away with ruining my evening, the good life I've worked hard to rebuild and enjoy?"

I reach for my big iron rake.

"Monkey King's my name," that monkey announces proudly, pulling out a needle from his ear. "Great Sage Heaven's Equal, Heaven's equal, heard of that?"

I guessed as much and still remember what Jade Emperor said during my trial:

"First there was that cheeky little monkey stealing longevity peaches and immortality beans, now this lecherous hooligan forcing himself on Chang'er. We've got to make an example out of him; otherwise, Heaven wouldn't be Heaven anymore."

"You despicable *bimawen*, stable boy!" I blurt out furiously. "Haven't you caused us enough trouble in Heaven, now you want to have more fun on Earth at others' expenses?"

"Blame me for your own trouble?" laughs my nemesis again, I'll just call him Monkey for now. "Why don't you take a pee and take a look at yourself in it, idiot?!"

Beside myself with fury, I go after him with my iron fork. Monkey, he just stands there, laughing, and lets me hit him on his head over and again, each time like hitting an anvil in a blacksmith's shop, my arms shaking with a thousand spasms.

I know I'm dealing with more than my match, so I flee and lock myself into a stone cave a few mountains away from Gao Village, my first home on earth as a demon, before I became a migrant worker and Gao's son-in-law, a secret refuge I've visited only once or twice since.

Monkey tries to talk to me through a little crack in the door:

"They shouldn't judge a book by its cover, I get that, believe me. The elder Gao, your father-in-law, does say you're a hard worker and all, although you do eat more than your share. The Gao family wouldn't have minded; it's just that they can't face the village folks with a son-in-law like you. You've got to put yourself in their shoes."

"Why don't you try to put yourself in my shoes?" I say, tears welling up in my eyes.

"They don't want to have this son-in-law anymore, you idiot, get it? Why don't you leave them alone and come with me and my master, Xuanzang, Buddhist monk from the great Tang Dynasty, on this grand journey to West Land?"

"What?" I can't believe my ears. "You're first disciple of that monk Guanyin, Goddess of Mercy, has told me about in a dream of mine? I thought it was just a dream. What took you so long? Why didn't you tell me in the first place? Take me to my master now!"

I open the stone door and step out.

"I will if you burn down this cave of yours!" demands Monkey.

"All right." I set my old demon home on fire.

"Give me that iron fork of yours, too."

"For now." I hand it to him the weapon I've used since my Canopy Marshal days in Heaven.

Monkey then twists my arms behind my back and ties me up.

"Is that necessary?" I protest.

Monkey does what he wants, it seems, and without another word drags me by my big ears back to the village.

"Easy, easy, Monkey!"

Me, once proud son-in-law of the Gao family, now being dragged home like this. Unlucky me, being dealt another bad hand by cruel fate.

I see a Buddhist monk, must be Xuanzang, sitting in a chair next to my father-in-law; behind them, next to the family altar, my mother-in-law tries to comfort my wife, who is sniffing with a silk handkerchief.

At the sight of me, Xuanzang frowns slightly and stiffens his back.

Once Monkey unties me, I prostrate before Xuanzang and pledge that I will henceforth set myself free from all earthly desires and follow my master to West Land, to the shore of salvation, nirvana, blah-blah-blah.

"You'll have to set this young woman free first," says Xuanzang. "The Gao family have been kind to you all these years, taking you in, giving you shelter, and home."

That's true and I'm grateful to them from the bottom of my heart.

I kowtow to my father-in-law, my mother-in-law, and then my beautiful wife one last time before my marriage is annulled there and then. I try to hold back my tears as a thousand feelings, bitter and sweet, wash over me. But what can I do? What choices do I have?

"If you don't want to rot in Hell," I remember Guanyin saying this to me in my dream. "If you want to be saved, you'll have to go with this Buddhist monk. The only way. The only hope."

"Now that you are a disciple of mine," says Xuanzang, now I call him Master, "you should have a religious name. How about Wuneng, Able Awakening, able to strive for salvation. How does that sound?"

"Thank you, Master," I bow deeply to thank him. "That's exactly what I've been doing my whole life."

"Now bow to your elder brother, my first disciple, Wukong, Vain Awakening, meaning he understands all is vanity in this world and beyond."

I turn to bow to Monkey, secretly pleased that my name is better, but worried that this elder brother will be on my case all the time. I'll have to learn to live with him and manage him to my advantage too. I catch Wukong winking at me knowingly when we bow to each other.

"By the way," says Master. "Your elder brother has a byname too, Monkey, just to make things easier." A faint smile plays around his lips and then disappears into blankness.

"How about one for you, say Pigsy? That seems to fit?"

It fits perfectly. What else can I say?

I bow to thank Master again.

"Now that I'm converted," I say to Master, perhaps trying to get in his good books. "I'll give up eating these five smelly vegetables as required by my new faith, no garlic, no scallion, no onion, no asafetida, no leek and none of these three meats—goose meat, dog meat, and turtle meat. A big sacrifice on my part, having been a meat-lover my whole life."

"How about no meat whatsoever?" says Monkey, winking at me again.

Master gives Monkey a look and says, "That's fantastic, Wuneng! Now, we can also call you Piggy Eight Nos, Zhu Bajie!"

We all burst out laughing. A rare moment of levity. What a relief!

Finally, time to say goodbye to my family and my home for the last three years.

I bow deeply to my ex-father-in-law who's given me a pair of new shoes, a new shirt, and a big bag of dry food for the journey.

I bow to my ex-mother-in-law, aunts, and uncles.

My teary eye searches in the crowd but can't find dear, sweet wife, my partner in so much joy, so many unforgettable memories we've made together.

"Please take good care of yourselves, and of my—" Here I have to hold back a sob. "I'll come back to be your son-in-law again if I fail to achieve salvation. There will be no other place I'd want to be failing nirvana—"

"Don't talk such nonsense!" says Monkey.

"I'm serious. I just want to make sure I have a home, a warm bed to return to if I fail."

"No more idle talk," my new master says to me and Monkey. "Let's get on the road."

Easy for you two, a monk and a monkey who have never tasted matrimonial bliss!

So, we get on the road: Monkey leading the way with that Gold-Banded Cudgel on his shoulder, followed by me, Pigsy, carrying the heaviest luggage, and Xuanzang, the Buddhist monk, riding that big, beautiful horse.

We went on for a long day. When it was getting dark, I felt so hungry and tired.

"Let's call it a day and see if we can find lodging in a nearby village," announced Master.

"Hurrah for that," I said. "I'm starved. Let's find a nice home and get some nice food so I'll be replenished and ready for tomorrow."

"Pigsy, you're just beginning and are already homesick and complaining?" said Monkey, half-jokingly.

"Elder Brother," said I. "You can live by drinking the wind or rain or whatever, not me. I need real food."

"Wuneng," Master said. "If you're indeed homesick already, this journey may not be the right thing for you. You might as well go back now. It's not too late yet."

I fell on my knees and kowtowed to my master: "Don't

listen to my elder brother. I was telling the truth and speaking from my stomach, is all. No homesickness whatsoever, none, nada, zilch. I'll go with you to West Land, all the way, whatever it takes!"

"All right," Master nodded. "Get up then and let's go find food and shelter for the night."

There was nothing more for me to say but to pick up the heavy load again and soldier on toward what looked like a house at the foot of a hill.

A crescent moon began to show her face in the early evening sky.

THIRTEEN
Old Steady

You may have already forgotten me. I'm one of those forgettable types after all. Other than the class clowns, smarty-pants, troublemakers, samosas and quarterbacks, the prettiest and the ugliest, and those boring nerds who win all the quiz bowls, whatever, who else do you still remember from your school days, anyone of those caught in the middle of the spectrum, nothing colorful, spectacular, or really disgusting, to remember by?

When you're steady, dependable, consistent, but don't shine in anything good or bad, who would bother to remember you? Yours is a supporting role, not much than an extra in a show starring others, is all.

No, no, don't get me wrong. I'm not jealous or envious or complaining.

I am all for Monkey getting most of the credit and glory. He earns it fair and square and deserves it all. He gets his share of the blame and punishment, too. Sometimes he's just a little bitty too good for his own good. He does the hardest work, the heaviest lifting, the go-to person whenever there's any danger, basically, no Monkey, no Master going to West Land, if you want my opinion, and gets punished the harshest, sometimes unjustly.

Pigsy is just being himself, having an enormous appetite for everything, easily fooled, easily tempted, that lusty heart of his never dies; not above playing a dirty trick or two, especially against Monkey to get even although I don't really know what exactly is the grudge, but he works hard, carries the heaviest of loads on his shoulders, does all the work assigned him too, most of the time, and is a lot of fun to be around.

As to Xuanzang, Master, he is kind, loving, gentle, and all, but sometimes I have my little bitty moments of misgivings, whether he is the right choice, is up to the job, but what do I know? I know enough to know I should keep that kind of thought to myself.

I've learned my lessons after all, having been punished so harshly for a little bitty offense, a little bitty accident really. I was born with an ambition to amount to something, a hero of sort known to every household in the world. I read all the books I could lay my hands on, travelled all over the place to learn from the best, and accomplished so many feats that I was awarded the grand title of Imperial Honor Guards Commander by Jade Emperor. Imagine the kind of glory I was basking in, in full shiny regalia from head to toe, part of His Majesty's entourage everywhere he went.

Then what? At one of Queen of Heaven's longevity peach extravaganzas I accidentally bumped a jade ornament on the altar, and it broke to pieces. Not a big deal, right? No, they made it feel like I had wreaked havoc in Heaven. Jade Emperor would have me dragged out and beheaded right away. Many tried to put in a good word for me, particularly Goldstar and Barefoot Fairy, begging Jade Emperor to have mercy on account of my accolades and this being my first offense.

I was given a much lighter punishment instead: my rear end

flogged eight hundred times, my chest being pierced through by spears and arrows one hundred times every seven days for forty-nine days. Then, I was kicked out of Heaven and sent down to a river of sandy water where I lived for years, killing whatever I could lay my hands on for food, humans, animals, what have you. What else could one do to survive under the circumstances?

One day, as I surfaced to get whatever catch for the day, I was met with this fellow. I am not the type fixated with my own shadow in water, I know I am not much of a looker, so what? A glance at this fellow, though, his ridiculously long nose, mouth, ears, and potbelly, I knew here comes one even less of a looker than me. And he'd make a real good supper, and last me for a week or two, being so fat and all. So, I raised my iron stick and went after him. I forgot to say this fellow was armed too, with a big iron fork.

You can imagine the kind of fight he and I put up together, round after round, sparks flying every which way, deafening clangor when metal meets metal, sending spasms down my arms. I knew this would not be easy catch, so I dived to the bottom of the sandy river to take stock of the situation.

I had barely had time to take a breather when I felt disturbance all around me and saw that pig coming at me again with that iron fork of his.

"You ugly darky!" shouted that pig. "You flatter yourself if you think those skulls dangling around your neck will make you look any prettier!"

"The pot calling the kettle black!" I shouted back. "Why don't you take a pee and see yourself in it?"

That only infuriated the pig more. "You cheek-less imbecile, you should've seen me in my last life, in my full regalia and glory as Canopy Marshal in Heaven!"

"Oh," I laughed. "You are the one who tried to force yourself on that beautiful Chang'er? Ever heard of the saying, an ugly toad wanting to eat a beautiful swan, way out of its league?"

I could see the pig's face become livid.

"And for your information," I continued. "The glory I enjoyed in my last life as Imperial Honor Guards Commander was not a little tittle less than yours, if not more!"

We went after each other even more furiously. After a few more rounds, the pig beat a retreat and I followed close behind.

When I popped my head above the water, I saw a monkey lifting a big Gold-Banded Cudgel ready to hit me, so I dived right back under water.

"You impatient *bimawen*, stable boy!" I heard the pig screaming at the monkey. "Why don't you wait till I've lured him out and then hit him?"

Bimawen? That rebel monkey who dared to call himself Great Sage Heaven's Equal and caused so much trouble up there that Rulai had to get involved, the last time I heard?

How life has a way of dealing out things! The three of us, all fallen angels of sorts, now meeting here and dueling it out. Isn't that strange? It's all karma, right?

As if on cue, I heard a voice calling me from the sky:

"Wujing, that Buddhist monk I've told you about has been here for quite a while. Why don't you come out and bow to your master?"

It was Guanyin, Goddess of Mercy.

I remerged to the surface of the sandy river right away.

Guanyin, in all her kindness and glory, was right there, perched on a cloud.

"Please forgive me for my tardiness," I bowed and apologized profusely. "But where's that Buddhist monk? I don't see him."

"Over there!"

I turned in the direction Guanyin was pointing and saw a

monk sitting on the east bank of the sandy river, next to him a white horse and that damned pig and monkey.

"Them?" I said incredulously. "That pig and I have been fighting like devils, and then that monkey almost got me. Nobody's said a word about the monk and the journey to the west."

"Now you know. Pigsy and Monkey are disciples of Xuanzang's, you elder brothers."

I hesitated, still fresh from the fight they'd given me, still a little bittle shy of them.

"You really want to give up this monstrous way of life and be saved?" asked Guanyin.

"Yes," I said. "I'll do everything and anything if I can turn a new leaf."

"Then, don't you worry about those two," said Goddess of Mercy, as if having read my mind. "They can't and won't hurt you. As a matter of fact, they're going to owe you a debt of gratitude right away, now."

"How?"

"You make them a raft out of those skulls hanging around your neck so they can cross this dangerous river safely. They've have been at their wits' end facing this insurmountable barrier."

That sounds like a great way to start, like hit the ground, or water, running.

I followed Guanyin to where the trio was.

"Meet your master and your two elder brothers!"

I bowed to Xuanzang, Master first, then to Monkey and Pigsy. As us three disciples bowed to each other, I caught my two elder brothers winking at each other and then me, so I winked back. I knew there and then that we were all good, a band of brothers protecting Master on the journey to West Land.

Seeing this, Guanyin beamed and soared into the cloud.

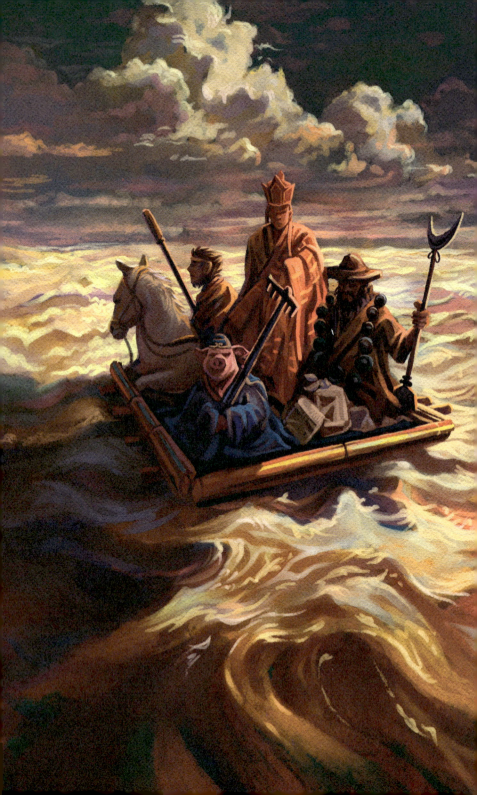

Master asked Monkey to cut and shave off my thick hair and messy beard and sideburns. I felt like a clean, newborn baby. A monk.

"Now that you're a disciple of mine," Master said. "How about me giving you a new religious name?"

"I already have one, Master. Wujing, Clean Awakening, given by Guanyin herself."

"Mmm, Wukong, Vain Awakening, Wuneng, Able Awakening, now Wujing, Clean Awakening. How neat! How about a byname, though, like Monkey, and Pigsy?"

I nodded. Can I say no? Of course not.

"Since this sandy river is where you're reborn," Master said, pulling his imaginary long beard, "becoming a Buddhist monk, let's go with Sandy then."

Sandy. Sandy. I turned it over in my mind. A little bitty down-to-earthy, nothing flattering or belittling, I'd take it.

As I bowed to thank Master, it occurred to me that he should have a byname too, like Monk, or Monky, if we were all in this together. Seeing the expressionless face of Master, I held my tongue. Humor is not really my thing after all, and I don't want to be taken the wrong way.

Nervously I set to work right away, cutting bamboos, tying them together, and then attaching the skulls all around as buoys to keep the raft afloat.

To my relief and jubilation, the raft turned out to be big enough to hold all of us, Master, his horse, Monkey, Pigsy, and me.

As the raft sailed toward the other shore, I knew I would be all right; we would get to our destination no matter what.

FOURTEEN
Damned Either Way

We're pressing forward in our journey to West Land, the three of us, Pigsy, Sandy, and me protecting Master from dangers across mountains, rivers, treacherous marshlands, endless stretches of wilderness, the best we can. Not a smooth sail, but we're making headway.

Sometimes, the real danger does not come from outside, but from within and we're our own worst enemy, is something I've learned the hard way.

One day, as we reached the foot of a tall mountain, the going got a teeny-weensy harder, what with narrow trails through thickets of bushes, rugged hills and steep cliffs, and animals of all stripes and shapes, tigers, lions, wolves, foxes, rabbits, snakes, whimpering, howling, mating calls, all kinds of bone-chilling noises. I could see the fright in the eyes of Master atop his big white horse.

As usual, I led the way beating about the bushes with my Cudgel as loud as I could, not realizing until a teeny-weensy too late that this was no different from whistling at night: it would attract wandering ghosts and demons instead of scaring them away.

Just when I thought we were lost as we struggled along a windy, sharply curved trail through the thickest of bushes, vines, and fallen trees sprawling our path, we found ourselves in a valley of barren, open space.

We were all thrilled and took a deep breath.

"Wukong," Master said, "I've been traveling all day long and I'm tired and hungry. Why don't you go and find some kind-hearted folks and get us some food?"

"Master," I said, somewhat irritated. "Can't you see for yourself that we're in the middle of a mountain, with no village or home in sight wherever you look?"

Master was taken aback by my response.

"You think you're such a hotshot, Monkey! Do I need to remind you that it's me who freed you from underneath that massive mountain and adopted you as a disciple of mine? How can you be so lazy and return my kindness like this?"

"That's an unfair accusation, Master," said I, feeling hurt. "I've been working my tail off every day since, you know that!"

"Then, why not go and find me some food? I'm starved!"

"All right, say no more and please do not pray that spell to punish me. You can get off the horse and rest and I'll go and see what I can find."

I somersaulted into the cloud and looked as far and wide as my Fire Gold Eyes could see—no villages, no homes, no chimneys with live smoke anywhere.

On a hillside, though, I saw a host of mountain peach trees, twigs loaded with ripening fruits. I was delighted and landed back where Master was sitting.

"Master, we've got food," I reported.

"What kind?"

"Mountain peaches."

"Okay, peaches are fine. We monks are not picky eaters anyway. Go get us some."

I somersaulted back in the cloud, hurried to the peach trees, and gathered as many good fruits as I could. As I rode the cloud back, I saw from distance someone approaching where Master, Pigsy, and Sandy were resting.

A beautiful young woman, dressed in long silky robe, carrying a willow basket filled with cooked rice, steam buns and what have you.

She would make a perfect pastoral scene except there is no sheep grazing or cuckoo birds singing anywhere. She can charm just about any man, catching his eye, capturing his heart, you know, but for me, this apparition from nowhere feels, even smells, a teeny-weensy odd. Something untoward afoot?

At the sight of the young woman, Pigsy jumps to his feet and hurries toward her.

"Greetings, kind lady!" Pigsy bows deeply, like a gallant gentleman. "May I ask where are you from and where are you going, alone in this wilderness between nowhere?"

"Oh, young master," says the young woman in a sweet voice, "I'm here to bring you food to show appreciation of Buddha's kindness."

Pigsy grins from ear to ear and leads her to where Master is. Master gets on his feet right away, bows, and queries about her family and such pleasantries.

"My parents are alive and well," the young woman says. "We live not far from here. My husband is attending cattle on the other side of the hill."

Perched in the cloud, I look around again and see no house or man attending cattle this side, the other side, any side of the hill, anywhere. I now know for certain what we're dealing with here.

"In that case," Master says, "you should take the food back home to feed your elderly parents and your hardworking husband. That's what a filial daughter and a virtuous wife is supposed to do. I don't want to be the one that ruin your reputation as a good woman. Besides, one of my disciples is getting us some peaches and should be back any time now."

"I've never seen a monk as wobbly as you are, Master!" says Pigsy angrily. "You want to wait when Monkey is back, so we have to split the food four ways? Let's share it now, three of us, you, me, and Sandy!"

With that, he takes the basket from the young woman and sticks his long mouth into the rice bowl.

I've seen enough.

I landed and lifted my Cudgel to hit the imposter.

Startled, the young woman darted and hid herself behind Master, crying heartbreakingly, "Kind master, please save me from this beast!"

"What're you doing, Monkey?!" Master stared at me furiously.

"Trying to kill this demon is what I'm doing, Master!"

"What demon? How do you know?"

"You may not know this, Master," said I as patiently as I could. "Back in the days when I was in Heaven, I was tempered in Laozi's *Bagua* Stove, that stove for making immortality beans. When I came out forty-nine days later, I got this pair of Fire-Gold-Eyes that can see thousands of *li* into the distance and see through pretty faces and thick skins, what have you, for what they really are."

Master stared at me incredulously.

"Besides," I continued, "before I converted to Buddhism and became a disciple of yours, I had done my share of such trickery, charmed, and snared quite a few greedy, lecherous men along the way. They all ended up on my dinner plates. That's what this young woman, this vicious demon, really wants, catching you and cooking you up for dinner so she, whatever she really is, will be immortal and never die."

"I don't believe you!" snapped Master angrily. "Look at her. So young and innocent!"

The young woman popped her head from behind Master and cried more heartbreakingly. "Protect me from this horrid monkey, kind master!"

She shot me a look and hid behind Master again. In that fleeting moment, in her glittering eyes I caught sight of a demon laughing at me, salivating, can't wait to sink its sharp teeth into the fleshy back of Master.

"Now I know, Master," I said, unable to contain my frustration. "You're not much different from those lecherous men. You're bewitched by this beautiful young woman and want to have her for yourself, is that it? How about Pigsy, Sandy, and me gathering some wood and making you a love nest so you can wed this young woman this very night? You can't wait, right?"

Master's face reddened with shame and fury, his lips trembling, but no words came out of his mouth.

I pushed Master aside and raised my Gold-Banded Cudgel again. Where my Cudgel fell, the beautiful young woman vanished; on the ground laid a stinky corpse.

Master would have crumbled on the ground if Sandy had not caught him in time.

"How can you kill a good woman like that?" screamed Master, pointing a shaking finger at me, "you bloodthirsty monkey!"

His pale lips began to mumble something, and I knew I was in big trouble.

"Wait, wait, Master!" I said, desperately. "Take a look for yourself, the food in the basket this young woman has brought you? Take another look!"

Master, supported by Sandy's strong arms, wobbled a few steps closer to the basket.

The mouthwatering sweet rice and steamed buns were gone,

in their place were six or seven ugly toads, all busy crawling out of the basket and then leaping away as fast as their legs could carry them.

Master looked half convinced and was about to let me go when Pigsy chimed in.

"Master, don't be fooled by Monkey! We all saw this good woman with our own eyes. How can she be a demon? It must be one of Monkey's tricks to cover up his crime, killing another innocent life, so you won't pray that spell to punish him again!"

Xuanzang, that master of mine, as fickle as he is gullible, flew into a rage again.

The moment he began to pray that damned spell, my head began to spin and hurt like hell.

"Please stop, Master!" I begged as I rolled on the ground, holding my head in my hands so it wouldn't explode. "Say whatever you wish to reprimand me, but please stop praying the spell!"

"What more for me to say, Monkey?" Master continued to fume. "How many times more do I need to teach you that we Buddhist monks shall never kill? What's the use of going on this journey for the scriptures if you keep killing innocent people? Go back!"

You'd have been killed, cooked up, and be churning in the demon's belly now if I hadn't killed it, is what I really wanted to say in my own defense, but what's the use arguing with him?

"Go back where, Master?" I asked weakly.

"Wherever you're from. I don't want you as my disciple anymore!"

"Without me as your disciple," I said, not to defend myself, but to tell him the truth, "I'm afraid you won't be able to complete the journey to West Land."

"My fate is in the hands of Heaven. I won't complain even if I will be killed and steamed for dinner by that demon. You think you're my savior? Go back! Now!"

"All right, if you insist," I said, my eyes moistening. "I only regret that I haven't been able to repay your kindness yet."

"What kindness?"

"Freeing me from underneath that mountain and giving me the opportunity for salvation, the kind of kindness if I do not repay, I'll suffer infamy into perpetuity!"

Upon hearing this gushing from the bottom of my heart, Master softened.

"All right, I'll give you a second chance. If you commit the same sin again, I'll put the spell on you a hundred more times!"

"Or a thousand more times, if you will, but I won't hurt anyone again."

I helped Master back on the horse, gave him a few of the peaches I'd gathered, and we got on the way again.

Before we'd gone much further, we saw an old woman wobbling toward us with a cane, wailing, wiping away tears.

"Trouble, Master!" exclaimed Pigsy. "That old woman must be looking for her daughter!"

"What daughter?" asked Master.

"That young woman Elder Brother has just killed, must be her daughter, her mother looking for her now."

Damn Pigsy, still holding a grudge against me for ruining his blissful life at the Gao's. No other way to explain this, being intentionally gullible.

"Are you blind, Pigsy?" I snapped angrily. "That young woman of yours was eighteen or nineteen years old, tops, this old woman is ancient, the way she walks and those deep wrinkles, must be in her eighties. You mean she gave birth to this daughter in her sixties?"

Pigsy shrugged, at a loss what to say.

I jumped in front of the old woman. She looked startled, then wailed more heartbreakingly for the whole world to hear:

"Where's my daughter? My poor daughter, where're you?"

In the old woman's tearful eyes, I saw the same demon, baring its teeth, salivating for Master's flesh.

What should I do? I'll be in big trouble with Master again if I kill this demon. If I don't, Master will be in big trouble, and the journey to West Land will end today, here and now. I'm condemned to choose, but don't really have a choice.

I lifted my Cudgel to strike again.

The old woman vanished and there, by the wayside, laid a stinky corpse.

Master was frightened off the horse and began to mumble that spell again before finding his breath, before Sandy helping him on his feet again. Eyes shut, Master kept mumbling, oblivious to how I rolled on the ground in excruciating pain, how pitiably I begged him to stop.

"Stop, Master, please," I cried, "say whatever you want, punish me however you see fit, but please stop praying that spell! It's killing me!"

"What's more to say, Monkey?" fumed Master. "You promised you'd never hurt anyone again only a short while ago, and now you've killed another innocent. I've tried so hard to save you, why are you so hellbent?"

"Master, I swear that was indeed a demon!"

"Such an egomaniac hotshot! Should never have agreed to take you under my wing. How can there be that many demons? If you do not aspire to be kind, why don't you just leave?"

Such a self-righteous, grandiose prig! That wing of yours can't even flap to fend off any attack, would've have ended up on a monster's plate a long time ago if I hadn't protected you the best I can. Small thanks I get.

"I don't mind leaving, Master, if you insist. Can you promise me one thing, though?"

"What? Say it."

"Master," Pigsy, that idiot, couldn't help chiming in again. "He wants to divide up the luggage with you. Why don't you give him a couple of the old rags and hats, what have you, and send him on his way?"

That really pissed me off.

"You ugly foul-mouthed pig! Have you ever seen me wanting any earthly possessions? I was born naked and would be happy to die and leave this world naked too, taking nothing with me to the never neverland."

"Why don't you leave then?" asked Master, as if not sure who to believe.

"Well, where should I begin, Master?" said I, grasping the opportunity to beg for a farewell gift I feel I've more than earned. "Before I caused trouble in Heaven and was duly punished, I was Monkey King living happily on Flower Fruit Mountain with a following of forty-seven thousand monkeys and enjoying respect and allegiance from everyone far and near. How can I go back and face them all with this thing on my head?"

I paused, and then continued.

"Can you have some mercy, remove it from my head, and put it on someone else, if you're so inclined? That's not too much to ask, Master, for having served you so loyally for so long, right?"

Master looked surprised by this request. "I wouldn't mind, but Guanyin never taught me how to loosen and remove that thing on your head."

I was so disheartened.

"In that case, why don't you keep me a teeny-weensy longer and see what happens?"

Master sighed.

"I'll give you one more chance, absolutely the last chance and absolutely no more killings!"

"Never ever again, Master, even if I had eaten leopard's gallbladders!"

Gratefully, I helped Master back on the horse, and we resumed our journey, me leading the way as usual.

Before we had gone for a few *li*, we saw an old man coming our direction, frosty-haired, long beard, a rosary around the neck, walking with a shaggy, serpentine cane, mumbling *amitofo* and some unintelligible Buddhist scripture.

I sensed trouble afoot again and felt a sudden tightness in my chest.

Master flew into a rapture at the sight of this old man.

"*Amituofo!*" enthused Master. "We are still thousands of *li* away from West Land and are already seeing such pious Buddhist believers. Amazing!"

"What's so amazing about this, Master?" said Pigsy. "That old man must be father of the young woman and husband of that old woman Elder Brother killed a short while back. He's here to seek reckoning, revenge. If they catch us, you'll be sentenced to death for sure, Sandy and I will be sent to ghost-wouldn't-lay-eggs frontier posts, and Monkey, well, he will play a trick and disappear into thin air, good for him!"

Damned Pigsy. He may look foolish and act idiotically sometimes, but he certainly knows what buttons to push and how to force Master's hand in getting his revenge. Payback time for him and he won't give up until he succeeds. Can't judge a book by its cover indeed.

I leapt in front of the old man and bowed. "Kind grandpa, where're you going, praying and walking alone at this late hour?"

The old man was startled but recovered quickly.

"Oh, I've been doing this all my life, as expected of a pious Buddhist. Today I'm praying an itty-bitty harder because my daughter left home to take food to my son-in-law quite a while ago and never returned; then my wife went to look for her and did not return either. I became worried, left home to look for them, oh horror, you know what I found? their corpses by the wayside! That's why I'm so heartbroken and praying so hard for their salvation, a better life for them in their next incarnations."

As I was listening to the old man lamenting, my Fire Gold Eyes saw underneath the frosty hair, long beard, and pious visage the same demon, salivating, baring its sharp teeth even more hungrily.

"You despicable demon!" I said. "Think you can pull the wool over my eyes? No way!"

The old man froze, shocked that I'd seen through him.

I was just about to lift my Cudgel again when I checked myself.

If I kill this demon imposter, Master will definitely pray that damned spell again. It'll kill me for sure. If I wash my hands off this, the demon will snatch away Master in the blink of an eye and have him steamed for an immortality extravaganza of sorts for sure. That's betraying the trust Guanyin, Goddess of Mercy, and Master has placed in me too. My job's to protect him, no matter what, yet if I do what I need to do to protect him, it'll be the death of me, and his death too, soon, because I won't be around to protect him anymore.

Damned I do and damned I don't. What a fix I've got myself into.

I murmured a spell, called up some local earth fairies, and asked them to bear eyewitness to what I was about to do. They all bowed affirmatively.

I lifted my Cudgel again and let it land on the old man's head so hard so there's no chance the demon could play the impersonating trickery again.

I saw Master swooning, caught in the arms of Sandy, and leapt back to where he was.

"You monkey!" Master fumed, struggling to be on his feet again. "Killing three innocent lives in a row!"

He began to pray that spell of his again.

"Don't, don't, Master!" I begged. "Why don't you take a look with your own eyes?"

I offered my hands, but Master ignored them; so, supported by Sandy, he wobbled to where the old man was and this is what he saw:

A pile of white bones and a skull covered with maggots busy feasting.

"Monkey," Master said, perplexed. "You've just killed this man, right before our eyes. How can he rot so fast?"

"That's what it really is, a demon! You can see the words carved on that skull!"

Master craned his neck to see and flinched as he tried to read out the words underneath squirming maggots:

Dame White Bones

"You see, Master," I said, and turned to the earth fairies for confirmation. They all nodded affirmatively.

An ironclad case, this time, I thought.

Master nodded slightly and was about to turn when Pigsy had to chime in once more. "Master, don't you see that's just another trick Monkey's playing on you, so you won't punish him for his vicious crimes?"

Master, this most fickle, gullible weakling of a monk, began to mumble that damned spell again. I fell on the ground and rolled in excruciating pain.

Master kept it on with his eyes shut, oblivious to my cries of pain as I wiggle and wriggle, tumble and fall and roll on the ground, like I was performing some crazy breakdance, my head hurting like a smashed melon, my brains being mashed by a bad cook.

"Please stop, Master!" I begged and begged. "Say whatever

you will to reprimand me, punish however you want, but stop this! I'm dying!"

"What more there's to say, Monkey?" Master paused. "You're a heartless animal, killing innocent lives like it's nothing!"

I was just about to put in a word in my own defense when Master waved to shut me up.

"Good thing that we're in a wilderness and nobody will report these horrific crimes to authorities. If we were in a town or city now and you kill again, what's going to happen to me when they catch us?"

So, it's all about you, Master, I get it, not really about the "lives" I've killed.

Would be too foolish of me to verbalize such a thought at this time, and at my own peril, too. If I have to leave, I would rather do so on my own terms.

"Master," said I, holding my head high, like giving a farewell speech. "It's god's truth that what I've killed is a demon who wants to harm you. So, this is what I get in return for having saved you from that demon, for having served and protected you all the way. If you can't tell truth from falsehood and so easily fall for Pigsy's lies, three times in a row, there's no use for me to stay anymore. I'm leaving. See who's going to protect you from dangers from now onward!"

"You insolent, megalomaniac monkey!" Master flew into a rage, trembling all over. "I still have Pigsy and Sandy? They don't count?"

"They do, but they can't protect you from real dangers, like that demon. I've served you the longest, too. That doesn't count? So, this is another case of tossing away the sling after shooting down the birds, killing the dog when there are no more rabbits to catch, is that it? I have news for you, Master: there are more dangerous dangers ahead than you can imagine!"

Tears gushed into my eyes as I were uttering those words, somehow.

The same blank look in Master's face.

"All right then. I'm leaving now. Do me one favor though: please do not pray that spell on me again."

"I will not," said Master.

"How can I be sure of that? When you run into real dangers again and when Pigsy and Sandy cannot save you, you'll certainly be thinking of me again, blame it all on me, and pray that spell again even though I'll be one hundred thousand *li* away. If I have to come back to save you, perhaps I should just stay with you?"

That last part of what I said really rubbed Master the wrong way.

He rolled off the horse, asked Sandy to get him paper and writing brush, and wrote something on it tremulously.

"You megalomaniac monkey, so full of it!" Master muttered through his teeth, handing the paper to me. "Here's my official dismissal letter: You are no longer my disciple and I swear that if I have to see you again, it'll be in Hell! You happy now?"

"No need to swear, Master," I said with a sigh. "I'm leaving now. Please accept my last bow as a disciple of yours!"

Master turned his face away. "I'm a good Buddhist monk and will never ever accept bow from someone as vicious as you!"

I pulled out a hair and murmured:

"Change!"

Three more me, Monkey, appeared, so, four Monkeys bowed to Master from four sides at the same time and there was no avoiding my farewell bow of gratitude, him accepting it or not a whole different matter.

"Sandy, brother," I said as I turned to leave. "I know you're a good man. So be wary of falsehoods spewing from Pigsy's big mouth and take good care of Master. If, in the unlikely event

that any demon catches him, tell that demon that Master's first disciple is Monkey King, Wukong, that should be enough to scare them away."

I saw Sandy's eyes moistening.

Pigsy stood there, like this whole thing had nothing to do with him.

"Why don't you just leave," Master said impatiently. "I'm a good monk and do not want to be associated with the name of someone as compromised, as foul as you. Go back to where you're from! Now!"

Heartbroken, nothing more I could say or do to change anything, I gave Master one last bow, somersaulted into the cloud, and sailed in the direction of home.

When was the last time I travelled this route? More than five hundred years ago? What've I done with my life since? What trouble have I caused everyone? What am I going to do from now? Am I going to amount to anything with this life of mine, at all?

I saw Flower Fruit Mountain appearing in the horizon. My heart skipped a beat.

I landed right outside Water Curtain Cave.

The whole place felt so abandoned and sad. Only seven or eight monkeys came out from the bushes, all so tiny, skinny, as if they hadn't eaten anything for years.

"Grandpa, you're back finally!" They hurrahed, hugging me, tugging at my clothes. and so on.

"Where's everyone else?" I asked.

"There's not many everyone else, grandpa," cried Little Mischief, now looking as old as a grandpa himself. "Old and young, altogether, about a thousand of us, is all."

What? When I left home for the glory of Great Sage Heaven's Equal, we had more than forty-seven thousand, all healthy, happy, well-armed, well trained. What happened?

As it turns out, many of them have been hunted down and captured by a gang of monstrous predators, some skinned alive for meat, some forced into circus, dancing, singing, putting on shows for the captors, some enslaved, sweating and toiling in the fields from dawn to dusk.

Old Sage, wise, having an answer for just about any question, is no more.

Square Head and many others like him have fallen, too, while defending our home.

Tears welled up in my eyes. My people, how they've all suffered on account of me, my vanity, my megalomaniac pursuit of grandeur in Heaven. Perhaps I've indeed sinned more than my share, especially when it comes to my own people, having abandoned them for so long and betrayed their trust, so I do deserve all the punishment I've received.

First order of business for me, to repent and recompensate, is to go and liberate all my people languishing in bondage in the hands of those atrocious predators.

I called up the thousand or so survivors amongst my people and asked them to gather piles upon piles of rocks on a hill.

"Grandpa," asked Little Mischief, smiling. "What kind of new game are you going to play with us?"

"Just you wait and see. It'll be fun."

With all the rocks gathered, I somersaulted into the cloud and looked around.

I saw in the distance a swarm of mean-looking cavaliers on mean-looking horses, armed with spears, knives, swords, you name it, charging toward Flour Fruit Mountain.

So those vicious predators have got the wind of my return and are now taking an offensive move as their best defense? Bring it on!

I landed back on top of our hill and waited.

When our attackers got to the foot of the hill, screaming

obscenities, spoiling for a dirty fight, I murmured a spell and then blew hard:

A fierce hailstorm arises from nowhere, sweeps up the rocks my people have piled up, and hurls them in the direction of our attackers, like a thousand gigantic slings shooting all at once; our attackers fall left and right like dead flies; only two or three turn around fast enough to escape.

All my people jumped for joy:

"What a game!"

"Grandpa, you did it!"

"Long Live our King!"

I've sinned again, killing so many lives, with just one hailstorm. Perhaps I've sinned beyond redemption and there is no hope for salvation anymore. But what can I do? Sitting around idly and watching my people being skinned alive, forced to do slave labor, entertaining their butchers with tears in their eyes?

I'm home again. That's all that matters now.

"Where's that flag of ours, you know what I'm talking about?" I asked.

Someone ran inside Water Curtain Cave and came back with an old, wrinkled flag. We had it cleaned and put these new words on them:

Make Flower Fruit Mountain Flourish Again
Build Water Curtain Cave Back A Grander Palace

FIFTEEN

Dream Visions

Life's been good since I returned home, Flower Fruit Mountain.

What do they say, east, west, home is the best? Especially when you're treated like somebody, feel like somebody, in my case, King.

It's like the good old days, partying, drilling, visiting neighbors to talk about anything under the sun, living freely and carefree, not kowtowing to anyone between Heaven and Earth, isn't that what I've always wanted, what I've been missing for more than five hundred years since I left for some vainglory elsewhere?

I've been sleeping soundly in my own bed in Water Curtain Cave, not exposed to the slings and arrows of the elements or worse human tongues.

Occasionally, though, I toss and turn and when I wake up in the morning, I recall having had some troubling dreams.

In one dream, I see three travelers trudging to the foot of a huge hill.

"I'm so tired and hungry," says one of them, a monk, on horseback. He looks like someone I know, but I can't place him.

"All right, Master," says the long-nosed, big-eared one of the trio, a fat pig, carrying a heavy load. He also looks familiar. "I'll go and find food. Why don't you rest here."

The third one is dark-skinned, donning a necklace of human skulls. What's his name?

The fat pig goes to look for a village or home, but doesn't see any, so he drops into the bushes nearby and begins to snore the moment his head hits the ground.

I see the monk, sitting by the wayside, getting anxious.

"Wuneng has gone for so long. Why isn't he back?"

Now I know who they are! I've all but forgotten about them.

"Don't you worry, Master," says Sandy, the dark-skinned one. "I'll go and look for him."

When Sandy does not return, Master looks even more worried. He gets up and goes to look for him and Pigsy.

He gets lost in some woods wrapped in some weird, unearthly light and vibe and becomes really frantic.

Out of the blue, there appears in front of him a magnificent temple with a golden dome basking in the glorious sunset.

Master, looking dazed, walks into this magnificent temple.

In a grand chair near the altar sits a big, yellow-robed demon, being served cup upon cup of wine. At the sight of the new visitor, the demon roars with laughter:

"Hahaha, this monk looks well fed, well fattened. His flesh must be tender and delicious. Coming to my place on your own, without me lifting a finger, like a fly perching on a snake's head, hahaha!"

Master's legs give way and he crumbles on the ground; he kicks and screams when a bunch of small demons come and grab his arms and legs.

"Don't kill me!" Master shrills desperately, "I'm a Buddhist monk traveling to West Land for true scriptures. I have two disciples who will revenge me if you do me any harm!"

Only two disciples? I don't count anymore even in a dream, nightmare of a dream. That hurts.

"There's three of you?" Yellow-Robed Demon roars heartily. "The more, the merrier!"

They dump Master into a hole in the back of the temple and put the chain lock on from outside.

Where're the two disciples Master depends on for his very life?

Sandy finds Pigsy in the bushes talking in his sleep, "Oh my god!... another kiss, a juicy one... one more squeeze before I go...."

Sandy pinches his big nose and wakes him up.

The two look for Master in the thick woods and see this golden-domed temple.

"Master is a lucky man," says Pigsy. "Must be enjoying feast upon feast in this place while you and I are starved to death. Let's go in and join him!"

"Luck or disaster, we don't know yet," says Sandy.

They walk up to the temple and see these words carved on the stone door:

Moon Ripple Cave

Alarmed, they raise their iron stick and fork to smash the door. It opens and a swarm of demons come rushing out, led by Yellow-Robed Demon: "My lucky day, more meat for dumplings!"

Pigsy and Sandy fight the big demon as fiercely as they can, but they are no match and have to beat a retreat.

My dream then shifts to where Master is. This happens in a dream, right?

Locked in the hole, tears in his eyes, Master mumbles the names of his two disciples:

"Pigsy and Sandy, where are you now? Why aren't you

coming and save me from all this? Oh, it's all so horrid, unbearable…."

Someone appears in front of Master. The monk, terrified, curls up into a ball in the corner, trembling all over.

"Don't you be scared," says the kind voice of a woman. "I'm the third princess of Golden Elephant Kingdom, three hundred *li* from here."

Master looks somewhat relieved and listens.

"I was abducted here thirteen years ago on the night of Mooncake Festival. We were all enjoying the moon-lit evening sky when a gust of dark wind came from nowhere and snatched me away. I've been forced to live like man and wife with the demon, giving birth to two kids, but not a single day has passed that I am not homesick."

Master sits up. In front of him is an elegantly dressed woman, sniffling, wiping away tears.

"Sorry to hear what's happened to you," Master says. "I'm but a poor Buddhist monk, any day I'll be butchered by that husband of yours and steamed for his enjoyment."

"Oh, kind master," says the woman. "I'll help you get out of here if you deliver this letter to my father, king of Golden Elephant Kingdom."

Master nods, tears in his eyes.

The woman helps Master on his feet; Master sneaks out of the hole and the temple.

As Master staggers into the thick woods, disoriented, his soft hands bruised by thorny vines and prickly twigs, I awoke.

What's going to happen to Master? Will he be able to get to Golden Elephant Kingdom and deliver the letter? What about Pigsy and Sandy?

Then I tried to dismiss all of this from my mind. Who am I to be concerned about Master, Sandy, and that bastard Pigsy? I have nothing to do with them now; I'm home sweet home enjoying life, carefree life. It's just a dream after all. Yet, dreams can tell us something, right? Can be a sign, an omen, a premonition, even a prophecy? The dream I have dreamed seems so real.

I drifted through the day, feasting, trying to have as much fun as usual, but my mind would be elsewhere sometimes, inattentive to what my guests were saying.

"Anything bothering you, grandpa?" asked Little Mischief.

"No," I said, trying to shake off whatever was on my mind and continue to enjoy life as loudly as I could.

I had a dream the next day and strange as it sounds, this dream picked up where the dream I had the day before left off.

Yellow-Robed Demon and his wife, one-time princess of Golden Elephant Kingdom, are in their bedroom.

"My dear husband," says the princess, "I've just had a dream while napping. In the dream an armored messenger told me that a wish I had when I was a little girl was yet to be fulfilled: to marry a handsome and kind husband. You've been such a loving and kind husband to me for the last thirteen years, but that wish of mine, to have a grand wedding, remains a dream."

"Oh, that can be easily arranged," says Yellow-Robed Demon heartily.

"I knew you'd do anything for me, for our love," says the princess. "So, I already let go that monk, to earn some quota of kindness so my wish will come true. I hope you wouldn't be upset."

"Upset?" says Yellow-Robed Demon, grinning. "Not a bit. I can always catch another young and fat monk to feast on another day. Delayed gratification, hahaha!"

Then my dream jumps to a different scene.

Pigsy and Sandy find Master moaning in the bushes and help him on his feet. The three, a wobbly monk supported by two disciples, hurry in the direction of Golden Elephant

Kingdom.

They finally come in sight of a magnificent city, capital of the kingdom, covered corridors, chirping streams, chimneys alive with cooking smoke.

I see Master prostrate before the throne and then present a letter to the old king, long beard, a majestic elephant roaring to Heaven scene on his golden robe.

Big drops of tears roll down his cheeks as he reads the letter.

He gives the letter to his Queen to read.

The whole place is a poodle of tears.

"Kind monk," says the old king, wiping away his tears. "Please go and subdue that demon and save and bring back my precious princess. I'll make you my royal brother and my coequal king in return so there is no need for you to suffer all the perils going to West Land."

"Your Majesty," Master kowtows, trembling. "I'm just a Buddhist monk and know nothing else but meditating and praying the scriptures."

"Incredulous! How can you have the guts to travel to West Land if you can't outpower all the monsters and demons along the way?"

"Oh, I have two good disciples protecting me from dangers. They're waiting outside as we speak."

Royal guardsmen drag Pigsy and Sandy to the throne. The old king is terrified at the sight of them.

"Are you pulling my leg, kind master?" the old king says, flying into a rage. "You call them your disciples, an ugly pig and a scary darky with that skull necklace? Was I born yesterday?"

Pigsy takes one step forward, prostrates, and says, smiling:

"Don't be frightened or upset, Your Majesty. My brother and I are not the love-at-first-sight kind of lookers, but you'll get used to us soon and find us actually quite lovable."

"Your Majesty," Master says. "I can vouch for their character. Both had their days of glory in Heaven before reborn in these less presentable forms on Earth."

"All right, then," says the old king. "Show me what you can do."

Now that I'm away, time for Pigsy to play, to show off.

"What would you like to see, Your Majesty?"

"How about becoming bigger?"

Pigsy murmurs something and grows to thirty feet tall, like a banana tree, grinning from ear to ear.

I know that fool knows thirty-six transmute tricks and would love to show off one by one, but the old king has seen enough.

"Any weapons you use? If not, my arsenal has all kinds, spears, knives, whips, swords, whichever you fancy."

"Thank you, Your Majesty! I've got this and it's all I need."

Pigsy shows a few moves with his iron fork, thrusting to the left, jerking it to the right, a backward somersault, and then landing with a strike on an imaginary opponent's head, his long, fat ears flapping, his potbelly bouncing the whole time.

Hilarious, not too shabby for Pigsy to pull this off. I could hear myself laughing in my dream, a teeny-weensy dismissively.

The old king, the queen, and all the courtiers look amused. Someone starts to applaud, and a scattered, half-hearted standing ovation follows.

Pigsy bows to the left and to the right and to the left again, like at the end of a stage show, his face glowing.

Festivity is in the air. Wine is served. Master turns it down when a beautiful young maid brings him a diamond-studded cup, Sandy sips, Pigsy gulps down cup after cup.

My dream shifts scenes again.

Pigsy and Sandy try to smash open the door of Ripple Moon Cave, home of Yellow-Robed Demon.

"What? Why are you back bothering me again?" shouts the big demon, trying to hold the door from collapsing. "Haven't I let your master go?"

"You don't know what crimes you've committed?" Pigsy shouts back. "Kidnapping the third princess of Golden Elephant Kingdom and forcing her to share your bed for the last thirteen years! Set her free, and surrender, or you'll have to deal with me again!"

Fuming with anger, Yellow-Robed Demon opens the door and rushes at Pigsy with his big iron knife.

The two fights for several rounds without either gaining the upper hand.

Sandy gets into the fray wielding his iron cane.

The trio leaps and bounds as if performing some kind of group dance, sometimes the fork and iron cane landing on Yellow-Robed Demon at the same time, sometimes the demon sending Pigsy and Sandy crashing to kiss the ground, sometimes Pigsy and Sandy hitting each other by mistake.

Pigsy, his face black and blue, flees.

Poor Sandy is caught by the big demon, tied up, and dragged inside the cave.

As you can imagine, I'm itching for some action, can't just let it end this way. I reach to my ear for my Gold-Banded Cudgel, but there's nothing; I poke in my ear again, frantically, and still feel nothing there. I am terrified: I've lost my Cudgel, and my mojo?

I woke up in a cold sweat, felt in my ear again: My baby, that magic needle, was still there. What a troubled dream.

I got up in the morning, tired, restless, worried. After a quick breakfast, I went to a quiet place on a hillside, pulled out the needle, murmured a spell so it grew to twenty feet long and rice bowl thick, and brandished it at lightning speed to fight imaginary demons only I know how; then I went through the seventy-two transmutations one by one until I was assured that I have not lost an iota of my old mojo.

When I returned to Water Curtain Cave, all the little monkeys came rushing toward me.

"Grandpa, did you hear the thunderous quakes all morning? We thought we were being attacked by some horrendous monsters again."

"Hahaha, it's just me taking a morning stroll. All is quiet now."

After lunch, I took a nap and had another dream. A daydream, literally.

"You woman, frail like water!" Yellow-Robed Demon screams at the princess. "I've been such a loving husband for the last thirteen years, clothing you in the best silk, feeding you the most delicious food, and giving you all the gold, jade, diamonds you want, yet you're still homesick and want to go back to your parents? You don't have any feelings for me?"

"My kind husband," says the princess, scared and sniffling. "Why are you talking such nonsense today?"

"Did you ask that Buddhist monk to take some secret letter to your father when you let him go? Otherwise, those two disciples of his, that ugly pig and that darky, would not have come here demanding me to set you free and let you go home. News for you: I've caught that darky and tossed him in that hole in the back."

"I swear I didn't write the secret letter you accused me of. Why don't you ask that darky yourself?"

"You're dead if that's true!"

The princess swoons.

Yellow-Robed Demon orders his little demons to bring Sandy in for interrogation.

I became worried. What if Sandy, being honest, tells the truth?

Poor Sandy. He looks so roughened up, hands and feet tied, bruises everywhere. Scared, too. At the sight of the princess on the ground, sniffling, he knows what is going on.

"You vicious demon!" Sandy says when the interrogation begins. "What secret letter are you talking about? When my master arrived at Golden Elephant Kingdom and was kindly received by the old king, he said a lady he had seen at your place looked exactly like a portrait of their third princess in the palace. That's why and how we were sent here to take her home. Don't you dare to lift a finger on the princess, a good woman! You can kill me if that helps you let out some steam."

Good Sandy, exactly as I've always thought him to be.

"In that case," Yellow-Robed Demon says to the princess, "Accept my heartfelt apologies!" He puts his arms around the princess's willowy waist; the lovely couple, eyes into each other, begins to walk toward their bedroom.

The princess stops, turns her head, and says, "Can you loosen the rope on that monk, my kind husband?"

"Sure, consider it done," says her demon husband lovingly. "I can go and meet my in-laws too, so they know their son-in-law is worthy of their daughter."

"No…no! my kind husband," the princess says nervously. "You can't go. In my eyes you're the kindest and the most handsome in the whole world, but they'd be terrified by your look."

"Oh, don't you worry. I can look as handsome as the next man in the world even in their eyes. See?"

Lo and behold, a tall, handsome man stands before the princess, sweet, smiling, his eyes lit up with adoration. I don't need to tell you how ecstatic the princess is, how she throws herself into his arms, and how the two lovebirds neck amorously, oblivious to Sandy, now unbound, looking a teeny-weensy perplexed.

I woke up when the demon husband carries his princess wife into their bedroom; got to give them some privacy, see what I mean?

After a quick breakfast, I called up my people and we paraded, drilled as hard as ever before, for peace, of course. What can one do in a troubled world like ours, filled with demons and monsters who want to harm you? Sitting around, meditating, and praying for peace will do the trick? I'm not so sure.

Take Master for an example. He's probably the kindest being on earth, wouldn't mind himself being killed and cooked up by demons desiring immortality. By the way, I never understand how the flesh of a mortal, an earthling like a Buddhist monk of Tang Dynasty, can work like Queen of Heaven's longevity peaches or Laozi's immortality beans. It's pure hype and nothing more, is what I think. This same monk wouldn't mind punishing me so harshly when I kill those demons in the nick of time to save his life. What good will that kind of kindness do if he dies? That kind of kindness is a teeny-weensy selfish, even cruel, if you ask me, 'cause for his own sense of moral superiority and purity he doesn't mind sacrificing the grand mission to West Land on which hinges the wellbeing of a great dynasty, from king to ordinary folks.

Am I being a teeny-weensy too hard on the monk, 'cause he's prayed that damned spell to punish me too many times and I hold a grudge against him?

My credo, if any, would not be unlike that practiced by Guanyin, Goddess of Mercy; she is the kindest in the world, but would not hesitate to put a condition, some constraint, on the recipient of her kindness, if necessary. That golden band on my head is Exhibit A. It's been my shame, my Hell, yet who am I to question Guanyin?

Tossing and turning in bed with these troubled thoughts

for a while, I drifted off to sleep again.

Yellow-Robed Demon, third son-in-law of Golden Elephant Kingdom, tall and handsome, arrives in the palace.

He prostrates in front of the old king and the queen and tells them this story:

Thirteen years ago, a tiger demon abducted their precious daughter on the evening of the Mooncake Festival, and it was he who had rescued their daughter and given her food, shelter, and love ever since.

The old king and the queen are not sure how to take this tale of chivalry from a son-in-law they've never met before.

"What proof do you have?" asks the old king.

"That tiger demon is right here," the son-in-law says, pointing at Master sitting next to the king and the queen as a distinguished guest.

All eyes turn and see in that chair a mean-looking tiger, baring its teeth and making menacing noises at them.

Fuming with rage, the old king orders his guards to bind up the tiger and toss him into a cage.

"Don't be fooled by the trickery of that demon!" I shout at the top of my lungs, but no sound comes out of my throat, as it happens in a dream.

Festivity everywhere in the well-lit palace of Golden Elephant Kingdom. The brand-new third son-in-law is the star of the night, basking in the loving gaze of the old king and the queen and the adoration of all the courtiers and revelers, especially the young among the fairer sex. There is so much drinking, dancing, long-sleeved dance, belly dance, you name it.

All the wine he has drunk getting into his head, perhaps, the third son-in-law begins to loosen up. He grabs a beautiful young woman playing *pipa*, a pear-shaped lute you must have seen before, and bites into her face. Poor girl cries in pain and

runs for her life. The third son-in-law, blood dripping from his mouth, grins from ear to ear and carries on.

It looks like that bloody bite breaks the spell he's put on himself coming to the royal palace. I can see him change, visibly, back to the shape of that hideous demon.

Realizing what's happening to himself, perhaps, the demon son-in-law wipes away the blood around his lips and runs into the maiden chamber of the third princess decorated exactly like it was thirteen years ago, pink colors, silk drapery, big mahogany bed with mosquito net.

Yellow-Robed Demon is just about to pour himself another cup of wine, to calm his own nerves perhaps, when a beautiful courtesan drifts in like a dream.

Somehow, she is not put off by the repulsive appearance of the demon.

"Your highness," she curtsies and says in her sweetest voice. "Let me pour it for you."

The demon royal son-in-law is so pleased. "Oh, beautiful, I was beginning to feel just an itsy-bitsy lonely here… hahaha!"

The young courtesan keeps pouring when the big cup is already full; somehow, the wine doesn't spill even when it is three or five inches over the cup.

"Amazing!" mumbles the demon son-in-law, his tongue a teeny-weensy stiff.

"Oh, your highness, you aren't seeing anything yet."

The young courtesan keeps pouring until the wine rises three or five feet high; not a drop spills over.

The demon son-in-law, so pleased, drinks greedily from the cup, his lecherous eyes fixed on the young courtesan's shapely figure.

"Can you sing and dance too?"

"Just a little," the courtesan says modestly. "Your highness wants to find out?"

"Of course! Show me all you've got tonight. I'm not going anywhere, hahaha!"

The young courtesan sings in her sweet voice, swings her slender body, and brushes the son-in-law's face with the tips of her long, soft fingers.

Excited, the son-in-law disrobes himself, removes his belt, hands his sword to the courtesan, and joins her in a duet-like sing and swing.

The courtesan now dances gracefully with the sword in hand, like a *wudan*, woman warrior, in an opera. Her movement picks up speed as she leaps and bounds and thrusts the sword at imaginary opponents from different angles when, rising to a crescendo, she suddenly turns and thrusts it to the chest of the demon son-in-law. Startled, the demon darts and is even more startled by what he sees only inches away from him:

A young dragon.

Right away, even in my dream, I recognize the young dragon as the former incarnation of Master's white horse. I'm elated and ready to shout "hurrah!"

The white horse has never as much said a word since joining us in the journey to West Land, quieter than Sandy, and has been a steady, dependable one, too. And I've never seen him engaged in a fight, and I'm rooting for him big time.

The young dragon and the big demon go after each other for many rounds, without either gaining the upper hand. The dragon fights the best he can, but the demon proves too big, too battle hardened for him to outpower, so he takes a retreat.

The young dragon, now in the form of the white horse, finds Pigsy sleeping soundly in the bushes somewhere and shakes him up.

Pigsy screams for fright upon opening his eyes.

"It's me, brother," the white horse says.

"Why, brother, you can talk?" says Pigsy, rubbing his eyes.

"I thought a demon wanted to slaughter me! Why are you here? Anything the matter?"

"Yes, Master is in danger, and we have to go and save him!"

"What happened?"

"Remember you and Sandy went to fight that yellow-robed demon and demand the return of the third princess and Sandy got caught?"

Pigsy nods.

"Well, that demon came to the court as a handsome royal son-in-law, turned our master into a disgusting tiger, the demon that had supposedly abducted the third princes. Our master is now a tiger locked in a cage!"

"That's terrible. That's terrible!" Pigsy mumbles, trembling. "If that demon is so awesomely powerful, there's no way we can beat him and save our master. Why don't you go back to the sea, and I'll carry all the luggage back to Gao Village and be the Gao's son-in-law all over again?"

"My brother," says the white horse, tears in eyes. "How can you come up with such a lousy idea? This is no time to be joking, or lazy, brother."

Yes, what a lousy idea! What a betrayal! I'm so mad at Pigsy and so want to go and pinch those two big fat ears of his and shake a teeny-weensy sense of loyalty into his big fat body. However, as in a dream, I can't even move a finger or toe of mine.

"Do you have a better idea then," Pigsy shrugs, "My brilliant and loyal brother?"

The white horse moans, thinks hard, and then says, "I know of only one person who can save our master. You should go and ask for help!"

I perk up my ears nervously, expectantly.

"Who are you talking about?" asks Pigsy although he understands exactly who the horse has in mind. "Me going and asking him for help?"

"Yes, you should go to Flower Fruit Mountain and ask Elder Brother to come and help. He's the only one who can subdue this demon."

Hurrah! At last, someone remembers me!

"What?" Pigsy protests in a whiny voice. "Don't you remember what happened with that White-Bone Demon? I was only playing a practical joke on Monkey, never thought Master would pray that spell that hard and then kick him out. I mean Monkey must hate me so much that one wrong word from me he would lift that big Cudgel of his and beat me to death."

Hahaha, Pigsy, now you know that practical joke of yours went a teeny-weensy too far and you'll have to answer for it.

"No, he wouldn't hit you. Monkey, Elder Brother, is the kindest and most loyal in his heart of hearts. If you tell him that our master really misses him, he'll definitely come and when he comes and sees our master in such trouble, he'll definitely take on the demon to free our master. Our only hope."

Our only hope for sure. I nod in agreement.

"Okay, I'm going," Pigsy says, reluctantly. "But don't you wait for me for too long. Who knows what's going to happen to me before I even get there."

A preemptive excuse for sneaking away if things do not turn out right for him?

Should never have thought this cunny Pigsy foolish.

Oh, that son-in-law dream of his, in his heart, never dies.

What about my heart? And what I've seen in my dreams? Are they real? Aren't they saying something about me, too?

SIXTEEN
Gracious Me

I woke up, confused, concerned, and elated all at once.
I called up all my people by a hillside to parade, drill, and feast again, trying hard to focus on enjoying life free from anxiety, not to worry about anything other than my own people.

A bunch of little monkey sentinels dragged someone to my presence and forced him on the ground. I knew who he was at the first sight but thought it wouldn't hurt to turn the tables on him and have some fun.

"Who on earth are you, stranger, having the balls to crash my party?" I asked.

"Not a stranger! An old acquaintance actually!" the captive said.

"An old acquaintance? I'm well acquainted with every one of my buddies and comrades and none of them looks like you. That big, long nose and mouth of yours, and those fat ears! Are you a demon, a monster, here to spy on us? Tell me your name or I'll kick your fat ass out of here now!"

"You don't recognize me, us having been brothers for several years for nothing?"

"Okay, lift your head so I can take a better look," I said.

"Surprise, surprise, it's Pigsy!"

"Yes, yes!" the captive jumped to his feet right away. "I'm he, old Pigsy!"

"Pigsy! Why are you here, not escorting Master on the journey to West Land? You must have offended Master and been dismissed too? Show me the dismissal letter!"

"No offense by yours truly and no dismissal letter either. I'm here because Master misses you so much, so he sends me here to ask you to come back."

"Liar!" I said, scenes of how I was dismissed flitting in my mind again. "You're not a good one for that. I am not going back."

"He really misses you. I'm telling the truth, I swear!"

"Misses me how?"

"The other day when Master called me and Sandy several times but neither of us heard him, he was upset and said if Monkey were still with us, he would have heard the first time and would have taken such good care of him. That's why he wants you back. Don't disappoint Master, Elder Brother, so I have not taken this long trip here for nothing."

Why am I such a softie when it comes to Master, even when I know what Pigsy says is not even half true?

"Why don't you tell me the sun rises from the West, uh? Okay, don't mean to give you such a hard time. You're my guest here, your first visit ever, why don't I show you around so you can have some fun?"

"Thanks, Elder Brother, but this is no time for me to have fun. Master is anxiously waiting for us."

"I have to do my duty as your host, a gracious host, so you won't complain about me in the future."

I took Pigsy's hand and showed him around Flower Fruit Mountain, the jaw-dropping view of sky-kissing peaks, rippling valleys, creeks meandering down ragged rocks, birds of all feathers and colors chirping in the thicket of bushes and tall pines and blossoming fruit trees everywhere.

"Elder Brother," enthused Pigsy. "To say this is paradise on earth would be an understatement!"

"I'm just getting by, brother."

"Are you kidding me? I'd give anything for this 'just getting by' life!"

When we wandered to a trail, a bunch of little monkeys presented us with baskets of freshly picked fruits, grapes, pears, loquats, berries, and melons of all kinds.

"Hahaha, kiddos, my Pigsy brother has an enormous appetite and is a voracious meat-eater. These fruits won't count as real meal, refreshment or dessert at the best."

"Oh, don't you worry about my big appetite, my good brother," Pigsy said. "As they say, when you're in Rome, do as the Romans do. Besides, these fruits look so fresh and delicious!"

Pigsy picked the biggest melon, sank his teeth in, and relished noisily, juice dripping from his lips, "Oh, good, so good!"

"Easy, easy, brother," I said, winking. "No one's racing you."

We all laughed.

"Elder Brother," Pigsy said, licking, having satisfied his tastebuds. "Let's go. Our master must be getting really anxious now."

"What's the big hurry," I said. "I haven't shown you inside our Water Curtain Cave yet."

"Another day, perhaps, Elder Brother. Let's get going. Our master has been waiting for too long."

"In that case, why don't you go? I am not going to detain you another minute."

"What? You're not going?"

"To where? I'm so happy where I am, free to go anywhere

and do anything I want without worrying about anyone bossing over me or badmouthing me to get me in real trouble, you know what I'm talking about? You can take this message to Xuanzang, your master: Once dismissed, forever dismissed, and don't miss me ever again!"

Pigsy looked stunned, and sad, at a loss what more to say. He shook his head, sighed, and turned to leave.

"Damned Monkey," he cussed when he thought he had gone far enough to be out of earshot. "Wanting to be a monster instead of a monk! May he rot in hell...."

Damned Pigsy! I sent a few little monkeys after him; they caught up and flipped him on the ground, tied him up, and carried him back to me, poor Pigsy howling like a pig being readied for slaughtering.

"You foul-mouthed pig!" I said. "How dare you curse me? I am not just your one-time brother from a long time ago. I am King here, in case you need me to remind you!"

"No, I didn't curse you, Elder Brother. I was only mumbling to myself how disappointed Master would be seeing me return by myself alone. You can cut my tongue if I had cursed you, I swear."

"You swear is worth nothing! I heard you with my own ears. For your information, when I give my left ear a gentle upward pull, I can hear everything said for the last thirty-three days, and when I give my right ear a gentle downward pull, I'll know the records of ten generations' worth of King Yama's judgements!"

"I know you smarty-pants must have changed into something to follow me," Pigsy mumbled, defeated.

"Let's not waste any more words," I said. "Little monkeys, let's give my brother here a more appropriate sendoff: hit him with a cane for twenty times first, and then flog him for twenty more times!"

Pigsy fell on the ground and begged for mercy:

"Elder Brother, spare me this send-off, please, on account of our kind master!"

"I know how kind our master is for sure!"

"All right, brother, on account of the Guanyin, then!"

The mere mention of Goddess of Mercy softened me a teeny-weensy.

"No beating then but tell me the truth. Our master is in grave danger, right?"

"No grave danger, brother. He really misses you."

"You're asking for a good beating again? Let me tell you this: although I am back in Flower Fruit Mountain, my heart is still with our master. There's been peril for him every step of the way. So, do me a favor by telling me the truth now, so you'll be spared a beating!"

"Oh, brother," said Pigsy in a more deferential tone. "You know and see through everything. Why don't you unbind me so I can tell you?"

The moment Pigsy was untied and got on his feet again, rubbing his sore arms and legs, his eyes darted left and right as if he wanted to bolt and flee.

"Don't get any ideas," I said. "I can catch you and drag you back even if I give you three full days of advantage. Tell me now because my patience is running out, fast!"

Pigsy began to tell me what'd happened since I was dismissed, confirming much of what I'd seen in my dreams, with only some minor details off here and there.

So, my dreams were more real than prophetic, or premonitions, workings of an overwrought mind. I was watching, live, like a fly on the wall, as things were unfolding.

"That's why the white horse, the young dragon really, asked me to travel all the way here and ask you to come back and rescue our master. He says you're the most kindhearted of all and will not hold the grudge against our master. As the saying goes, one should love his teacher, even teacher for just one day, as he would love his father for the rest of his life. You've got to come and save him, Elder Brother!"

"You fool!" I said. "Didn't I tell you when I was leaving that in case Master is caught by any demon or monster, just mention that Monkey King is his First Disciple?"

"I did, Elder Brother," Pigsy said, his eyes fixed on me. "That's what made it a hundred times worse!"

"How?!"

"Well, this is what I said to that demon: Don't you dare to lay even a finger on our master. His First Disciple, by the name of Monkey King, Great Sage Heaven's Equal, is so great that no demon or monster is his match. You'll die a horrible death when he catches you. You know what that demon said in response? He said: Never heard of that little monkey, whatever. If he dares to pop up here, I'll skin him alive, cut his heart out, chop him into a thousand pieces, grill, deep fry, boil, what have you, for a big feast…."

Imagine how mad I was upon hearing this. No one has ever dared to insult me with such foul language. It cuts to the quick.

"What demon is this, having eaten the leopard's gallbladders?!" I asked, although I already knew.

"It's Yellow-Robed Demon! I was only repeating what he said."

In the back of my mind, I sort of suspect this is Pigsy playing some kind of reverse psychology on me, but somehow I do want to go and rescue Master although I don't know why. All I need is a good excuse.

"All right, Pigsy," I said. "Let's go and catch this foul-mouthed demon and give him the death by ten thousand cuts! I'll return here once I've had my revenge."

"Of course, Elder Brother! Whatever you do afterwards is completely up to you."

As I was getting ready to leave, all the little monkeys came rushing out and tried to stop me.

"Where are you going, Grandpa," said Little Mischief. "Why can't you stay so our fun life can continue forever and ever?"

"Kiddo," I said, my eyes moistening. "The whole world knows I'm a disciple of Xuanzang and I've pledged to protect him on the journey to West Land. He's given me a few days' leave, out of his kindness, so I can come back and spend some time with you all. Now that Flower Fruit Mountain is made glorious again and Water Curtain Cave is built back even better, you should all be safe from any outside attack. Have as much as you can, do some useful work when bored, planting some trees and growing vegetables, what have you. I'll be back when mission is accomplished and enjoy the free, carefree life with you all again. That's a promise."

With that, I held Pigsy's hand and somersaulted into the cloud.

When passing East Sea, I halted and said to Pigsy: "Brother, you go ahead first. I need to go down and cleanse myself."

"What's there to cleanse, Elder Brother? We've got no time to waste."

"Well, much to cleanse 'cause I may have taken on more than a teeny-weensy of demon aura since I left Master. He is fastidious, you know, and one faintest whiff can knock him out."

After a good bath in East Sea, I took off again and caught up with Pigsy in the blink of an eye.

We saw a golden-domed temple down there in the thicket of woods, exactly like what I've seen in my dreams.

"That's where Yellow-Robed Demon lives, brother! Sandy's still being locked up somewhere in it."

"I know," I said and landed outside the golden-domed temple.

Two kids, eight or nine years old, were playing some game with crooked clubs.

Without a word of warning, I snatched them up, took them on top of a ragged cliff not far from the cave, and dangled them over the edge, threatening to drop them off at any moment; they kicked, screamed, and cussed like hell.

Their mother, looking exactly as I remembered, came rushing out and shouted:

"Hey, that monkey up there, I've never done anything to you, don't even know you, why are you hurting my sons? You don't know how powerful their father is. When he is back, you'll have an earful from him for sure!"

"You don't know who I am, First Disciple of that monk, Xuanzang?" I shouted back from the cliff. "You go and let go my brother Sandy and I'll give back these two bastards of yours, two for one, a very good deal for you!"

That was a quick and easy exchange.

When Sandy came out, a freed man, he gave me a deep bow, his eyes glistening with tearful joy: "Elder Brother, you're truly a godsend! I can't ever thank you enough for coming to my rescue!"

"You sweet-lipped monk!" I snapped. "Did you ever put in a good word for me when Master was praying that damned spell to punish me?"

"Let bygones be bygones, brother," said Pigsy. "Let's go and rescue our master!"

"All right. Let's do it this way," I said to Pigsy and Sandy. "You two take these two kids to Golden Elephant Kingdom and threaten to smash their brains against the marble steps of the palace. That'll definitely get the attention of Yellow-Robed Demon, their royal son-in-law. He'll then follow you here so I can take him on. That way, we will not be fighting in the palace causing so much collateral damage, hurting so many innocent people."

"Easy for you to come up with such a crazy idea!" Pigsy said. "You send us there with the two kids you've just returned to their mother, and if anything happens to them, if somehow with a slip of hand we get them killed, we'll have blood on our hands and have to pay with our lives while you're so far away, safe and sound and clean."

"Who says you'll really smash their brains against the marble steps?" I said as patiently as possible. "All you need to do is to lure that demon out, pretend to fight him, and then get him here so I can take him on in a vast open space."

"That sounds like a good plan, Pigsy," Sandy said. "Let's go and do this!"

Once they were gone, dragging between them the two boys kicking and screaming, I turned to address their mother.

"How did you end up here?" I asked, in a much softer tone, to confirm what I already knew from my dreams.

"Well, a long story," said she, tearing up. "What else could I have done when I was taken here thirteen years ago? To live, to return home one day and do my filial duty to my father and mother, I had no choice but to put up with the demon. There's not a day, an hour, a minute, that passes by that I do not think of my parents."

"Don't you cry, my lady. I'm here to subdue the demon and get you home so you can be reunited with your parents, and who knows, find yourself a much better husband."

"Are you looking for death?" said the lady incredulously. "Your two brothers, they are much bigger and stronger, were no match for that demon husband of mine. You, such a little skinny thing, want to take on that demon? That's crazy talk!"

"Don't you underestimate me, my lady," I said. "Have you ever heard of this from Laozi, what that old sagacious Daoist says, about how the small and soft can beat the big and strong? You know what I think? Those who look big and strong only eat more and waste more cloth and nothing more."

The lady smiled through her sniffles. "You think so, little monk? I mean you really think you can beat that demon?"

"Yes! I have power second to none between Heaven and Earth. You haven't seen anything yet."

I should have learned enough lessons to brag like that again, but somehow just can't help it.

"Really?"

I nodded, beating my chest confidently: "It's all on me, you have not a thing to worry about."

I then told her my plan. She nodded, half convinced, and went to find a quiet place to hide.

With a quick murmur, I became Yellow-Robed Demon's beautiful young wife waiting in the bedroom of their marital bliss for the last thirteen years. I relish a moment like this, as I did with Pigsy when he was old Gao's son-in-law, if you still remember.

Before long, I heard a gusty wind and sensed the vibe of a demon.

"My husband," I cried, tears washing down my rouged cheeks. "You're finally home!"

That demon husband of mine gathered me in his arms, kissed me hotly with his bloody-red tongue, and asked urgently: "What's the matter, crying your heart out like this?"

"Oh, my husband," I said between sniffles, "you enjoyed staying in the palace of my father and mother so much that you didn't want to come back? This very morning, Pigsy and Sandy grabbed our two sons and, no matter how I begged them to let go, took them to see their *waigong* and waipo. It was supposed to be a quick visit. That's why I'm worried to death, like a thousand daggers jabbing into my heart…."

I whimpered and howled, crying my heart out.

"So those bastards have indeed killed my sons!" Yellow-Robed Demon muttered through clenched teeth. "I thought they were bluffing. Wait till I lay my hands on that Buddhist monk and have our revenge! Don't you cry, hon. How's your heart? Still hurts a lot? Should I go and get you a doctor?"

His hot tears mingled with mine.

Oh, such heartfelt tenderness from a demon, a teeny-weensy more than I'd expected, more than I could handle.

"I feel much better now you're here, my kind husband," said I, sobbing. "It still hurts though, 'cause I've been crying so hard and my heart's broken."

"Oh, I have a remedy," enthused the demon husband. "A panacea. All you need to do is to gently rub it where you hurt, and you'll be cured. Be careful not to press it hard with your thumb. If you do, my real self will be revealed."

Hahaha, gotcha! A self-incriminating confession without being tortured.

I looked up into his eyes glistening with loving kindness and nodded appreciatively.

He led me into the inner recess of the cave and then spit out something from his mouth, a pearly, bead-shaped thing, the size of a baby chicken.

One glance and I knew this is something really special, must have been tempered in Laozi's *Bagua* Stove for years and years.

I rubbed it ever so gently on my chest and then suddenly pressed it hard with my thumb.

"Don't!" that loving husband of mine cried out and tried to grab it back.

I tossed it into my mouth and gulped it down.

My husband raised his fist to hit me, which I blocked, and with a touch of my face, I changed back to my real self.

"Honey, why are you looking at me with such a face?!"

"Don't you honey me, you monstrous fool! Don't you recognize me?"

"No," said Yellow-Robed Demon. "You do look somewhat familiar, your name is on the tip of my tongue, but I cannot place you. How dare you come and seduce and then impersonate a good woman? Where're you hiding her?"

"You insolent bastard!" I snapped angrily, "don't even remember who I am, Monkey King, Great Sage Heaven's Equal—"

"Oh, *bimawen*, that stable boy, I do remember now, thinking you're equal to Heaven, causing so much havoc there, you thick-cheeked monkey, coming to the rescue of that monk who's dismissed you like a dog—"

"That monk is my master and whatever happens between him and me is none of your business. Besides, you've insulted me behind my back!"

"What? Says who?"

"Pigsy, remember that pig of a monk? He told me so."

"That disgusting pig dares to call himself a monk!" fumed the demon. "How can you believe that pig who talks out of both sides of that long, ugly mouth of his all the time? You should know better!"

"Regardless," I said, knowing what he said about Pigsy is more than half true. "I'm a guest coming from afar. If you don't have good food and good wine to treat me, like a gracious host, why don't you stick your head over so I can smash it open and have something to drink tea with?"

"Hahaha," that demon burst out laughing. "That's foolish talk, coming to my home to provoke a fight. I have a hundred and a dozen little demons and even if you have arms growing all over your body, you won't be able to fight your way out!"

"It's you who're talking nonsense!" I laughed. "Even if you have thousands, tens of thousands of little demons, I'll still prevail and wipe them all out from the face of Earth!"

As my words still resounded down the corridors of the cave, swarms of little demons, brandishing knives, spears, swords, what have you, came charging at me, raising a battle cry at the top of their puny lungs.

Imagine how thrilled I was to have this opportunity to fight the evils of the world again.

I pulled out my Gold-Banded Cudgel, murmured "Change!" and voila, I now have three heads and six arms, wielding three big Cudgels at once. I charged into the little demons and smashed left and right; they dropped like chickens with broken necks, torn bellies, blood splashing everywhere.

Yellow-Robed Demon charged at me with his big knife. We fought like two devils, on the ground, in midair, bouncing, somersaulting, him coming down from above hoping to split my head in halves, me sweeping my Cudgel against his midsection to break his back....

We went on for fifty rounds without either gaining the upper hand.

I executed a High Pat on Horse move, which he dodged; he nosedived on me brandishing his big knife, which I blocked with my Cudgel; I then executed a Snatch Peach from Underneath Leaf move and hit him on the head really hard. When I lifted the Cudgel, though, the demon was nowhere to be seen.

I knew then this demon was not some nameless nobody, an earthling. Didn't he say he somehow recognized me?

I somersaulted into the cloud and sailed toward Heaven at lightning speed.

I pounded open Heaven's gate and marched to where all

the records are kept.

All the stars and planets in all the constellations, Hydra, Virgo, Cetus, Hercules, Eridanus, Pegasus, Draco, Centaurus, Aquarius, you name it, can be accounted for, except for one:

Kui Xing, "spoon" of the Big Dipper.

"He must have gone down to Earth," Chief Registrar, a snow-haired old man, said nervously. He reported this to Jade Emperor right away.

"How long has Kui Xing gone?" asked Jade Emperor.

"Thirteen days," answered Chief Registrar.

"That's thirteen years on Earth," Jade Emperor mused aloud. "Time to go and take him back, now!"

A detachment of Heaven Commandos went down to that golden-domed temple, Moon Ripple Cave, where Yellow-Robed Demon had called home for the last thirteen years, apprehended him without much trouble, and brought him back to the presence of Jade Emperor.

At the sight of him, I reached for my Golden-Banded Cudgel in my ear and then thought the better of it. After all, I didn't want a repeat of what happened the last time I was in Heaven, more than five hundred years ago.

"Kui Xing," Jade Emperor said. "Life in Heaven is boundlessly blissful and beautiful, that's not enough for you, so you had to sneak down to Earth?"

"I deserve a thousand deaths, Your Majesty," Kui Xing fell on his knees and said. "The third princess of that Golden Elephant Kingdom was originally a beautiful altar girl in Heaven. She and I, you know, fell in love, and had a few trysts on the sly. Feeling ashamed, she left Heaven and was reborn as a princess on Earth. I followed soon afterwards, and we lived happily together for thirteen years, until, you know."

Jade Emperor pardoned him and sent him to work as a charcoal man for Laozi, that ancient, sagacious Daoist.

When this demon business was taken care of, I turned to leave.

"You don't bow and thank His Majesty before leaving?" said Chief Registrar.

"Oops, I almost forgot," I said and bowed slightly to thank Jade Emperor.

"Once a monkey, always a monkey," Chief Registrar said. "He can never learn proper manners."

"No offence taken," Jade Emperor said dismissively, "so long as he doesn't cause us any disturbance again."

I sailed back to Earth at lightning speed, landed at Moon Ripple Cave, and found Pigsy, Sandy, and the princess exactly where I'd left them.

We traveled to the palace of Golden Elephant Kingdom right away.

Once there, I told the old king who his third daughter and son-in-law were in their former incarnations in Heaven, how they fell in love, and came down Earth, and so on.

The old king, teary-eyed, thanked me profusely.

The king and the queen helped the princess, their long-lost daughter, on her feet. They huddled together and had a good cry, their tears of joy mingling. There was not a dry eye in the palace.

As if remembering something, the old king turned and said to me:

"Why don't you go and see your master now?"

I was taken to a dimly lit place in the back of the palace. There I saw in the cage a tiger, its paws holding onto the bars, its whiskers and spotted skin soiled, its eyes dull and caked with discharge, not a pretty sight for the usually proud king of the jungle.

"My kind master," I said, as a wave of sadness and other feelings washed over me. "What's happened? You, such a merciful monk, kicked me out for my sins, how come you ended up like this? I can't even bear looking at you, terrible!"

The tiger stared back at me blankly.

"Elder Brother," said Pigsy. "What good there's talking of personal grudge? Save our master now!"

"You're his favorite disciple," said I. "Why don't you save him? I said I'd return to Flower Fruit Mountain once I've subdued that demon you and Sandy can't handle."

As I turned to leave, Sandy fell on his knee and grabbed my hand.

"Elder Brother, on account of Guanyin, Goddess of Mercy, save our master. If Pigsy and I could, we would have. You wouldn't be able to live with yourself if—"

"Say no more," I said, helping Sandy on his feet. "Get me a bowl of water. Hurry!"

Pigsy ran as fast as his two legs could carry him and came back with a bowl of water.

I murmured a prayer and spat a mouthful of water into that tiger's face.

Lo and behold, in the cage was now our master, Xuanzang, that monk sent by Emperor Xuanzong on a journey to West Land to seek true scriptures of Buddhism.

We opened the cage and helped our master out.

"Gracious me! Is that you, Wukong?" exclaimed my master, rubbing his eyes. "When did you come back? From where? How? Why?"

Sandy gave a quick account of how he, Pigsy, and the white horse fought the hardest they could but came up short and had to go and get me back to outpower Yellow-Robed Demon and save him.

"I owe you a big one, Wukong, my worthy disciple," Master said in a tremulous voice and was about to bow to me when I held him with both of my hands. Master bowing to a disciple?

What'd people say if the word gets out?

"When we are back home, after securing the true scriptures from West Land," Master said. "I'll report to Emperor Xuanzong how you outshined everyone else for this grand mission and therefore should be rewarded the most!"

"Don't mention it, master, don't mention it," I said sheepishly, a teeny-weensy embarrassed by the outpouring of heartfelt gratitude from Xuanzang. "Your loving kindness is reward enough for me."

Indeed, what else do I want for me, for my life? I mused quietly as we resumed our arduous westward journey, me leading the way, followed by Pigsy and Sandy, both carrying heavy loads of our most basic supplies, food, water, clothes, what have you, Master riding the white horse.

Whatever I, we, have gone through, is behind us now. Tomorrow is another day.

SEVENTEEN
Comic Relief

It seems that Xuanzang, our master, never fully recovered from the horror of being turned into a disgusting tiger. He is irritable, jumpy, easily frightened, suffering from some kind of syndrome, PTSD? Oh, don't ask me what those letters stand for, please. All I know is he sees vicious tigers, wolves, and demons at the sight of any old trees, dark woods, or rugged hills in the distance.

"Master," said I, "you're a Buddhist monk and supposed to be free from all these earthly desires and fears, right? Didn't some ancient sage say desire nothing and fear nothing, and if you clean out all the dirt and dust in your mind, you'll able to live pure and free? A teeny-weensy of hardship is unavoidable if you want to be a superior being, it's part of the deal, right? What do you have to fear, Master, other than fear itself. Now that I'm back, even if the sky collapses, you'll still be safe and sound, not a tree leaf will fall on your head."

Imagine me being the one giving a pep talk to Master.

He seems to hear what I say, but does not actually listen, quietly nursing some private thoughts of his own.

One day, we reached a mountain of pointed summits and

perilous canyons and as we got ready to rest for the day, an old charcoal man, donning a straw hat, a sharpened ax in hand, came shouting in our direction.

"Kind monk, you can't rest here. There is a vicious demon in the area making noises about capturing and eating humans coming from East Land."

Master was so terrified and could barely stand on his trembling legs.

"Don't you worry," I said to Master. "Let me go and find out what that old man is talking about."

I leapt in front of the charcoal man and questioned him.

"Why are you cooking up such a story to scare my master? He is on a grand mission to West Land for the true scriptures of Buddhism. You must be a kinsman of that demon, an uncle, a nephew, a distant cousin, whatever, in it for some crumbs?"

"Absolutely not," said the old man. "So, that master of yours is indeed the monk everyone here has been talking about? Then, he's exactly what that demon has been waiting for."

"Let the demon try me first." I said, mirthfully. "If they begin with my head, I'll be dead right away and will not feel a thing when they boil or stir fry me. If they begin with my feet, well, that'll be different. They can work their way, from my toes, ankles, knees, thighs, up to my backbones and chest, what have you. It'll be death by a thousand bites, you see what I mean? That'll be horrible."

"They don't have that kind of time to waste on you," said the charcoal man, looking me up and down. "Once they catch you, he'll tie you up and put you in a steamer and eat you when you're so well cooked, so tender—"

"So much the better," I laughed. "The only drawback is it'll be hard for me to breathe inside that steamer."

"You slick-tongued monk, monkey! That demon is not a nobody and dealing with him is no child play."

No child play, I know, but it's playtime, perhaps?

Should I tell Master what the charcoal man has said? If I do, he will be scared the living light out of him; if I don't and he is snatched away by the demon, it'll be so much trouble getting him back.

I thanked the old man and, rubbing my eyes red with tears, leapt back to where I'd left Master, Pigsy, and Sandy.

"Brothers," I whispered to Sandy and Pigsy, loud enough for everyone to hear. "Why don't we divide up things here and now, so Sandy, you go back to that river of yours and be that demon again, and Pigsy, you go back to the Gao's and relive your dream of being their son-in-law."

They looked at me incredulously.

"We can sell the white horse," I continued, "and buy a coffin for our master. We go our separate ways now, too much trouble going to West Land, still thousands and thousands of li away."

"What nonsense you're talking about," Master overheard what I said and was visibly upset.

"Don't you see he's crying?" said Pigsy. "Monkey has been through Heaven and Hell, not afraid of being burned by fire or deep fried in oil, but he is now crying like a baby. He must have news of some horrible demons. If he is scared, what about us?"

"Wukong," Master said. "Why are you crying like that? Trying to scare me?"

I told him what the charcoal man had said about the demon. "We've got to go back and find another way."

"Going back?" Master shrilled. "We haven't made much headway for the last three days! You've been goofing off, not trying your best, and now trying to find an excuse, is that it?"

"I'm no lazybones, you know that, Master. It's just that my best may not be good enough for this demon. Even if I am made of iron inside out, I can only be melted into a few nails and there's not much more I can do."

"I see what you mean, Wukong, but you are not alone. We also have Pigsy and Sandy here. You can lead them however you want, and I can't believe there's any mountain we can't cross."

"All right, Master, that's what I like to hear! To cross this mountain before us, Pigsy has to do two things my way. Otherwise, not a chance."

"Elder Brother," said Pigsy, looking alarmed. "If you don't want to go forward, let's go our separate ways. Why make it all on me?"

"Pigsy," said Master. "Why don't you listen and see what your Elder Brother has to say?"

"Actually," I said to Pigsy. "You have to do only one thing: either you stay here and take care of Master, or you go ahead and do some scouting in the mountain."

"Can you be an itsy-bitsy more specific about each, so I can make an informed choice?"

'Well," said I, like a teacher explaining a class assignment, "taking care of Master means you're fully responsible for him. When he wants to walk, you support him with your arms; when he is hungry, you go and find him food; if he suffers from a single pang of hunger, you'll be punished with a beating; if his face shows a teeny-weensy hint of being famished, there's beating for you; if he looks an ounce skinnier, there's a beating for you, too."

"That's mission impossible!" Pigsy said in a whiny voice. "To say the least, if I go to a village to find food for Master, all they'll see is a pig, an almost fattened one, so they'll catch me, slaughter me right away for a big feast! In that case, our master will have to go hungry and how can I be held responsible for that? I'll already be churning in the bellies of some villagers. What about that scouting option, brother?"

"I don't blame you for not liking the first option," I said

sympathetically. "The other option, well, you go into the mountain and find out how many demons are hidden in it, waiting to jump on us, what caves they live, what weapons they have, etc. etc. etc., so we can strategize accordingly and cross—"

"That sounds manageable! I'll go scouting then."

With puffed up chest, and the big iron fork on his shoulder, Pigsy marched into the mountain for the scouting mission.

I couldn't help chuckling.

"You bad monkey!" Master said. "You have no feelings for your brother at all, tricking him into this scouting errand and then laughing at him!"

"I am not laughing at him, Master. I'm laughing 'cause I know Pigsy will not do any scouting at all, being so scared of the demons. He'll find a place to rest up and then come back with some lies to fool us."

"How do you know?"

"Well, you just wait and see."

I changed into a tiny cicada, caught up with Pigsy, perched on the hair behind his big right ear, and went for the ride.

Pigsy went on for a few *li* and became breathless. He put down the fork, turned a backward look, and mumbled to himself:

"That pitiable weakling of a monk, that smarty-pants of a monkey, *bimawen*, and that good old useless Sandy, they're all resting comfortably while poor me alone having to do this scouting business. Was I born yesterday? I know how to take care of myself, for your information, if anyone happens to be listening!"

I am listening and it is all I can do not to burst out laughing.

He walked on for a few more minutes and then threw himself into a thicket of soft bushes, yawned deliciously, and dozed off.

I changed into a big hornet, landed on his fat lips, and gave him a good sting.

Pigsy bolted up. "Oh, mama! That hurts!"

He felt his swollen lips and took a look. "Blood? Must be demons!"

He looked up and saw a woodpecker, me, hovering around.

"Hey, you," shouted Pigsy angrily. "That stable boy picking on me is not enough and you have to pile on? My mouth is not some rotten tree and there are no worms for you, all right?"

With that Pigsy fell back and began to snore again.

I landed on his face and pecked on lips hungrily.

"This damned bird," Pigsy sat up and felt his lips again. "Want to make a nest in my mouth so you can lay eggs and raise a family here? No way!"

He got up, put the fork on his shoulder, and continued the scouting errand. A few *li* deeper into the mountain he saw a big rock and bowed.

"My kind master," he mumbled incoherently, what with swollen lips and nonstop drooling. "Pigsy, me, did some fearless scouting deep in the mountain and did find some demons. They're made of earth, no, of iron, no, of wood, no, of paper. Why, these all sound ridiculous. How about stone, yes, they're made of stone, this is a stone mountain after all...."

Rehearsing the lies you'll be telling Master?

I was ready to give him a good thrashing there and then but had to wait and see how it would all play out.

"The caves have what kind of doors? Just say iron framed doors. Don't know how deep the caves are, but they have three levels, right? Oh, how many nails in the doors? Who can notice and remember that much detail? Good stuff, and even that smarty-pants *bimawen* won't be able to tell, hahaha!"

Let's see who laughs last, can't wait to compare notes with you when you're back!

Pigsy was still rehearsing the lines when he was yards from

where Master was.

"Are you getting ready to give a big sermon, brother?" I said, appearing next to him in my true form.

"You give me a fright, Elder Brother!" Pigsy said, looking at me suspiciously.

"Did you find any demons, Pigsy?" asked Master.

"Well, I did, Master," said Pigsy smoothly. "A whole nest of them."

"How did they treat you?"

"Mmm, they called me great-great-grandpa! They cooked some real nice vegies and soup for me to eat. They said they'd organize honor guards with banners and drums to cheer us as we pass through the mountain."

"Pigsy," I chimed in. "Were you napping in that nest of soft bushes when the demons were talking to you?"

"What do you mean?" said Pigsy nervously. "Don't try to lie under the broad daylight and get me into trouble."

I grabbed an ear of his and asked him about the demons, the door, the caves, and so on. Pigsy answered with the lines he had carefully rehearsed.

"Liar! You never got deep into the mountain. All you did was catching some sleep in those bushes and then tried to come up with these lies to fool us. I can recite every word of your lies."

"How do you know?"

"Should I remind you of the sting you had from that hornet? And the woodpecker?"

Pigsy's swollen lips twitched and mumbled something unintelligible.

"You'd have gotten our master in some deep trouble, you know that?" I said, working up a big fury. "Let me thrash that fat ass of yours five times so you will never lie again!"

"Oh, no, have some mercy, Elder Brother!" begged Pigsy. "Just a gentle caress, okay, a slap, is good enough. With that lethal Cudgel of yours, I'd be dead if you beat me five times."

"How about three times?"

Pigsy crawled to Master and grabbed his sleeves.

"Wukong says you tend to lie when it is convenient to do so and I didn't believe him," said Master. "Now I know he's telling the truth and you do deserve to be punished. However, we need all hands on deck if we want to cross the mountain. So, Wukong, spare him now and we'll deal with him afterwards."

That's how Pigsy avoided a good thrashing this time.

We picked up our things and slogged into the mountain, Pigsy taking the lead as our scout.

Every few steps of the way, Pigsy would turn and see if I had changed into something to keep an eye on his every move and read every thought of his. At the sight of a tiger charging downhill toward us, he would raise his fork and be the first to go and fight it; every old tree or trunk he saw, a Methuselah or Jōmon Sugi look-alike, oh, these two names are quite a mouthful, he would be so jumpy and scream "Demon!" and he would chase every gust of wind and the shadow of every bird hovering over us.

"Can't you see I'm losing my mind, brother?" Pigsy said, crying. "Don't torment me anymore. I've promised that I'd never lie again."

"I know you mean to keep your promise," said I. "So, stop tormenting yourself anymore."

That calmed him down a teeny-weensy.

We continued our journey deeper into the mountain.

A bunch of little demons lurched out of shadowy bushes, followed by a giant demon, armed with a big seven-star sword.

"Who goes there?" they shouted at us.

Before Pigsy could answer, one of the demons exclaimed, "See that thing, the first one, big nose, long ears, the ugliest, must be Pigsy, exactly like in this sketch."

Boy, these demons have done their homework and mean business.

"Absolutely! And that one riding the horse," exclaimed another demon, glancing at the scroll in his hand, "must be Tang Monk, and that hairy-faced monkey—"

"Hey, what've I ever done to you," said Pigsy when we faced the demons, literally, "insulting me like that?"

"Show me your tongue, then," said the giant demon, "so I can take a better look."

"Open your mouth and say ahhh," a little demon instructed Pigsy, a sharp iron hook at the ready in his hand.

"You puny bastard!" shrilled Pigsy, mad as hell. "Here's my ahhh for you!" He knocked down the little demon with his big iron fork and charged at the giant demon.

A fight ensued. For a while we all looked on like spectators of an engrossing show. They fought for twenty rounds without either gaining the upper hand.

With a wave of hand from the giant demon, all the little demons piled on. In a moment of panic, Pigsy turned to run, tripped, his long mouth hitting the ground hard. As he struggled to get up, a bunch of demons got on top of him. They grabbed his hair, his ears, his feet, his tail, and his whatever, and right before our eyes, carried a howling pig into their cave. It all happened so fast.

Master trembled like a malaria patient.

"Don't be afraid, Master," said I reassuringly. "I am here."

"What's going to happen to Pigsy?"

"Don't really know. Let's get through this mountain first."

I pulled out my Gold-Banded Cudgel and pointed it forward.

A clear pathway pierced into the mountain like a beam of light.

We pressed on.

Before long, we saw a grizzly old man in a black robe, like a Daoist priest, sitting by the wayside, whimpering pitiably, "Help! Help!"

Getting closer, we could see that one of his legs was broken, bleeding badly.

Master got off the horse and tried to help the old priest on his feet.

"It hurts! It hurts!" the old priest winced in pain.

"What happened?" asked Master. "How did you get hurt?"

The old priest said he and a disciple of his were on their way to the temple for sermons when they were attacked by a spotted tiger. It snatched his disciple and disappeared into the mountain.

"Please help, kind master. I must get to the temple now. I'll be indebted to you forever if you can help me!"

"Of course!" Master said. "Although you're a Daoist and I'm a Buddhist, we are both men of faith, cut from the same cloth. But how can I help if you can't even stand on your feet? How about you taking my horse?"

I've seen and heard enough. This old Daoist priest is none other than the giant demon in disguise.

"Oh, Master," I proffered. "Let me carry the old man on my back."

Reluctantly Master climbed on top of his horse again and the old priest climbed on my back.

We trudged deeper into the mountain.

"You stinky old relic!" I whispered to the burden on my back. "You can pull a fast one on my master, but not me! Think you can have him for a feast? You're daydreaming!"

"I was born and raised in a good family," whined the old priest. "And I'm a good Daoist priest. Accusing me of being a demon is blasphemy!"

"You a Daoist priest?" I muttered through my teeth. "Why

don't you recite for me some scriptures from Laozi, Zhuangzi, Mozi?"

"Wukong!" Master called out from atop the horse, having overheard my chitchat with the old man on my back. "Why are you tormenting the good priest like that? Just because you're doing him a favor? That's unbecoming us Buddhist monks!"

"All right, Master," I said, and then dropped my voice to a murmur again. "My master is too kind to tell, but you can't fool me! If you dare to pee or poop on me, and soil up my clothes, I'll reckon with you until you regret you've ever crawled up on my back!"

"I know how to be grateful if I've learnt anything at this old age."

After a while, even someone as strong as me began to feel the weight on my back. I was thinking how to smash the demon against a rock and kill him when I felt something like a massive mountain was falling on my head; I darted in time so it landed on my left shoulder.

This stinky old Daoist monk is a mentalist too and one step ahead of me?

"Hey, no big deal," I muttered, trying to put up a good face. "Only that the weight now feels imbalanced, tilted to one side, making it—"

Those words had barely rolled off my tongue when another mountain dropped on my right shoulder. So now I had to bear two mountains at once. Damn. I struggled to make a few big strides to catch up with Master, but the mountains I was carrying became unbearably burdensome and began to cut into my shoulders. Breathing became much harder.

What can I do to rid this dead weight on my shoulders? Me, who knows so many tricks and has such magic power, being outpowered, outsmarted by this old demon?

I was still thinking what to do when I saw a gust of dark

shadow flitting from me, and catching up with Master and Sandy, its crooked claws reaching down to grab and snatch Master.

Sandy put up a fierce fight to protect Master. They fought like hell, the seven-star sword and big iron stick knocking at each other, sparks flashing every which way. They fought for eight or nine rounds when Sandy was knocked onto the ground. The old demon snatched him up with one hand, grabbed Master from the horse with another, opened his mouth and took hold of the white horse by its mane, and dragged all three into the cave.

All this happened in the wink of an eye. I was so mad and so sad, tears washing down my cheeks like flooded rivulets, but I could barely move a limb of mine, déjà vu, like when I was buried under that Five-Element Mountain more than five hundred years ago. I thought I am peerless, invincible, yet this demon got better of me. How come? Oh, Heaven, this makes no sense at all. Is it some grand scheme of things that I am yet to understand?

Two earthly fairies appeared in front of me.

"How dare you lend the mountains to that demon?" One of them whispered to the other. "This is Monkey King, that Great Sage Heaven's Equal that caused much disturbance up there hundreds of years ago. You've eaten leopards' gallbladders?"

"Well," the other fairy said. "That demon threatened to put a spell on me if I refused him."

"So, you're not afraid of what I would do to you?" I couldn't help chiming in. "You don't know how lethal my Gold-Banded Cudgel is?"

That fairy, a mountain spirit in charge here, apologized profusely and worked to lift the two mountains from my shoulders.

Upon being liberated from the deadly weight, I cracked

my fingers, kicked, stretched to loosen up my limbs that had gone somewhat stiff, and somersaulted into the cloud. I looked around and found a weird-looking Daoist temple on the other side of the mountain. That must be the home of the giant demon. I landed, changed into a grey-haired Daoist priest, and marched toward the temple.

On the way I saw two little demons hurrying along and tripped them with my cane, my Gold-Banded Cudgel, really.

"What the f—!" one of them cussed as they picked themselves up fast. He was about to strike me when he checked himself. "I'd be happy to have you pay for this with more than a few silver coins if you were not a Daoist priest yourself!"

"Much obliged," I said. "What's the big hurry?"

"Oh, to finish off that monkey of a monk put under two big mountains by our king, so we'll have nothing to worry about when we steam that monk from Tang for a big feast. Can't wait. Hahaha!"

"Who's invited?" I couldn't help asking.

"Granny, I mean Queen Mother, is the first on the list, of course!"

I let these two go on their way, changed into a little demon, and hurried toward the old granny demon's home.

When I was led in and saw this old demon dozing in a grand chair, frosty hair, wrinkled face, only a few half-rotten teeth left in the mouth twitching and drooling uncontrollably, my eyes welled up for no reason at all.

Me, Monkey King, Great Sage Heaven's Equal, second to none, escorting Xuanzang on a grand mission to West Land, my whole life, I have only bowed to three, Rulai, Guanyin, and my master who freed me from under Five-Element Mountain. What an unpalatable disgrace for me to bow to this hideous old relic, yet I have to swallow my pride for Master's sake, for now. Oh, Heavens, it's so hard.

I threw myself on the ground in front of the old demon; she was startled and woke up; I gave her the invitation from my king, her son, to the feast featuring the monk from Tang.

"My filial son," the old granny exclaimed in joy. "Giving me this gift of immortality, finally! Can't wait!"

When with much help she finally climbed into a fragranced wicker sedan chair carried by us little demons, we got on the way.

We had gone for five or six *li* when I said. "My shoulder hurts, why don't we take a breather here?"

The other three little demons all liked the idea. As soon as we put the sedan chair down, I pulled out my Gold-Banded Cudgel and smashed two of them into meat pies and one halfdead, moaning in pain.

That demon granny stuck her head out to see what was going on and was met with a blow from my Cudgel. Her skull cracked up, her brains and blood splashing every which way. When I dragged her out of the sedan chair, that old granny showed her real self, a nine-tailed fox demon.

Now it's my turn to be old granny, no, Queen Mother, riding the fragranced wicker sedan chair carried by four little demons, a little trick of my magic power, of course, to the feast featuring the flesh of my master.

Imagine how thrilled I was, being welcomed by my son, that giant demon, that fake old Daoist, who'd taken a joyride on my shoulders, and a whole bunch of little demons; they all kowtowed to me over and again.

"My good son," I said, grinning. "I'm so blessed. Where's that monk from Tang?"

"My good son my butt!" I heard Pigsy mumbling; he was dangling up there from a beam, hands and legs all bound up.

"What're you talking about?" asked Sandy, dangling from the same beam.

"You didn't see that granny's monkey tail when she bent to greet her son? That's *bimawen*!"

Damned Pigsy.

"My kind mother," said the demon king jubilantly, "who else would I think of inviting when catching that monk from Tang if not you? Your health and immortality is my happiness, mama."

"My good son," said I, beaming, "That long, fat ears of that pig of a monk, hanging up there, steamed, grilled, or deep fried, will make real nice appetizers before the main course."

"Whatever you wish, mama!"

"Damned *bimawen*!" Pigsy muttered through his teeth. "I'll scream hell when they try to cut my ears. That's what you wanted?"

I chuckled, enjoying the show I was putting on.

The two little demons I had encountered earlier came back howling.

"Your Majesty, disaster! That monkey has gotten away from the two mountains you put on his shoulders, killed Queen Mother Her Majesty, and is on the way here."

Shocked, now knowing what was going on here, the demon king charged at me with his big seven-star sword.

Me, back in my real self, met him blow for blow with my Gold-Banded Cudgel.

It was a well-matched fight and we fought for thirty rounds, on the ground, in midair, without either gaining the upper hand.

Then, out of the blue, the demon tossed a noose in the air, murmured a spell, and it fell on my head, and stuck to it like hell. It feels as bad as that damned headband and hard as I try I can't seem to shake it off my head.

The demons dragged me to a stone pole and had me tethered to it like an animal, using a magic rope of his.

"Hahaha, Elder Brother," jeered Pigsy. "Looks like you can't have my ears for appetizers after all."

"You're not tired of dangling up there yet?" I snarled. "I won't let you down then when I'm done here."

"How can you talk about saving me if you can't even save yourself? We're all going to die, master and disciples, and will continue our journey in Netherland!"

"Just you see!" I said, pulled out a hair, murmured something, voila, me still tethered to the pole, but the real me is now a little demon guarding the captives.

"Look! Look!" Pigsy hollered. "That monkey tethered to the pole is a fake!"

"What's the fuss?!" asked the demon king, still drinking to recover from the death of his mother.

"Your Majesty," reported I, the little demon guard. "That pig was calling you names!"

"What?!" fumed the demon king. "I thought he was a stupid fool, turns out he's worse. Give his fat, foul mouth a good thrashing, twenty times!"

"Easy, easy, brother!" begged Pigsy when I began to hit him with a stick. "Otherwise, I'll holler again 'cause I know who you really are."

"How can you tell?"

"Well, that monkey butt of yours, like two rouged cheeks. Isn't that tell-tale enough?"

I dropped the stick and hurried to the kitchen in the back, wiped clean the bottom of a big wok, and applied that smoke stain all over my butt.

When I sauntered back, Pigsy laughed again. "Now you're a little black-cheeked monkey!"

I gave him a dirty look and walked up to the demon king.

"Your Majesty, that monkey, tethered to the pole, has been wiggling and wriggling nonstop, trying to break free. Why don't we use something stronger to bind him up so he can't even move?"

"Good idea," said the demon king. He loosened his belt of lion hair braid, handed it to me. "Nothing beats this," he said and went on drinking.

I hurried to the other me, untied him from the pole, and tied him up again with a replica of the demon king's lion-hair belt. I hid both the magic rope and the real lion-hair-belt up in my sleeves, and sauntered back to the demon king, as myself, Monkey King.

"Wake up, you cheeky rascal!" I said, poking him in the chin. "See who's here?"

The demon king looked up, his eyes popping out in shock.

"Another monkey monk here?!"

"Hahaha, the one tied up there is my brother. I'm here to free him."

"I know what you're up to," the demon king said, now fully awake from the wine-induced stupor. "You and I don't need to fight it out, though. Here's the deal. When I call your name, if you answer correctly, I'll let your brother go."

"Deal!"

"*Bimawen!*" hollered the demon king.

Bastard knows. I don't want to be associated with that insulting title ever again.

"Monkey!"

That's me, but not my name.

"Great Sage Heaven's Equal!"

That's a title I gave myself, but not my name.

"Wukong!"

"Yes," I said before I realized what I'd done. That's the name my first master gave me when I set out to learn the secret of life and the world, so I can't help it, can I?

I was sucked into something shaped like a sandglass, a big

calabash. It was total darkness inside. I tried to hit my head against the roof and kick the sides, but nothing gave. It was tight as hell and red hot like a blacksmith's furnace.

I've been tricked by this old hand demon again, yet I've been through Heaven and Hell, being grilled in Laozi's *Bagua* Stove for forty-nine days and coming out even more powerful. So, I just sat there and waited, and waited. Somehow, they did not seem to be in a big hurry.

"Oh, mama!" I howled at the top of my lungs. "This hurts! I'm melting into some meat smoothie, oh, horror!"

I wasn't sure if demons outside could hear me, the walls of the calabash being so thick and strong.

To my pleasant surprise, the lid was opened, and I saw a pair of eyes staring down, silhouetted against lamplight in the cave.

I pulled out a hair, murmured something, and it changed into a half-melted me moaning in pain; the real me changed into a teeny-weensy cicada, flit to the mouth of the half-opened calabash, and landed outside as a little demon.

"Your Majesty," the little demon me reported. "That monkey monk is cooked halfway through, almost ready."

"Fantastic! Close the lid and let it cook some more until that monkey is nothing but a bowl of soup and bones!"

Hahaha, you old fool. I'm already out.

I pulled out a hair, gave it a gentle blow, and it became a replica of the calabash. That real thing? It went up to my sleeves to join the magic rope and the lion-hair braid of belt.

I poured more wine for the demon king and then changed back to my real self.

"Your Majesty, your appetizer is here!" I flicked my middle finger on the demon king's forehead and snapped.

He looked up, eyes popping out in shock again.

"Another Wukong? How many brothers do you have?"

"Hahaha, countless!"

"That calabash of mine, you know, can hold a thousand of you!"

"Oh yeah, I have a calabash too!" I took out the calabash from my sleeves and shook it in his face; his eyes darted between his calabash, inside which I was supposed to be melting fast, and the one in my hand.

"What? Looking exactly the same. How come? Where did you get it?"

"Well, where did you get yours?"

"You really wanted to know?" the demon king said. "Mine goes back to time immemorial, Pan'gu creating Heaven and Earth from chaos, Nüwa refining colored stones to repair the collapsed sky. There grew on Mount Kunlun a single vine, from that vine grew this magic calabash, which Laozi has kept ever since."

"The same story for my calabash," I said, thinking fast on my feet. "Except that two, not one, calabashes grew from that vine. Mine is male and yours is female, hahaha!"

"What? Never heard of that!"

"Ever heard of *yin* and *yang*, you ignorant dullard?"

He mumbled something incoherently, confusion written all over his face.

"Don't believe me? How about doing another round of this, you call my name and see if I'm sucked into your calabash, and then it'll be my turn?"

The demon king's eyes lit up again. "Sure!" he said, and then called my name:

"Wukong?"

"Yes," I answered, standing firm where I was.

He called again, more frantically, and I answered again, and nothing happened.

This went on for seven or eight rounds.

"What's going on?" howled the demon king. "My boy calabash meets your girl calabash for the first time and suddenly becomes bashful and loses its mojo?"

"Possibly!" I said, laughing. "Now my turn. My girl calabash may not be shy though."

The demon king rolled his eyes.

"My king," I said in the softest, tenderest voice I could muster and curtsied like a singsong girl.

"Yes?" answered the giant demon in spite of himself and was sucked into my calabash.

Got-cha!

I could hear the muffled sound of him kicking and screaming in pain as he began to melt in the calabash hot as hell. But I had more urgent matters on hand and had to let him mellow on his own for now. The calabash is secure in my sleeves anyway.

I searched in the cave and in a pantry behind the kitchen found my master, Xuanzang, his hands and feet bound in ropes, looking so famished, too tired to keep his eyes open.

"Master," I called gently.

"No, no, have mercy!" he cried out, shaking worse than a malaria patient.

"Don't be afraid, Master," I said, my eyes moistening. "It's me, Wukong."

I unbound my master with frantic fingers, helped him on his feet, and hurried to where Pigsy and Sandy were still hanging from the ceiling.

Wait. I stopped myself in my tracks. One last trick from me.

I pulled out a hair, gave it a gentle blow, and two little demons ambled toward where my two wretched brothers were.

"Hey, brother, see that fat pig hanging from the beam there?" One of them said. "We can get him down and steam him into some smoothie, so we can eat and then fight that monkey thing?"

"Oh, that disgusting pig," the other little demon said. "His skin is so thick and rough, must be hard to cook."

"You're right, that little brother down there," Pigsy chimed in from the ceiling. "You're really smart!"

"Oh yeah," said the first little demon. "That's easy. We can skin you first and then steam you."

"No…no!" Pigsy sounded really scared now. "I don't taste good either!"

"No worries," laughed the first demon. "We can spice you up with chops of ginger, pepper, onion, garlic—"

"Wukong!" I heard Xuanzang muttering from behind me. "That monkey in you never rests, right? Haven't Pigsy and Sandy suffered enough, hanging from that ceiling for so long?"

"Sorry, Master," I said, recalling the two little demons. "I thought a little levity would do no harm."

I cut Pigsy and Sandy down from the ceiling right away.

"You *bimawen*!" said Pigsy once his feet touched solid ground, more amazed than mad, rubbing his half dead limbs. "Let me take a look at that thing, that calabash, and see if the demon king is still there."

"Oh, he is still in it for sure," said I gleefully, "melting like a snowman under a hot summer sun, hahaha. But no, I can't open the lid for you."

"Just a quick glance," begged Pigsy.

"No way! You know what'll happen if I open the lid just a little."

"Yeah, brother," Sandy said to Pigsy. "Didn't we see what happened when they opened the lid when he had Elder Brother inside that thing? Curiosity can get a pig killed too, hahaha. We'll all be dead for sure."

"All right, my disciples," Master said, reassuming authority.

"Enough child's play. Let's get on the road again."

Pigsy, Sandy, Master, and I hurried back to the kitchen and made a pig of ourselves, sorry Pigsy, just can't resist it. We then loaded up with whatever was still left, got outside the cave, and were ready to resume our journey when we heard a raspy voice rumbling overhead.

"Monkey, give back my treasures!"

I looked up. It was Laozi, Father Daoist. All the memories of being grilled in that hell of a stove of his more than five hundred years ago came rushing back.

"What treasures?" I said resentfully.

"That magic calabash and that lion hair braid belt up in your sleeves?" said Laozi solemnly, as if giving one of his deep sermons. "They're mine!"

"How?"

"Well, that demon now being cooked in that calabash? He was once a boy attendant of my *Bagua* Stove, fell to temptation, stole that calabash used to hold my precious immortality beans, and fled to Earth. And that belt? It is made with a segment of that vine growing on Mount Kunlun. You already know the story. The thief has been at large for so long and I owe you a big one for catching him for me at last."

What else can I say, and do?

I tossed both treasures into the air; they soared into the wide-opened arms of Laozi. In the blink of an eye, they were all gone.

I don't know why, but I felt much relieved, and it was with a much-lightened heart that I got on the way again with my master, Xuanzang, Pigsy, and Sandy, between star-lit Heaven and Earth where everything, trees, flowers, grasses glistened with the first hint of morning dew.

EIGHTEEN
Seriously?

So we've been journeying for days and months, have covered I don't know how many *li*, only Wukong knows the exact number, perhaps, and overcome I don't know how many more perils, again only Wukong knows.

I wasn't sure of that monkey when I first saw him under that mountain and wondered how could they, Rulai, Guanyin, have put the success of the entire mission not only on my shoulders, but also in the hands of a monkey.

Don't get me wrong. He has proved very useful to me. Scouting. Getting food. Fighting off demons. Snatching me from the devouring mouths of animals and monsters. Indispensable? Mmm, well, I won't go that far. There is only one who can be characterized as such, you know. That's why the mission is known as Tang Monk Going to the West—in perpetuity!

It's just that he sometimes gets carried away, an itty-bitty too cocksure of himself, too quick with his Cudgel, for his good and for my good, when the latter happens, I have to use the ace up my sleeve to reassert my authority.

I know he nurses a grudge against me for having done

so perhaps more often than necessary. I have to be a strict disciplinarian, an enforcer, a tough love kind of father figure although in terms of real age, I am not even thirty yet, I am of Monkey's great-grand-grand-grand-grand-, okay I lose track, grandson generation. He has been around for I don't know how long, centuries? I'm the one in charge here, period.

One time he used his Cudgel to draw a circle and told me, Pigsy, Sandy, and the horse to stay inside that foolproof protection dome, and then went to look for food for us. After we sat in that circle for a while, I listened to Pigsy and stepped outside to stretch my arms and legs. What harm could that do, right? Well, it broke the magic of our protection, and we were snatched up by some vicious demons right away, would have ended up in their dinner plates if Wukong had not returned in time and rescued us. He wasn't thrilled, as you can imagine.

Pigsy, my second disciple? Well, pigs are pigs are pigs is all I can say. You can't blame him for being who he is, having too big an appetite, falling to temptations easily, especially when it comes to sensual indulgences, and being an opportunistic liar, but he is a hard worker and throws himself, everything he's got, into whatever he does. He's fun to have around, but as their master, I keep a straight face when he tells racy jokes. Propriety is the best policy, I think.

As to Sandy, my third disciple, I don't have much to say other than to say he is a steady, loyal, hardworking straight shooter, unassuming, never a star in anything, good or bad, always playing his supporting role quietly, the best he can, like carrying loads of our luggage, setting up camp, and so on.

I stepped up when Emperor Xuanzong called for the grand mission, would not have done so if I had a shred of doubt of my intelligence, character, and worthiness. Who else in the entire great Tang Dynasty, anyways?

Yet, sometimes, I do have my misgivings. Okay, only when

the going gets an itty-bitty too hard; when I fall into some hopeless traps; when I feel an itty-bitty homesick, when I get real sick, like with malaria. This letter of mine addressed to Emperor Xuanzong I've turned over in my mind many times:

Emperor Xuanzong Your Majesty:

Your loyal subject Xuanzang, basking in your boundless glory, kindness, and trust, has been progressing in the journey to West Land to secure true scriptures of Buddhism for the spiritual welling of the great Tang Dynasty, although the journey so far has taken a toll on my health, and I may not be able to complete… to return alive even….

In the darkest moment, caught in a dark mood, I confided in Wukong about this self-doubt. He laughed.

"I can deliver this letter of yours if you write it. It'll be in the hands of Emperor Xuanzong before the ink is dry, yet what nonsense is this talking of dying, self-pity, when I am here? I can go and even get King Yama to erase your name from the Book of Life and Death…."

That monkey, he has a way of talking that makes me feel much better.

I said sometimes I have my doubts, an itty-bitty, mind you. For one, I understand that the journey to West Land, long and tortuous, cuts through some difficult terrain, exposes us to the elements, rain, snow, thunderstorm, swift rivers, let alone countless demons and monsters. I have a hunch that all these barriers along the way were set up by Rulai, Father Buddha, to test me over and again, to see if I am the real deal, if I am up to the task, worthy of the true scriptures, but haven't I proved myself already through all the exams in front of the greatest, most erudite, sagacious of Buddhist scholars of the great Tang Dynasty? As if, as if Rulai enjoys seeing us being so tortured during the journey, having fun at our, my expense?

And more tortures, harsher, even more ridiculous, are

awaiting us, me? Is there any way to avoid, avert the purgatory and get us straight to our destination?

One day, being so parched under brutal sunshine for too long we drank from the river we happened to be crossing to quench our thirst. The water looked clean enough.

The moment we reached the other shore and set foot on land, my stomach began to make funny noises. Soon it began to swell and hurt so bad that I couldn't help moaning. The same thing was happening to Pigsy. I could see big drops of sweat rolling down his long face too.

"It must be the water you've drunk," Sandy suggested.

Where on earth in this ghost-wouldn't-lay-eggs place can we get medicine to take care of this?

We soldiered on, Wukong walking close by my side in case bulge-bellied me fell from the horse, Sandy helping Pigsy pushing forward his monstrous belly a few times its usual size. It was quite a sight, if anyone happened to be watching us.

We finally reached a town. Strangely, everyone we saw everywhere in town was female, old and young, not a single male, boy or man.

We entered a small cottage, was received by an elderly woman, and asked her for help.

"Can you make us some hot soup to ease the pain, our kind benefactor?" I begged. "It's killing me."

"Hot soup won't do any good," the elderly woman said. "This is Land of Women (*Nüerguo*), you've never heard of us? There's not a single menfolk amongst us. That river from which you drank? It's called Mother Baby River. Girls here, when they reach the ripe age of sixteen or seventeen, when they are ready to be mothers, they go to that river and drink from it, and three days later, they go to Baby Reflection Pond in town, and if they see a double shadow in the water, it means they'll give birth soon! So, soup or no soup won't do you any good now!"

Seriously?!

I am pregnant?

Just by drinking a bowl of water from that river?

Me, a monk, a man, being pregnant?!

The most ridiculous thing I've heard.

"Oh, mama! I am about to give birth to a baby!" howled Pigsy. "Look at me, is there an opening in my body for the baby to come out? And me being a single daddy, or mommy raising the baby all by myself?"

"Hey, brother," Wukong said, laughing. "You've never heard the old adage that when a melon is ripe, it'll fall from its vine by itself? No worries!"

"I'm dead. Dead!" Pigsy moaned pitiably. "Brother, can you ask that old woman if she can find me a midwife who has a light and nimble hand, so it won't hurt that bad?"

"Don't twist your body so much, brother," Sandy said, half joking, half seriously. "In case your water breaks prematurely, before the midwife arrives."

I was in so much pain and in no mood to join the levity. It'd be unbecoming anyway.

"My kind benefactor," I said to our host. "Is there a drugstore here so a disciple of mine can go and get some abortion medicine for us?"

She shook her head. "Look at your bellies, so bulged already, no drugs could do any good. The babies are ready to burst out anytime, you have an opening for this or not."

Pigsy began to howl again. And I moaned helplessly too.

"Well," the elderly woman said. "There's only one remedy. Deep in the mountain there's a broken cave, in this cave there is this Dissolution Spring. Drink a bowl of water from that spring and the fetus inside you will be dissolved."

Really! What a godsend!

"Master," Wukong said. "You hear that? I'll go and get that

water and you'll feel good as new!" Then he turned to Sandy: "Brother, take good care of our master while I'm away. Don't let anyone get close and get any ideas, you know what I mean?"

"No worries," the elderly woman said. "You're lucky to be staying with me. At my age, I am not interested in this sort of thing anymore. Been there and done that. Hahaha. If you were with a family of younger females, they'd have jumped on you right away to copulate with you. You say no? They wouldn't hesitate to cut you into pieces to make fragrance sachets!"

"Our master," Pigsy said, pointing at me, "would be perfect for fragrance sachets. Me? I'm so stinky people can smell it a *li* away."

Wukong gave Pigsy a dirty look. "Why don't you keep quiet so you can save some breath for a smooth birth?" With that, he was gone to fetch that dissolution water.

Every second we were waiting felt like the end of the world. Oh, God, why're you punishing me like this? My belly is ready to burst anytime, my heart is all but broken, I've cried my eyes out. I didn't sign up for this when I stepped up for the mission, did I?

When Wukong was finally back, with a bucket of water from that spring, I was ready to fall on my knees to thank him, my savior, if it were not for my bloated waistline.

Pigsy, half paralyzed on the ground, his head slumped against the door frame, tried to kowtow without success, only managed a gush of "thank you thank you thank you!"

The elderly woman gave me and Pigsy each a bowl.

"I can drink from the bucket directly!" said Pigsy.

"Don't be greedy," said the elderly woman. "One big mouthful is enough to do the trick. If you drink just one drop more than that, all your intestines will melt into smoothie, and you'll cry bloody murder like hell!"

"Oh, mama!" said Pigsy, wincing.

Minutes after drinking the magic water, my stomach hurt even worse, like all my organs, my heart, my lungs, my liver, and yes, my intestines, were put in a churn and some naughty boy was turning it round after round after round, for fun. I rolled on the ground and couldn't help wailing.

Oh, God! What in God's name! You call this tough love? I call it cruelty, pure and simple!

Pigsy? He was rolling, wailing, and cussing like mad, too.

Then, I felt hot things spurting from the two holes down there, soiling my robe. It stinks like hell, but what do I care about smell now? All I want is for that excruciating churning to be over.

Pigsy made an even bigger, nastier mess, as can be imagined.

When that ordeal was all but over, the elderly woman said: "Don't you feel much relieved now? Now go and wash yourself clean, boys. I'll make some nourishing porridge to help you recuperate."

Wukong carrying me on his back, Sandy supporting Pigsy with both arms, we went to a little creek nearby and took a good bath in it.

When we came back, the place was cleaned, and the porridge was ready. It smelled so good. I ate two full bowls, twice my usual portion; my belly, still tender from the hell-like trauma, felt an itty-bitty better, okay, a lot better.

Pigsy? He asked for more even after having gulped down ten bowls.

"Care for more water, brother?" Wukong asked Pigsy, winking. "That bucket is still more than half full."

"Thanks, but no thanks, brother, I'm not pregnant anymore," said Pigsy, licking his lips.

"Give that bucket to me," said the elderly woman. "There's still enough in it to buy me a coffin when my time comes. I'll bury the water in a pot in the backyard and put up a sign: No Dissolution Spring water is buried here!"

"And your next-door neighbor, after stealing it," quipped Wukong, that smarty-pants, "will also put up a sign: Me your next-door neighbor did not steal it."

We all laughed heartily, for the first time for a long time.

We bid farewell to our kind host and got on the way again.

The moment we found ourselves in the main street of town, we were hurrahed by women on both sides, like some carnival, circus is in town:

"The breeders are here! The breeders are here!"

Seriously?

They mean us?

They mean to keep us here to propagate all these women?

Do I look like a stallion that can keep at it forever, if I can do it at all?

Okay, what do I know about this, raised within the walls of monasteries all my life, having never seen and done anything morally compromising, okay, other than that one time I stumbled upon some embarrassing drawings in an old, illustrated book hidden in the deep recess of a library? You didn't hear me saying this.

"Hey, I'm a champion breeder!" Pigsy waved to the cheering crowds, grinning from ear to ear.

"Shut that big, fat mouth of yours!" Wukong said harshly. "Let's try to get out of here alive!"

So, Wukong, Pigsy, and Sandy tried to knit their eyebrows, curl their lips, and screw their faces to make themselves look uglier, scarier than their normal selves, but to no avail. All eyes of the women were on me. I could feel their blistering heat.

Why me?! Poor me?!

A small cavalry, led by a royal banner, came ambling in our direction.

They stopped before us; their leader, a matronly courtier elegantly dressed, got off the horse, and curtsied to me.

"My apologies for being late in coming to meet our distinguished guest. Congratulations!"

"Thank you," I bowed and said. "But can you enlighten me about the congratulations?"

"You'll find out soon enough," said the matronly courtier, smiling. "Just follow me!"

"Their Queen Her Majesty must have prepared a pleasant surprise for you," said Pigsy.

I knew what he meant and almost fell off the horse.

"Don't you worry, Master," whispered Wukong reassuringly. "Just play along."

Just play along? Easy for Monkey to say, 'cause nobody is asking him to her playmate.

We followed the matronly courtier and after a few turns were led into the palace of Queen of the Land of Women. It was as grand as any palaces I have seen with the only exception that all the courtiers and guards are women. Once again, all eyes are on me.

"Welcome, my royal brother!" said the Queen from the throne, looking as beautiful as regal, her eyes glistening with warmth and pleasure.

I bowed, thanked Her Majesty for her hospitality, and explained that we were only passing through on our way to West Land for the true scriptures of Buddhism.

"So we've heard," the Queen said, her warm gaze on me. "But we have a proposition here: You stay here as my King, and I'll be your Queen. That'll make us all happy, happiest in the world."

Me being King?

King of Land of Women, and staying here forever with my Queen?

That has never entered even my wildest dream.

"Hey, Your Majesty," Pigsy proffered. "If my master does not object, you can have me instead. I can be as good a husband as anyone!"

The Queen was annoyed and gave him a dirty look. All the courtiers and maids laughed.

"Don't believe me?" boasted Pigsy, beating his chest. "Anyone of you want to check me out? I'm a champion, you know."

They all flinched and laughed even harder.

"Thank you so much for your kindness, Your Majesty," I finally found my tongue. "I'm a Buddhist monk entrusted with a grand mission from Emperor Xuanzong. If I stay here, that'd not be in the interest of the spiritual wellbeing of all the people of our great Tang—"

"We understand," said the Queen charitably. "What we meant is you alone stay with us; your disciples can continue the journey and complete the mission."

"Say yes, Master," Wukong whispered to me. "Otherwise, we won't get our passports stamped and will never get out of here."

"What'll happen if she wants to consummate," I whispered back, blushing, "and I end up losing my essence, my *yang*, how can I face the world again?"

"Don't you worry, Master. Say yes, and I'll take care of the rest."

Easy for Monkey to say, but do I have a choice?

Inevitably, a grand banquet followed as part of the celebration.

"What's your pleasure, Your Majesty?" the royal chef asked me before we were all seated. "I mean, are you vegan or carnivore?"

"Vegan, of course."

"I'm a meat-lover!" announced Pigsy although no one asked him.

Everyone burst out laughing, including the Queen.

It was during the banquet, when so much wining, dining, chitchatting, and cheering was going on that the Queen put her royal zeal on the passports of Wukong, Pigsy, and Sandy. She still had the presence of mind to exclude mine, though.

I was finally alone with the Queen in her royal chamber, young, beautiful, her face rosy, her gaze so warm.

"Our royal brother," she said, "my King. I've had a dream recently, dreaming of this very moment, and it's come true! We're meant for each other, right?"

I stood there, a nervous wreck, watching her untying her tall beehive like hair before a mirror, having never been alone with a beautiful young woman, knowing yet not really knowing what'll happen next.

"Hahaha," said the Queen, finishing her toilet. "Your first time? No need to be shy. Such a gorgeous evening, full moon outside, star-lit sky, a handsome young man and a beautiful young woman together. What're you waiting for? Let's taste the joy of becoming husband and wife, becoming one!"

She came up to me, rich long hair falling on her shoulders, her face flushing with joy and excitement, and took my hands.

"Are you cold? Let mama warm you up!"

She kissed my forehead, then my lips, moaning so pleasurably.

I stood there, stiffened, not knowing what to do.

She led me to her grand royal bed of ivory, unbuttoned herself, revealing her creamy, bouncy bosom. I tried to avert my eyes, but somehow couldn't, like when I stumbled upon that old illustrated book in the temple so many years ago, when I was still a youngster.

"See this pair of pillows of lovebirds?" she murmured

tremulously, "and silky beddings and everything? That's all for you and me."

We sat on the edge of the bed. She put her arms around my neck, kissed me again, and tried to help me undress but without success, because I wasn't cooperating.

I lied there, still in my monk's robe. She climbed on top of me, kissing, squirming, moaning. This would be a dizzying dream-come-truth moment for perhaps every other hotblooded young man, they'd be on fire and paint this chamber red, you know what I mean? Yet I am lying here like wood, not feeling a thing, cold as fish. I can see the whole thing playing, like watching it like a fly on the wall, on the ceiling, and finding it all so ridiculous. Am I cut from a different cloth than everyone else? Something amiss with me? Of course not! I'm entrusted with a grand mission. I was born for that mission and nothing else.

I do feel ashamed, though, an itty-bitty, not for myself, but for the young Queen, working so hard on me, on her hands and knees, trying to pull off my robe and coax some response from me, but receiving nothing, nada, not an iota, in return. It all gets so embarrassing, and exhausting that she finally gives up and goes to sleep on her side of the bed. Me, I just lie there, praying all the scriptures that I can still recall to my mind, not getting a wink of sleep.

I'm also grateful. The young Queen could have given the word to have me dragged out and beheaded. My head would be rolling on the street or being hanging outside one of the city gates. But she did none of that. When she got up in the morning, the young Queen looked tired and sad; she didn't say a word to me while her maids were preparing her toilet and get her ready for the day.

Wukong, Pigsy, and Sandy were waiting for me when we stepped out of the Queen's chamber.

"Look at our master, the bridegroom," I heard Pigsy

whispering to Wukong. "He looks so tired, must have been indulging himself all night! Who'd blame him, hahaha!"

"You fool," said Wukong. "See the Queen? Does she look like a happy, satisfied bride to you?"

The Queen marched to her throne, sat down, and extended her hand to me.

I was going to ask what she wanted when Wukong stepped forward and handed my passport to her. She put her royal zeal on it without looking and waved for us to leave.

I thanked her profusely, feeling relieved, albeit being dumped like an article of useless clothing, ashamed yet proud all the same.

I knew that I'd be safe in this regard from then onward, no need to worry about losing my essence, my *yang*, thank God, because I'm cut from a different cloth, having no interest in the man and woman business so many in the world willing to risk everything for. No, not me. I'd encounter such things a few more times during the journey ahead, queens, nymphs, demons, what have you. One time a hot demon of queen, breathing wine and desire all over my face, even reached down there and tried to excite me. No response. Nada. Sorry. What can I say? Hahaha. she had to give up.

Of course, Wukong has to come to my rescue, each time, so they will not kill me, cut me up, and steam my flesh for their longevity.

Even when we finally set foot in Tintu, West Land, our destination, I'd have to go through such absurdity one more time, almost a formulaic variation of the same story. By this time, I have left my great Tang for fourteen years! Didn't I promise to be back in two or three years?

Imagine how thrilled I was to breathe the air of Tintu, heavenly, where everyone was dressed like a Buddhist monk, pious, pure, all living life the simplest, minimalist way, untouched by earthly desires, unburdened by anything superfluous, ornamental.

The first night we put out at a temple, where we were warmly received, we heard a heartbreaking cry from a young woman, so sad that tears welled up in my eyes. So, Wukong and I went to look and found a young woman, disheveled, in dirty rags, locked in a dark room in the backyard. She said she was a princess of Tintu, kidnapped by a demon she doesn't remember how long ago. She had to pretend to be crazed and crawled like a pig to survive, not to be harassed by any monks.

I was dumbfounded, never thought such things could happen in a holy land like Tintu.

"We'll get you out of here and back to your father and mother," Wukong said. "Just you wait."

The next morning, when we found our way into a main street, it happened to be the day the princess of Tintus tossing the embroidered ball from a big stage set up for the purpose in a town square, flowers, flags, and loud music everywhere. The streets were throbbing with throngs of young men, all so handsome, dressed in their best, parading themselves back and forth in front of the stage, hoping to be the lucky one.

I don't know if I was so blessed or cursed, but that ball tossed by the princess passed all those eager young men and landed on my head, like what had happened so many years ago, when a similar ball landed on my father's head, when he was being paraded through the streets after winning the first prize in the imperial exam. The beginning of my long story was seeded right there and then.

In my case, though, I was a mere bystander, an unwitting party crasher of sorts, yet the ball hit me!

Seriously?

What're the odds?

"Why are you always the lucky one, Master?" asked a rather

envious Pigsy. "Why not me? I would make the princess so happy and be the best imperial son-in-law they could ever dream of!"

"Hahaha, brother," Sandy said, "Just take a look at yourself! If the ball had hit you, the princess would cry and pray for three days and nights to have it back."

"You don't know what you're talking about!" Pigsy said boastfully. "I'm big-boned, fit and strong, and have much to offer, hahaha!"

"That lecherous pig in you never dies!" rebuked Wukong jocularly.

With the princess's ball in my hands now, I have too much to worry about to listen to them bantering.

"It hit a monk! It hit that monk!" All the young men hollered and rushed toward me. If it were not for Wukong protecting me from the jealous mob, I would have been torn to a thousand pieces.

"Don't you worry, Master," whispered Wukong confidently. "Just play along."

Play along, again? How? Pray to God that I'll be able to get out of this one with my skin, my essence, my *yang*, intact.

We were soon led to the presence of the King and the Queen. They looked me upon and down, asked me a few perfunctory questions, and had me compose a few poems impromptu, I mean with prompts given there and then. I am not much of a poet, not even a closet one, but I have in my memory at least three hundred Tang poems, can recite them backwards, if I have to do so to save my life, so that'd make me a poet of sorts. The prompts the old King gave me? The four seasons. That's it. I mulled it over for a few seconds and verse lines began to roll of my tongue:

Spring
Heaven turns a full circle in its orbit,
Earth bustles with ten thousand new things.

> *Peaches and plums dance in a sea of blooms,*
> *Swallows paint the beams in rosemary dust.*
> *"Not bad, not bad," says the King, nodding approvingly.*

> *Summer*
> *Smoky wind blows and thoughts are slow,*
> *Sunflowers in the palace shine brightly.*
> *Jade flute melody awakens midday dream,*
> *Fragrance of lotus drifts into the courtyard at night.*

A long "O…," not sure an expression of joy or sorrow, escapes the lips of a beautiful young courtesan not far from the king; she covers her mouth with her hands.

> *Autumn*
> *Sycamore leaves in imperial garden turn golden,*
> *Frost creeps through pearl curtains at night.*
> *Swallows know it is time to leave their nests,*
> *Wild goose fold reed flowers flying over other places.*
> *There glitters in Wukong's eyes a dreamy, faraway look*
> *as he listens and watches me. Monkey understands and*
> *appreciates poetry?*

> *Winter*
> *Sky is rainy flying clouds dark and cold,*
> *Wind blows snow and covers thousands of mountains.*
> *Deep palace has its own red stove to warm it up,*
> *Plum blossoms brighten jade balustrade everywhere.*

"Wonderful! Wonderful!" enthused the old King when I was done. The Queen and all the courtiers cheered, too.

I know I have passed the literary test with flying colors, as you'd say, and have dug myself into a deeper hole, all Monkey's fault.

"Don't you worry, Master," Wukong whispered to me again reassuringly. "Just play along."

Until I play myself into the hands of my intended, I mean the princess, like with the young Queen of Land of Women, or that hot female demon, not too long ago? I'd be damned if that happens again.

"Time for a big feast to celebrate!" Pigsy shouted.

I was so embarrassed and had to bow and apologize.

The moment we returned to our guest house, I raised my cane and gave Pigsy a good thrashing.

"Hey, hey, master!" Pigsy cried, running for cover. "Just because you're now imperial son-in-law doesn't mean you can beat me like that?"

"No more nonsense, brother!" Wukong said to Pigsy. "Say sorry and then go to bed!"

An auspicious date was set for the bridegroom, me, and the bride, the princess, to meet for the first time, like a blind date, get betrothed and wedded at the same time. Double happiness ceremony on a really fast track. Imagine how flustered I was.

On the auspicious day the whole palace, courtiers, courtesans, maids, imperial guards, chefs and cooks, deep courtyards of deep courtyards and passageways, what have you, all throb in buoyant festivity.

Finally, the moment arrives: the King's parade rolls in, followed by the parade of the Queen and the Princess, my bride.

She is so gorgeous, impeccably gorgeous any way you look at her, her face, although veiled, her figure, her gait, what have you. Pigsy's mouth is agape with admiration; he would be thrilled to be in my shoes.

Poor me, in my shoes, is a nervous wreck, déjà vu, variation on the same annoying theme.

"I smell something fishy about this princess," Wukong whispers to me. "Demonic."

"What?" I'm flabbergasted. "What's going to happen to me? All your fault, Monkey!"

"Just you wait, till the princess gets a teeny-weensy closer."

And when the Queen, the Princess, and their entourage get close to where we are, the bride lifts her veil slightly to have a glimpse of me, her bridegroom.

"You demon!" I hear Wukong muttering. "Want to pull the wool over my eyes? No way!"

He pulls out that needle from his ear and charges at the Princess.

"Don't, Monkey!" I cry out. "If you kill anymore innocents, I'm going to pray that spell on you again!"

"Don't, don't, Master!" Wukong stops himself in the tracks for a second or two, and then continues, and lifts his Cudgel, now twenty feet long and rice bowl thick, above the bride's head. Where the Cudgel lands, the gorgeous Princess vanishes into thin air; in its place is a crumbled bundle of crown, veil, and bridal dress.

Imagine how dumbfounded the King, the Queen, and everyone else are.

Wukong chases a dark cloud and fights that demon in the air. It is like an airshow the whole kingdom is watching live. For a moment, I forget this has anything to do with me and I am in no mood to pray that spell to punish Wukong either.

When Wukong finally subdued the demon, it turned out to be a white-haired jade rabbit from the Moon, not happy with life up there, an itty-bitty too quiet and lonely for her, so she stole down to Earth, abducted the Princess of Tintus, and then impersonated her to enjoy earthly pleasures.

What lengths people in Heaven or on Earth are willing to go to to live the kind of life that I turn away from again and gain. Something wrong with them, or me?

When Wukong led the King and the Queen to that dark

room where their real Princess had been languishing, and opened the chain lock, she was terrified and crawled back to the corner.

"No, no, don't!" she whimpered, shielding her eyes with her dirty hands.

"It's us, remember?" Wukong said. "Your father and mother are here!"

I don't need to tell you how the King, the Queen, and the Princess hugged together and cried their eyes out, tears of sorrow and joy, and how sad the royal family was when we bid them farewell; they were all teary-eyed, watching me, their would-be son-in-law, albeit for only one day, go.

As for me, my mind and heart are already elsewhere, where I set my sights on fourteen years ago.

NINETEEN
Altered Ego

I thought it'd never happen again, but it did, déjà vu all over again, only worse, much worse.

It was a beautiful day in May, Dragon Boat Festival, a holiday to remember that exiled poet, Qu Yuan is the name, I think; he threw himself into a river out of despair. Poor man, why ending your life like that, without one more fight?

We had been going for most of the day uneventfully until we saw a big mountain standing in our way.

"Wukong," Master said. "Why don't you go ahead and see if any demons are lurching in the bushes ready to jump on us?"

"Master," I said half-jokingly. "Didn't I tell you that you're a Buddhist monk and should be free from such earthly fears? Besides, I'm here so you have nothing to fear."

Master nodded, so we pressed on. After clearing the summit, we saw a large opening, a valley of flat farmland. Pigsy became excited and gave the white horse's butt a nudge.

"Hurry, brother!"

The horse ignored him and maintained the same gait as before.

"Hurry, brother!" Pigsy nudged the horse again, a teeny-weensy harder. "I'm so starved and tired. Let's hurry and find some kind villagers so we can have food and shelter for the night."

The horse still ignored him.

In a mood for a teeny-weensy levity again, I took out the needle from my ear, shook it gently, and before I had time to utter the word "Hurry," the horse broke into a trot and then a wild run as if fleeing from a ghost.

"Hahaha, you *bimawen*!" Pigsy said. "He still remembers that high and mighty Imperial Stables Assistant Steward."

I laughed too.

On the horseback was our poor master, terrified, holding onto the reins for his very life. The horse kept the wild run for about twenty *li* and then, feeling safe again perhaps, slowed down to its regular pace.

We ran as fast as we could, with all the loads on our shoulders, and soon caught up with our master. He was mad as hell, but before he had time to scold me and let out some steam, a gang of bandits jumped out from nowhere and stopped us, all armed with knives, spears, what have you.

"Your life or your money!" bawled the fiercest looking one among them, apparently ringleader.

Startled and terrified, Master fell off the horse.

"Your Highness," he beseeched, barely able to pick himself up. "Have mercy!"

"Your life or your money!" the ringleader bawled again.

"Oh, that's what you wanted, Your Highness?" Master said, somewhat relieved. "We're just poor monks and have nothing valuable other than the clothes on our backs."

"All right, let's have your clothes, and that horse too!"

A few of the bandits grabbed Master's arms and tried to disrobe him. Other bandits laid their hands on Pigsy, Sandy, and me; two of them seized the reins of the horse and tried to drag it away; the horse stuck all four hoofs into the ground refusing to go.

Mad as hell, I pulled out the Gold-Banded Cudgel and charged into the bandits, wielding it left and right; wherever it hit I heard backs broken, legs fallen off, skulls cracking and brains squishing every which way. The first of them to fall was that fierce ringleader.

The moment he was freed, Master climbed onto the horse and was ready to run when he was stopped by Pigsy and Sandy.

"Where're you going, Master?" asked Pigsy.

"You'll get lost, going alone," said Sandy.

"No matter," Master said. "Just tell your Elder Brother to have mercy and not to kill any of the bandits."

"Asking Monkey to have mercy?" shrieked Pigsy, pointing at the bodies sprawling around us. "Don't you see those cracked skulls, squashed brains?"

"What?!" Master rolled off the horse and walked around to see for his own eyes, his face ashen, mumbling incoherently.

He had us dig a big hole and bury all the bodies in a makeshift grave. Then, he sat down and began to pray:

"Oh Heavens, please forgive my disciple Wukong. I thought we've tamed that monkey in him and apparently, we've failed. What horrific crimes he has committed. As his master I am certainly responsible. Nonetheless, the ultimate responsibility should lie with him and him alone, so please do not drag me into the court for the trial."

"Hey, Master," said Pigsy. "Now you've washed your hands off the whole thing, what about us, me and Sandy? We're innocent too and are no partners in the crimes Monkey has committed."

So, Master included Pigsy and Sandy in his prayer, vouching for their innocence.

I found the whole thing ridiculous and couldn't help laughing.

"Master, how can you be so senseless? I killed those bandits all on account of you, to protect you. You think they'd really let you go if you gave them your clothes and the horse? So, this is what I'm getting for protecting you from harm?"

"Wukong," Master said. "I'm praying for your own good, so you'll be a more merciful, more virtuous being. That's all. Don't take every word I said too seriously."

How can I afford not to? I'd be rolling on the ground like hell now if you pray that damned spell just once. Perhaps, I should be grateful.

We went on our way again, Master, disciples, and the horse, each nursing some private sentiments of our own, jealousy, resentment, even anger, whatever.

Before long, we saw a country villa and were all delighted. We would have food and shelter for the night for sure.

The patriarch of the family, a kind elderly man, welcomed us. His wife and daughter-in-law busied themselves preparing food for us right away. His five-or-six-year-old grandson was thrilled to have unexpected guests in the house and amused by our appearances too.

"You look weird, ugly," the boy said to Pigsy, playing with his long nose and big fat ears. Pigsy grinned and made some funny noises through his nose and obliged as much as he could.

"Manners!" The patriarch reprimanded his grandson mirthfully.

We all laughed, and I could hear pangs of hunger in my belly as aroma from the kitchen permeated the place.

At the dining table, as we tried not to devour our food, to have manners, of course, Xuanzang, our master, explained why we were going to West Land and the kind old man told stories of his childhood and youth.

"Speaking of youth," Master said, "where's your son if you don't mind me asking?"

The old man put down his cup and sighed.

"It breaks my heart to even think of him, so much shame and

disgrace on our family name. One day I'll have to face the spirits of all my ancestors for having brought up such an unfilial son."

He sighed profusely again and shook his head. "What I'm going to say at this table stays at this table, though?"

We all nodded solemnly.

"My son, my only son, has fallen into banditry."

Master, Pigsy, Sandy, and me—we all looked at each other and understood what this meant.

"I wish I had never had this son," the old man broke into a sob. "And…I wish, I wish he were dead!"

That upset me more than a teeny-weensy. "Don't you cry, kind benefactor. I could take care of that easily."

The old man looked up, surprised, and said, "Oh no, I didn't mean that literally. He may be an unfilial son, but he's my only son and I need him to give me a proper burial when I'm old, real old."

Master gave me a harsh look.

We heard a big commotion from outside.

The doors were pushed open; in walked a man in his thirties, his face and clothes covered in blood stains, followed by seven or eight men; all looked like they had just escaped death.

"Pop, I'm back with some friends!" the man announced, gesticulating at the men behind him. "We're so starved, so—"

He saw us at the table.

"Pop, I don't know you're having some guests tonight!" our kind host's son said. "Guys?" he hollered to his friends. "I thought we'd have to make do with vegies for supper. Turns out some choice meat has delivered themselves to us. Get them, their hearts, their lives…."

In the blink of an eye, the bandits had their knives on our necks. I could feel the bone-chilling edge of the one on mine and could see Xuanzang, my master, trembling in terror.

"My son," the old man fell on his knees, grabbed his son's

hands, and begged. "These are monks, our guests. Why do you want to kill them?"

The son's old mother, wife, and young son were all crying and begging him not to hurt us.

"Pop," our host's son said. "They've killed our leader and a whole bunch of my buddies. Eye for eye! Blood for blood!"

He brushed aside his old father and hollered at his buddies again: "What're you waiting for? Let's get on with it so we can have a feast soon! I'm so starved!"

Time to act. Now.

I pulled out the needle from my ear and murmured a spell; the needle grew to twenty feet long and rice bowl thick instantly. With one sweep of my Cudgel, I knocked off the knives on our necks and sent the bandits crashing on the ground; Master, Pigsy, and Sandy seized the opportunity and bolted out.

I finished off the bandits one by one and then went after the old man's son, apparently the new leader of the gang. With one hit from me, his skull cracked.

The old man, old woman, and the young mother howled. The young boy crawled under the dining table, his eyes popping out in terror. I mouthed a "sorry" to him and bolted out, too.

When I caught up with my people, I heard Pigsy saying this to Master.

"Did you see what I saw? He did it again!"

"Are you sure, Pigsy?" Master said, still recovering from the narrow escape from death.

"Sure as hell, I saw with my own eyes!"

You couldn't have seen with your own eyes, you pig, 'cause you were already out running for your life, but—

Master turned and gave me such a dirty look that I trembled. The moment he felt out of danger, Master stopped the horse and began to murmur that damned spell again.

That band on my head began to cut into me instantly; it

hurt so bad like I could explode into a thousand teeny-weensy pieces any moment. I rolled on the ground and begged:

"Oh, Master, please stop, please have mercy!"

"Mercy? Why didn't you have mercy for all the lives you've killed?"

"Master, if I had mercy for those demons and bandits, you would have been dead how many times over by now?"

"You slick-tongued monkey," Master fumed. "Go. I don't ever want to see you again. Ever! Never!"

I have finally had it too.

"All right," I said. "Please stop praying that spell so I can go in peace and in one piece, but how can you get to West Land without me protecting you by your side?"

"You ruthless, egomaniac hotshot!" Master muttered through his teeth. "How many times have you got me in trouble, tarnishing my impeccable name? If you don't leave me alone this minute, I'm going to pray that spell until your skull cracks and your brains squish!"

Such a shiny example of mercy, Master!

Without another word, I somersaulted into the cloud and soared away.

I was free again, sad, miserable like hell.

Where should I go now?

Back to Flower Fruit Mountain, only to be laughed at by my own people for coming back in such disgrace?

Back to Heaven, only to be kicked out by Jade Emperor, or suffer the infamy of being *bimawen*, stable boy, again?

Pay another visit to any of those dragon king friends, only to overstay my welcome?

Where's my dignity? My pride? What exactly is my destiny, from here onward?

And the injustice I've suffered in the hands of none other than my own master, over and again.

There's perhaps only one that I can go to, the one and only between Heaven and Earth who does have mercy.

When I was in the presence of Guanyin again, tears welled up from my heart, my soul, and I cried uncontrollably, like a baby.

"Wukong," Guanyin said in her kindest voice. "What's going on? Tell me what's happened so I can help you."

Between sobs, I told Guanyin my story.

"That Tang Monk you've picked for the grand mission to West Land, he's kind and merciful all right, but he's a teeny-weensy too rigid. How should I put it? Okay, his feeling good about himself being kind and merciful and his impeccable reputation all come at a deep price tag for me 'cause I have to be unkind and unmerciful to those vicious demons and bandits who want to kill him for his flesh. How many times has he punished me for snatching him away from perils and saving his life? Oh, believe me, Your Highness, when he punishes, he can be harsh, cruel."

"Is that so," Guanyin said, thoughtfully. "People of our faith should never kill, period, under any the circumstances, yet…. Let me see what I can do, Wukong. In the meantime, why don't you go and get some food and rest, be a guest of mine, now that you're here?"

I thanked Goddess of Mercy profusely, feeling a teeny-weensy better.

"Your Highness, I—" I said before leaving.

"I know," Guanyin said, smiling. "You're still worried about Xuanzang. He'll need your help soon and will be happy to have you back."

I was led to a guestroom where I ate, took a bath, and went to bed, the first time for a long time to sleep in a real bed, ivory frame, a puffy goose down pillow, and all, and fell into dreamland instantly.

I am on my knees by a wayside in the middle of nowhere, a bowl of water in my hands above my head.

"Master," I say. "You don't even have a drop of water to drink when I am not with you. Have this water to quench your thirst first, clean, cool water. I'll then go and get you some food."

"Why are you back?" says Master, angrily. "I'd rather die of thirst than drink your water. Go! Leave me alone."

"Master, you know without me by your side going to West Land would be mission impossible."

"Possible or impossible is none of your business, your megalomanic monkey! Stop pestering me, will you?"

That's the last straw that breaks the camel's, no, the monkey's, back.

"You hardhearted hairless blockhead!" I cry out, unable to hold back pent-up anger anymore, and throw that bowl of water in his face; he darts; and it hits his chest; he falls from the horse, faints, and not another word comes from his lips again.

What a weakling of a monk Master is.

I pick up his bags and somersault into the cloud. As I soar in the sky, I cast a background glance and see Pigsy and Sandy helping Master on his feet and then pointing in my direction, cussing, beating their chests.

I am sitting on a big rock outside Water Curtain Cave and reading something aloud, as if I were issuing a proclamation from the throne:

"Whereas we care about the spiritual wellbeing of our subjects in the boundless central kingdom and whereas we sense a dire need of correct moral compass, blah-blah-blah, we hereby commission Xuanzang, a monk by the surname of Chen, to travel to West Land for the goal of securing true Buddhist scriptures, accompanied by his First Disciple Wukong, Second Disciple Pigsy, and Third Disciple Sandy, blah-blah-blah...."

"Elder Brother," I hear someone hollering from way down below. "That official document by Emperor Xuanzong is not meant for your eyes! How dare you?"

I stop, upset that I'm thus interrupted, unceremoniously.

"Bring that rude, ugly thing up to me, little ones!"

A bunch of little monkeys get hold of the interrupter, grab his arms and legs, and carry him up to where I am.

"Who the devil are you, daring to barge in like that?" I demand to know.

"You don't recognize me, Elder Brother? I'm Sandy!"

"Sandy who? Why are you here?"

"I'm here because since you left, our master has had a hard time. He was even beaten up and robbed. I know Master is an itty-bitty temperamental, sometimes, but we are his disciples and can't hold that against him, can we? He needs your help badly! Besides, you want your salvation, too, right? If you don't want to come back to us, at least give me his bags. You enjoy your free life here and we go on our way."

"Hahaha, my brother," I laugh. "I can go to West Land myself and achieve my own salvation."

"You're so off, Elder Brother. The whole world knows that Xuanzang is the one, not you, commissioned by Emperor Xuanzong to travel to West Land for the true scriptures. Even if you get there, you think Father Buddha will give you the scriptures? In your wildest dream, brother! And if you don't come back and protect our master, this grand mission will certainly fail, all we've done so far will be for nothing. You know that too well, don't you?"

Never thought Sandy could be such a good talker.

"It's you who are so off, brother!" say I. "You think I'll be going to West Land by myself? I can have my own Tang Monk too. Don't believe me?"

I give the cue, a snap of fingers, and my little ones lead out of Water Curtain Dave a magnificent white horse; on its back sits Xuanzang, followed by Pigsy and Sandy, both carrying heavy loads.

"Blasphemy! Blasphemy!" Sandy hollers furiously. "Where on earth did you get a fake copy of me?" He raises his stick to hit the other Sandy, who falls and reveals himself to be a little monkey impersonator.

I charge at Sandy wielding my Gold-Banded Cudgel. Somehow, he manages to get away and I am in no mood to pursue him.

It was morning at Guanyin's abode in South Sea. I was chitchatting with Goddess of Mercy when I saw Sandy hurrying up the steps. He prostrated before Guanyin and was about to speak when he saw me sitting at the feet of the goddess. He jumped on his feet and charged at me with his iron stick.

"You devil of a monkey! How dare you come to Guanyin when you've committed so many horrific crimes?"

"Hold your weapon, Sandy!" said Guanyin, "and take your time to explain what's happened."

Like a prosecutor making the opening statement in court, Sandy recounted all the offences and disobediences I have allegedly committed. "He even dared to hit our master last night, almost killed him, and robbed his bags with important official documents in them!"

"Wait a minute," Guanyin said. "You said last night? Wukong has been at my place here since yesterday, so he's innocent of this charge of yours, to say the least. I can vouch for him."

"I saw Wukong outside Water Curtain Cave with Emperor Xuanzong's official document. Strike me to death with thunder if I'm lying."

"All right," Guanyin said. "That's easy. Wukong, why don't you go with Sandy to Flower Fruit Mountain and see if what

Sandy said is true or not for your own eyes?"

So, when we got there, I mean when I returned to Flower Fruit Mountain for the first time for quite some time, I saw me, Monkey King, sitting on a big rock outside Water Curtain Cave drinking, laughing, fooling around with a bunch of little monkeys! A picture-perfect copy of me, down to the cheek-less face, red buttocks, what have you.

I was perplexed and mad as hell.

I pulled out my Gold-Banded Cudgel and confronted me, I mean the other Monkey King.

"You imposter!" I shouted. "How dare you come and usurp my throne, take all my little ones, and lord it over here? Take this from one!" I went for him brandishing my Cudgel.

Me, the other Monkey King, met me with a Cudgel of his, an exact copy of mine.

It was a well-matched fight, blow for blow, somersaulting into the cloud, nose-diving to earth, flitting to the left, only to twist and turn and tumble to the right, like a pair of dragonflies, or rather, identical twins, chasing each other for fun, except that we were both dead serious and fighting for our lives.

"Don't just stand there and enjoy the show," I hollered to Sandy. "If you can't help me, why don't you go back to Guanyin and tell her what's happening here?"

"Don't just stand there and enjoy the show," the other me hollered to Sandy. "If you can't help me, why don't you go back to Guanyin and tell her what's happening here?"

Imagine how puzzled Sandy was, his eyes darting between me and me; shaking his head, Sandy somersaulted into the cloud and left.

We continued to fight tooth and nail, cussing like hell, all the way to South Sea—to be adjudicated by Guanyin.

"You two stop fighting and stand apart from each other," Guanyin said in her kind and calm voice of infinite wisdom,

after listening to Sandy's confused and confusing report, "so I can tell which of you is real and which is fake."

"I'm real," I said.

"I'm real," the other me said—the same words, not the slightest difference in tone or pitch.

Guanyin took a long and hard look at me and me and could not tell.

She thought for a moment and began to murmur something.

The band on my head began to tighten, cut into me, hurt me so bad that I rolled on the ground in pain.

The other me dropped on the ground and rolled, too, his face and body contorted in pain.

"Please have mercy and stop that pray!" We begged in unison.

Guanyin stopped and then said: "Wukong?"

"Yes?" we answered in unison again.

Guanyin shook her head.

"Why don't you go back to Heaven and ask Jade Emperor to adjudicate? He should know if anyone does."

We somersaulted into the cloud and sailed to Heaven.

After the usual hassles of Heaven Guards, we were led to the presence of Jade Emperor, sitting high and mighty in his throne.

He was not too thrilled to see me, and me, having been aroused from another of his long naps.

"Trouble from *bimawen* never ends," said Jade Emperor. He took a good look at me and then the other me and knitted his eyebrows. "Get me the Demon-Detecting Mirror!"

When Heaven Guards handed him the mirror, Jade Emperor shone it on me and then me and shook his head.

So, we were both dismissed and kicked out of Heaven again.

We both laughed.

"Why don't we go to Netherland and see King Yama?" said I. "He should know if anyone knows at all."

Verbatim from the other me.

We fought again like devils as we descended, cussing, kicking up waves of bone-chilling air, waking up dead souls crying for mama, and sending guards and commandos running with hands on their heads, until we reached the lowest level of Netherland, in the presence of King Yama, high and mighty in his throne.

"Long time no see," King Yama said, looking at me and then me, a little perplexed. "I thought you'd never want to come back and visit again. So, to what do I owe this pleasure?"

I bowed and explained why I was there.

"From what I can tell," I concluded, "you're the only one who can tell."

The other me also bowed and gave the same story, verbatim.

"All right," King Yama said. "There's only one way to find out."

Guards carried out volumes upon volumes of the Book of Life and Death; they turned the pages and searched up and down and left and right but could not find a single monkey in them.

With a pat on his forehead, King Yama exclaimed angrily. "Is this a joke or something? You think I'm getting senile? You erased yourself and all the monkeys from our book some years ago. Get lost and don't ever come back and pester us again!"

So, we were kicked out of Hell too.

There was only one place left to go.

We found our way back to Earth, somersaulted into the cloud, and sailed to the West, every move of ours the same, as in synchronized dance, swimming, whatever.

Once again, we had to deal with the hassles of going through gates upon gates, stopped, pat searched, by stern, smartly dressed guards, before we were finally led to a grand, incense-filled hall; Rulai, Father Buddha, was giving a big sermon:

.... *somethingness of nothingness, nothingness of somethingness, absence of presence, presence of absence, emptiness of fullness, fullness of emptiness, desire-freeness of desire-fulness, desire-fulness of desire-freeness, one-ness of all-ness, all-ness of one-ness, being-ness of nonbeing-ness, nonbeing-ness of being-ness, blah-blah-blah-ness of non-blah-blah-blah-ness....*

Noticing the two new arrivals, Rulai paused, took a quick glance, and continued to address the large congregation of pilgrims.

"This," Rulai said, pointing at us, me and the other me, "is a perfect example of one being torn by two hearts, one true, kind, loyal, destined for salvation, and one false, consumed by vanity, trying to lead the true heart astray. They each know in their heart of hearts who is true and who is false, the false one knowing only too well that he shall meet his imminent damnation."

I looked at the other me and he looked back, and then before I knew it, the other me changed into a bee to flee, only to be caught by Rulai in a teacup. He turned the teacup upside down and left it there on the podium. The bee buzzed frantically inside but could not get out.

I thought of me more than five hundred years ago being caught by the same Rulai in his palm and being put under that humongous Five-Element Mountain.

Will anyone ever come and free this poor bee, a me too?

"Now," Rulai said to me. "You can go back to your master and protect him on the journey to West Land."

I saw an opportunity here and wanted to grab it before leaving.

"Since I'm here, Your Majesty, can I ask—"

"Don't even think of it, your smarty-pants," Rulai said, eyeing the band on my head. "Follow that true heart of yours and you'll be richly rewarded."

My true heart?

The heart that has been throbbing inside me since I, that little stone monkey, was born hundreds upon hundreds of years ago?

What does that heart really want?

Have I, my heart, my ego, been battered so much by things I've been through, been splintered into two, if not more, mes that even I can't tell which me is true me and which me is false?

"What took you so long?" asked Xuanzang, my master, upon seeing me back.

"I thought you would never want to see me again, Master," I mumbled.

"Well, you can imagine how hurt I was when you hit me, your master!" said Master, barely able to control his feelings. "Now I know it was not really you."

Who's told him? Guanyin?

"Now I know," Master continued, hesitantly. "I know being that hard on you, punishing you like that, is unbecoming a Buddhist monk, unbecoming me."

Oh, I'm such a softie. A kind word can vaporize all the anger I've boxed up in me. I was just about to say something when we saw Pigsy landing from a whirlwind of cloud, carrying two bags on his back, Sandy close behind.

"Master, master!" said Pigsy breathlessly. "I found these inside Water Curtain Cave!" He then turned to me: "What say you, brother?"

I was still struggling for words when Master answered the question for me by telling Pigsy and Sandy what had really happened. Imagine how amazed they both were.

There and then, we, master and disciples, patched things up, packed up, and got on our way again.

TWENTY
Third Time's The Charm

It was smooth sail from then onward for days and days. Our hearts were beating for the same purpose as we pressed on, rain or shine, getting up at the first hint of sunrise and settling down for the night long after sunset, climbing rugged mountains, crossing swift rivers, forging through hot, throat-parching desserts.

Yes, it was getting hotter each day, unbearably hot. Even Master, the usually uptight one, all buttoned up, used his hat to fan himself; sometimes he stripped to the waist and revealed his hairless chest and pale skin.

"Wukong, why don't you go and find out why such heat?" Master said, breathing heavily.

"We're getting so close to where the sun sets is the reason why, I think," quipped Pigsy. He had been sweating so much that his thick skin looked dry and wrinkled with rows of furrows, his tongue hanging from his long mouth gasping for air; oh, his bad breath I could smell a full *li* away.

I leapt into the cloud, looked around, and saw a lone cottage not too far away. I landed there as a cleanly dressed little monk and knocked on the door. It was opened by a grizzled old man.

I bowed deeply and explained who we were and where we were going.

"You're all welcome to stay here for the night," the old man said kindly, "although I do not have much to offer."

Master, Pigsy, and Sandy were all thrilled to have shelter for the night to cool off.

They bowed and thanked the old man profusely.

"Our kind benefactor," Master said to the old man when we all had tea and bread and caught our breath. "It's already late autumn, how come it is so hot here, hotter than mid-summer, if I may?"

"Oh, you don't know?" the old man said. "We're not far from Flaming Mountain, a humongous pit or peak of fire, like a volcano erupting nonstop, and we, folks living in an eight hundred *li* radius, are all under its spell. Your only path to where you're going cuts through this hell-like mountain. I'm afraid there's no getting around it."

Master paled upon hearing this.

"How could you live here," I asked, taking another bite of the bread served by the kind old man, "if nothing grows here, see what I mean?"

"Hahaha," the old man laughed. "We burn incense and pay tribute to Iron Fan Princess; she has a magic bansho fan, one wave of that fan of hers can stop the fire; another wave of the fan can send us wind; a third wave of the fan can send us rain, so we can plow, seed, plant, and have enough harvest for the year. It all depends on whether she is pleased or not. If not, we'll all go hungry and there's nothing we can do about it."

"How do you pay tribute to please this Iron Fan Princess then?"

"Well, give her the best we have, the choicest meat, sweetest fruit, tastiest wine, whatever we've got. She lives very far from here, in Bansho Cave on Green Cloud Mountain.

Our pilgrimage there and back takes a full month, walking a distance of one thousand four hundred and fifty-six *li*."

Master looked even more nonplussed.

"You can see we are poor monks, with only our clothes on our back."

Now I know who we're dealing with here, the mother of a boy demon I had a difficult time subduing and had to ask Guanyin for help. Too many demon fighting memories to keep track of, and too many such stories to tell all at once, right?

"Don't you worry, Master!" I said and stood up.

"Where're you going, Wukong?"

"You all carry on without me. Will be back in a sec."

I somersaulted into the cloud and sailed in the direction of Green Cloud Mountain.

In the blink of an eye, I landed outside Bansho Cave covered in ivies, trees, flowers, what have you, a heavenly place although it pales when compared to my Water Curtain Cave.

I knock on the door, a clean young maid opens it, I explain who I am and why I am here, she goes back inside and before long, a most gorgeous yet fierce-looking woman comes out, wrapped in the fanciest silk and donning shiniest gemstones, a sharp sword in each hand.

"Where's that monkey?" she demanded.

"Here, my kind sister-in-law!" I bowed, "Wukong at your service!"

"Don't you dare to sister-in-law me!" snapped Iron Fan Princess.

"Well, back in my Heaven days, your husband, Bull Demon King, and I are the thickest of brothers. That makes you my sister-in-law, doesn't it?"

"If that's true, why did you get our son Red Boy in trouble? How do you explain yourself? Now that you dare to show up here, time for some revenge!"

She raised her swords and was ready to charge at me.

"Hold, hold, my sister-in-law, let me explain. That precious boy of yours, he had the same magic power with fire like his mother, he captured my master, Xuanzang, and wanted to steam him for feast. I had no choice but to save my master. Besides, where he is now, an altar boy for Guanyin, is quite a good deal. He'll remain young forever and will never die."

"That may be true, you slick-tongued monkey, but I'll never get to see my son again!"

"Oh, that can be easily arranged, sister-in-law, if you lend me your fan. I'll return it to you when the fire stops, and my master has crossed Flaming Mountain. That's a promise."

"If you stick your neck out and let me cut it, I'll lend you my fan. That's a promise, too."

I stuck my neck out and she hit it as hard as she could, using the two swords in turn, and I did not feel a thing.

Frightened, Iron Fan Princess turned to run inside. I blocked her.

"Hey, sister-in-law, you promised!"

"Sorry, my fan is not for lending! Why don't you take no as the final answer?"

"Well, this is my answer to your answer!" I said and pulled out my Gold-Banded Cudgel.

We began to fight, blow for blow, and before long Iron Fan Princess began to lose her strength. She pulled out her fan, from nowhere, gave it a shake, and a powerful gust of wind sent me swirling, dazed like hell until I landed I don't know where.

I picked myself up, somersaulted into the cloud, and sailed right back to Bansho Cave, changed into a tiny flea, and slinked in through a little crack.

"Damn that monkey," Iron Fan Princess said, taking a tiny bite of a cake and placing it back on the ivory table, "giving granny such a fight! More tea, dragon oolong tea. My throat still feels like on fire!"

A maid hastened from the kitchen with a fresh pot and poured into the big cup on the table. When Iron Fan Princess picked up the cup, I jumped in, and the next thing I knew, I was tumbling down a water slide tube into that gorgeous princess's belly; it felt warm and tender all around; I could hear her heart beating like some church bell.

"Sister-in-law," I hollered at the top of my lungs. "Please, let me borrow your fan for only once. Please!"

"Where's that monkey?" I heard Iron Fan Princess shrieking. "How could he get in when the door is shut?"

"Your Highness," her maid said, timidly. "I think he is inside you."

"What nonsense?! How?!"

"Yes, sister-in-law," I hollered again. "I am inside you as I speak! You want to find out whether I'm lying?" I knocked my head against her heart a few times. It twitched, beating faster and more thunderously.

"Stop, please stop!" cried Iron Fan Princess, rolling on the ground in pain. "You're killing me!"

"If it were not for my brother Demon Bull King, I wouldn't mind kicking your liver a few times too! Lend me your fan, now!"

"All right, I'll hand it to you when you come out."

"Let me see it first," I said, climbing up to her throat.

She told a maid to bring out the fan. I could see it through her mouth as she spoke.

"Keep your mouth open so I can come out," said I. "Don't even think of trying any trick. If you do, I'll kick a big hole through your ribcage."

"I promise!"

Iron Fan Princess kept her sweet mouth open, like for a doctor to see and examine her, and waited.

"Why don't you come out now?" She mumbled, trying not to close her mouth while speaking.

"I'm already out," I said, back in my real self, holding the fan in my hand.

Iron Fan Princess turned and looked so surprised and beaten that I almost felt sorry for her.

"I'm much obliged, my good sister-in-law!" I bowed and marched outside the cave.

Imagine how thrilled Master and everyone else were.

"Never thought I'd have a chance to see it this close in my lifetime," enthused the old man, our kind host.

We bid good-bye to our kind host and got on our way again.

About forty *li* onward, the heat became unbearably hot.

"Oh, my feet, like walking on burning charcoal!" complained Sandy.

"Me too," moaned Pigsy, "like being barbecued alive!"

"All right," I declared excitedly. "Time to use the magic fan."

To my chagrin, after I waved the fan once in the direction of Flaming Mountain, the fire burned even more fiercely.

Shocked, I waved it a few more times and the fire only got much worse, and I waved it more frantically until it shot up a thousand feet into the sky, some flames exploding over our heads and burning off a few hairs of mine.

"Run! Run!" I shrieked.

We all turned on our heels, literally, and ran and didn't stop until we were out of imminent danger.

"Brother," complained Pigsy. "That fan of yours, almost got us all cremated alive!"

"I must have been had by that Iron Fan Princess," I said, crestfallen.

Upon hearing this, Master wimped, "What can we do

now, Wukong?"

"We can go East, North, or South, where there is no fire, Master," Pigsy suggested.

"But our destination is West. I don't mind walking through fire if I can get there!"

"What a fix we're in," said Sandy, with a deep sigh.

I sighed too. "Why don't you all put out for the night here? I'll be back in a sec."

With that I somersaulted into the cloud, and in the blink of an eye I landed outside Thunderous Cloud Cave, the abode of Demon Bull King.

A gorgeous woman, as gorgeous as Iron Fan Princess but about ten years younger, robed in the fanciest of silk and donning shiniest of gems, was taking a leisurely stroll outside. Upon seeing me, she fled inside, screaming as if she had seen a ghost.

I followed her in.

The gorgeous young woman flew into the arms of a big, husky man, thick sideburns, veins visible on his forehead, sitting at a big table loaded with plates of steamed pig ears and paws, fried leopard's gallbladders, you name it.

"Oh, hon, my baby," Demon Bull King kissed the woman in his arms. He looked the same as I remembered, fiercely handsome, having a big appetite for everything, and so on, except for going a teeny-weensy gray at the temples. "What's wrong? Tell daddy and I'll take care of it."

He looked up and saw me.

"Hey, you, *bimawen!*" He muttered through his teeth, standing up. "Why're you here? Haven't you caused me enough trouble?"

I bowed and explained why I came to visit.

"You started that hell of a fire yourself and have the thick face to come and ask me for help?"

Me the arsonist who started the fire? I'm to blame for Flaming Mountain, that damned wall of fire between us and our destination in the West?

"Don't you play that innocent I don't know card with me!" fumed Demon Bull King. "When you leapt out of Laozi's *Bagua* Stove more than five hundred years ago, it fell on its side and some live charcoal scattered. That's what started it all. I was a security guard there and became a fall guy for you, condemned to where I am now. All the good things you've done, stable boy! So, don't you dare to my brother me again!"

Damn. All my chickens are now coming home to roost.

"I had not the slightest idea, my brother, honestly. All the more reasons I have to repent and strive for salvation with this journey to West Land."

"So I've heard," Demon Bull King grunted through his nose. "To what do I owe the pleasure, anyway?"

"Well," I hesitated, "as Iron Fan Princess' ex, you should still have her ear, I assume, you two having shared the same lovebirds pillow for many years after all."

I regretted the moment those words rolled off my tongue because upon hearing them, that "hon" "my baby" of Demon Bull King threw herself into his arms again, whimpering, beating his thick chest with her fists, "no, no, no...."

"You *bimawen*!" Demon Bull King flew into a rage again. "You caused my fall from Heaven, you've harassed my ex, and now you're messing with my babe here! If I don't take care of you now, I am not worthy of being called a man!"

He picked up his big stick and came after me.

We fought like two devils, blow for blow, round after round, without either gaining the upper hand.

In the thick of fight, I heard a messenger boy calling somewhere in the sky:

"Grandpa Bull King, our king is waiting for you to begin

the banquet. The other guests have all arrived!"

"Oops, I almost forgot," said Demon Bull King and hollered back to the messenger boy. "Tell your king my friend I'll be there in a sec."

After a few more half-hearted rounds with me, Demon Bull King said: "Don't you dare to bother my babe again when I'm gone."

He blew a kiss to his babe down there, outside the cave: "Just a few drinks, hon," and was gone.

"Hon" stomped her feet unhappily and walked back inside the cave.

What do women see in this guy, this heartless lover? Just because he's handsome?

An idea came to me.

I turned and sailed in the direction of Green Cloud Mountain and landed outside Bansho Cave again, this time a picture-perfect copy of Demon Bull King.

The news of my arrival was reported inside immediately.

When I was led to the presence of Iron Fan Princess, a maid was still frantically helping her fix the hair and makeup.

"So, tired of that fresh meat of yours already?" she said nonchalantly although I could sense some nervous excitement underneath.

I was tongue-tied. Women. They will be a mystery to me forever.

"What wind has blown you here, anyway?" she asked in the same matter-of-fact tone.

I recovered quickly.

"I've heard that *bimawen* came to bother you about the bansho fan and almost got away with it. That damned monkey, having done us so much harm and having the balls to come and mess with us again! I'll skin him alive if he shows that cheek-less face of his here again and cut him into ten thousand pieces!"

"The way you talk big!" Iron Fan Princess turned around and sniffled. "Since you abandoned me for that fresh meat, life has not been the same for me, alone, lonely, with no one to share my bed, no one to protect me...."

Such sorrow from such a beautiful woman can break just about anyone's heart, although I'm just roleplaying—not for fun, but for a serious purpose.

"That monkey could have killed me when he tricked his way inside my belly," she continued, sobbing.

"That sly son of a gun!" said I furiously. "Can't wait to catch him and let him know who he's dealing with!"

"But I outsmarted him," Iron Fan Princess said proudly, breaking into a smile, "sending him away with a fake fan. Hahaha!"

"So I've heard," said I. "You're the smartest!"

"Smarter than that stinky fresh meat of yours?"

"Of course, and sexier, spicier, too!"

"You sweet-tongued liar!" snapped Iron Fan Princess, her eyes glistening with joy.

She had her maids set up the table with wine and delicacies and we began to eat and drink together like a coup, a reconciliation dinner, see what I mean?

After a few cups, Iron Fan Princess looked a teeny-weensy tipsy, her face flushing, her eyes looking into mine with longing. She sat next to me, and then simply in my laps, snuggled her head in my shoulder, moaned with pleasure, squirmed deliciously, had me drink from her wine cup, fed me sweet and juicy fruit, what have you.

As I played along, kissing her hot, fragrant lips, burying my face in her rich cloud of hair, my hands exploring the curves of her body, I felt a strange excitement swelling up in me like a tide that kept rising, dizzyingly, ominously, threatening to break the strongest of dikes; I could have surrendered and died there and then—happy.

Is this why Pigsy still dreams of going back to Gao Village and be their son-in-law again?

Why Kui Xing, "spoon" of the Big Dipper, willing to give up Heaven and followed that altar girl down to Earth, even if the price to pay was to be reborn a demon?

But this is no time to let this tidal wave, whatever it is, wash me away. I have to hang on for my dear life, for our journey to West Land.

"Hon, my babe," I murmured, extricating myself from the heart-melting arms of Iron Fan Princess. "Where do you put the real fan? Make sure it is in a safe place so that monkey cannot steal it."

"Aha, my man cannot stay focused," she said, half-annoyed. "What else is new?"

She opened her mouth and showed me the fan, perched on the tip of her tongue, the size of an apricot leaf. "Happy now?"

No wonder her lips have remained zipped when we neck like a pair of hungry doves.

I picked it up and turned it around to take a good look. "Amazing! To think that this small fan can have such humongous power!"

"My lord," said Iron Fan Princess reproachfully. "You've been relishing that stinky fresh meat of yours so much that you've clean forgotten how this thing works? All you need to do is to twirl it between your left thumb and index finger and it will grow and do endless magic!"

That's all I need to know.

I tossed the fan in my mouth, changed back to my real self, and bowed. "I'm much obliged, sister-in-law!"

"Horrible! Horrible!" sister-in-law let out a heart-piercing howl and crawled under the dining table.

I tore myself away from the scene, marched out of the cave,

somersaulted into the cloud, and landed when I got closer to where Master, Pigsy, and Sandy were waiting for me.

I saw Pigsy hurrying towards me.

"Elder Brother!" he hollered, out of breath. "Our master is worried about you to death and has sent me to see what took you so long. Everything good?"

"What do you think, brother?" I said proudly, opened my mouth, and spat out the fan.

"Amazing, Elder Brother! Let me take a look."

I handed him the fan.

The moment Pigsy had the fan in his big paws, he morphed into someone else, taller, handsomer, fiercer. Demon Bull King.

Damn, smarty-pants outsmarted by a simpleton!

"You stupid stable boy!" Demon Bull King laughed, "think you'd have gotten away with this?"

We fought again, Gold-Banded Cudgel vs. big iron swords, blow for blow, each bursting with pride, fury, and righteousness, kicking up big clouds of dust into the sky.

We were in the thick of fight when I saw Pigsy, this better be the real Pigsy, hurrying toward us.

"If you had come sooner, this thing," I shouted, pointing at Demon Bull King, "would not have succeeded in having me fooled, pretending to be you!"

"What?" Pigsy was mad as hell. "That disgusting face of yours, Demon Bull King, daring to impersonate me? Why don't you take a pee and see yourself in it?"

With that, he raised his big iron fork and went after Demon Bull King, too.

Caught between me and Pigsy fighting him from left and right, front and back, Demon Bull King was fast losing steam, his blows becoming weaker and weaker.

Then, we saw a thousand little demons coming to his rescue, brandishing swords, knives, spears, what have you. Pigsy and I fought off waves upon waves of these little demons charging at us, but Demon Bull King got away, with the fan.

I somersaulted into the cloud, took a quick look, and sailed in the direction of Green Cloud Mountain, followed by Pigsy.

Upon landing outside Bansho Cave, I pounded on the door with my fists.

No response.

Pigsy hit the door hard with his iron fork.

The door opened and out stepped none other than Demon Bull King himself, a shiny big sword in each hand. Without a word, he went for Pigsy's throat, which I blocked with my Cudgel.

The three of us began another round of fight, two against one, an unfair fight if you ask me, but what do I care about fairness when what's at stake is so big, whether we can shut down the fire on Flaming Mountain and get on our way to the West?

This Demon Bull King, strong as he is, may have indulged in sensual pleasures a teeny-weensy too much over the years and therefore lost a teeny-weensy of his *qi*, so he soon became out of breath and sweated like a broken steamer.

As he jumped around dodging our blows, the big guy tripped and fell. As he struggled to pick himself up, I placed my Cudgel squarely on his head, Pigsy his iron fork on his chest. I hit him so hard on the head that it was knocked inside his body.

To my shock, a new head popped out right away, darker, more grotesque, eyes rolling like a clown, as if daring me to hit him again.

This I obliged and knocked this head inside his body again.

Another head, even uglier, popped out from his body, laughing at me contemptuously.

I was mad as hell and hit it frantically; each time the same thing happened.

I knew what to do, for good. I knocked that ugliest of heads into the devil's body again with all my might and thrust my Cudgel in. I could feel the devil struggling and pushing at the other end of my Cudgel, but I held firm.

I heard a heart-piercing cry from a woman running toward us.

A familiar voice that has recently cooed and confided her loneliness and sorrow in my ears, its owner snuggling and squirming in my arms, causing a smashing, take-no-prisoner kind of disturbance in me.

"Please spare him!" begged Iron Fan Princess on her knees, tears streaking down her rouged cheeks.

"Only if you lend me the fan," I said as firmly as I could.

"You can have it for all I care," said Iron Fan Princess, sniffling.

She took out a little silky pouch from her bosom and held it out to me.

The moment I pulled out my Cudgel, another ugly head of Demon Bull King popped out.

"Don't, babe!" that head screamed.

"I only want you, my lord," cried Iron Fan Princess, "and don't care about anything else in the world."

Demon Bull King looked confused, not sure what to say.

I placed my Cudgel on this head of his again.

"What say you, you lucky bastard?" said I, "want me to knock this ugly head of yours back in so it will never see the light of day again?"

"You've had your fling, hon, my baby," said a tearful Iron Fan Princess, extending her arms to Demon Bull King. "Now time to come back to mama, and do not ever play truant again!"

Did I see Demon Bull King's eyes moistening as he nodded, and staggered to his "mama"?

Did I see Pigsy's eyes wide open, as if wonderstruck, a tear

or two rolling down his long face, as we turned to leave?

I wasn't sure 'cause my vision became a teeny-weensy blurry for no apparent reason at all.

I don't need to tell you in detail how we crossed Flaming Mountain after extinguishing the fire with the magic fan.

Oh, before I forget, we gave the magic fan to the old man who had kindly hosted us as a farewell gift so the people around here could have good harvest year after year and live happily, hunger-free, ever after.

TWENTY ONE

In the Land of Nirvana

The farther we went, the more different people looked, their eyes, their clothes, the tongues they spoke, even the aromas from their kitchens, but we understood each other somehow, like the more different we are, the more we are the same. As before, we encountered temptations and perils of all kinds and benefited from the kindness of so many strangers.

Before we knew it, we found ourselves in West Land, where, we've been told, there is no suffering, 'cause there's no greed, no desire, and we are all released from karma and the cycle of death and rebirth, where we indeed see monks everywhere, long robes, shaved heads, all looking so pious, quietly reciting scriptures as they come and go. We've arrived at the destination of our long journey to obtain the true scriptures of Buddhism and take them home to great Tang so all Tang people can begin their journey toward nirvana.

When we passed a big temple with a tall stature of Rulai, Father Buddha, Xuanzang, my master, was awestruck and stopped the horse to admire.

"Master," I had to remind him. "You've bowed so many times in front of fake, imposter Buddha temples and statures.

Now you're in front of the real deal and you forgot to show respect?"

Master rolled off the horse and bowed and murmured his joy and gratitude profusely.

I have been here a couple of times before, not as a pilgrim, tourist, or anything, but to get Rulai's help in subduing demons and monsters and making me, my battered ego whole again. I had no time and was in no mood to enjoy the sights and sounds of this heavenly place. Now, here I am again, with my master, my charge, his safely arriving here having been my mission, I am thrilled, but I have to check that celebratory impulse. I still have a job to do—mission almost accomplished, but not quite yet.

We came upon a river, about eight or nine *li* wide, turbulent currents tumbling onward, wilderness on both sides, not a human soul far and near.

"Are we lost? Is this the right way?" Master said, worried. "How can we get across without even a boat?"

I looked left and right.

"There's a bridge!" I exclaimed, pointing toward something upstream, like a rainbow silhouetted against the sunset-lit sky. "That's how we'll reach the other shore!"

We trudged to that bridge and were surprised by what we saw:

A single log arching across the swift river, long, narrow like a balance beam, a tightrope.

How can we walk on that bridge, not to lose our head, our balance, and reach the other shore?

"What will happen if I fall?" said Master. "Let's find another way."

"I will not step onto that thing even to save my life!" said Pigsy.

"There is no other way around this," I said. "Let me show you!"

The moment I stepped onto the thin single log bridge, gingerly, my head began to swirl with the tumbling waters underneath; I almost lost my balance and fell. Keep your eyes straight and don't look down, monkey! I told myself and regained my balance. Soon I became oblivious to the perilous danger underneath and felt like I was walking on any other regular bridge, going faster, surer.

"See? Easy!" I hollered back when I reached the other shore.

I saw Master shaking his head, Pigsy and Sandy trying to push each other onto the bridge, neither daring to venture a single step.

I ran back to where they were and grabbed Pigsy's arms. "Just follow me. Really easy."

"Can't do it, brother, spare me! Let me somersault into the cloud and leap over!"

"What nonsense! None of our usual tricks will do here. You have to walk across if you want to reach the other shore, for salvation!"

"Salvation or not," cried Pigsy, throwing himself on the ground, "just can't do it!"

I tried to help Pigsy on his feet, but he kept his butt on the ground and refused to budge.

"Leave him alone, Elder Brother," said Sandy. "I wouldn't walk on that thing to save my life, either."

We were all standing there, Master, Pigsy, Sandy, me, and the white horse, staring at that thin arch across the perilous river, the only possible link between us and the other shore, salvation, eternity, whatever, mesmerized, terrified, at the end of our wits.

"Look!" exclaimed Master, pointing wildly. "A boat! A boat is coming!"

We all turned to look.

IN THE LAND OF NIRVANA

Against the early evening sky, lit by the last rays of the setting sun, where shimmering water and firmament blending into one jaw-dropping magnificence, a small boat is gliding fast toward us.

On that boat is a lone ferryman, who looks like an old monk. I recognize who he is right away, but know it is not my place to say anything. Not now.

When the boat reached us, we could see that it had no hull. A bottomless boat.

"How can we get on this broken, bottomless boat?" said Master, disappointed, falling into despair again.

"Trust me," said the old ferryman in his deep voice. "This boat of mine has helped countless multitudes across the river. Have faith and you'll be fine."

I bowed deeply to thank the ferryman, grabbed Master's hand, and led him to the boat. He was still hesitating when I gave him a tug, he staggered, and fell into the bottomless boat, splashing, trying to stay afloat. The ferryman gave Master his hand and pulled him up on his feet. Master stomped a few times to shake off the water on his robe, mumbling about me being rude, rough, and so on.

I had no time to mind my master's complaint and hurried to help Sandy, Pigsy, and the white horse onto the boat too.

Once we were all onboard, the old ferryman used his long bamboo pole to push the boat away from the shore.

"Look!" Master exclaimed, pointing wildly, his face ashen.

We all turned to look.

A body was drifting on the water not far from us, an exact copy of Xuanzang, our master.

"Don't be afraid," the old ferryman said calmly. "That was the old you."

"It is you, Master!" Pigsy clapped his hands excitedly.

"Old you!" exclaimed Sandy rapturously.

"Congratulations," the old ferryman said to Master again, "you've arrived."

When we finally stepped ashore and turned to look, the boat was gone, a star appeared in the evening sky, then a few more, and then a whole galaxy of them, all twinkling, the whole world a dreamy, glimmering splendor.

Master bowed deeply to the river, to the star-lit infinity, awestruck, mumbling incoherently, and then turned to bow and thank us for protecting him all the way to the land of nirvana.

We were all so thrilled for our master, congratulated him for having shed his old self and been born anew, and thanked him for taking us along the journey—in protecting him we found our salvation too.

We all but sang and danced our way to Thunder Sound Temple atop the majestic Mount Sumeru, where we were met by the famed Four Heavenly Kings, champions of the four corners of the world respectively; they led us through doors and corridors into a magnificent hall, palace like, in the presence of Rulai seated in a grand chair, lotus posture, flanked on both sides by the famed eight Bodhisattvas, Guanyin, Goddess of Mercy, you've already met her quite a few times, aka Avalokiteshvara, and Manjushri, Maitreya, Vajrapani, Mahasthamaprapta, Samantabhadra, Kshitigarbha, Sarvanivarana Vishkambhin, each name quite a mouthful, right? Five Hundred Rohan, those who have achieved Nibbana and are freed from the cycle of life, death, and rebirth... you get the drift.

When all the official papers were checked and identities confirmed, Rulai addressed the huge assembling. I can only give a gist of what he said:

Great Tang is a great country of rich natural resources, hard-working people, yet it has been plagued by greed, lecherous desires, frauds, and become a land of unkindness, disloyalty, unfilial betrayal, murders, natural disasters, you

IN THE LAND OF NIRVANA

name it. Therefore, great Tang needs the true scriptures of Buddhism, namely, classical scriptures in the Big Wheel canon, to enlighten the people, guide them out of the hell of ignorance, indulgences, irreverence:

Tripiṭaka, three baskets, the doctrine of karma, the four jhanas, ten courses of wholesome action and the five precepts, nirvana, the highest good and final goal, the complete and final end of suffering, a state of perfection, the end of all rebirth....

The Five Hindrances to meditation: sense desire, hostility, sloth and torpor, restlessness and worry, and doubt....

The Four Noble Truths about suffering, craving being the cause of suffering, removal of craving to end suffering, the path leading to this suffering-free state of being....

The Middle Way between extreme asceticism and sensual indulgence....

Rulai droned on and on in his deep voice and my head swirled in this sea of exotic sounding words. When the sermon was finally over, Father Buddha gifted copies of these sacred texts to Xuanzang, my master, hundreds of volumes of them:

Blessed are the people of great Tang herewith and blessed are those who see hope for liberation from physical bondage and are ready to abandon their earthly desires and begin their journey for the shore of salvation.

After bowing and thanking Rulai, we began to descend the majestic Mount Sumeru to return to our quarters, the white horse loaded with the scriptures.

We were about halfway down when we saw a Buddhist monk diving on us from mid-air and in the blink of an eye snatching all the volumes of scriptures from the horseback.

What? Day robbery even here, in the land of nirvana, Rulai?

Flabbergasted and mad as hell, I pulled out my Gold-Banded Cudgel and somersaulted into the cloud to chase after

301

the scripture snatcher. Before I could hit him, the culprit let go and all the volumes scattered down like snowflakes. It took us forever to find and collect all the volumes, one page at a time. What shocked us more was that all these pages were blank. Without a midge of ink on any of them.

We have been had by Rulai?

"My disciples," cried Xuanzang, our master, crumpled on the ground. "Never thought this could happen here, of all places in the world. How can I return to our great Tang with these wordless, worthless blank sheets?"

We all stood there, dumbfounded.

"How can I face Emperor Xuanzong again?" Master continued to lament, beating his chest. "I've betrayed His Majesty with empty promise, a capital crime!"

"Don't cry, Master," said I. "Must be a practical joke from those two senior monks, Ānanda and Mahākāśyapa are their names, I think? They were not too thrilled because we didn't give them any gifts in return for the scriptures. Remember?"

"The scriptures are for sale?" Master sounded incredulous. "That'd be abuse of power and a blatant case of corruption!"

"No," said Rulai, Father Buddha, when we hurried back to him and asked for help. "All they need is a good-faith gesture, token of sincerity."

"I am a poor monk, Your Majesty, with only clothes on my back," said Master. "There is nothing that I can give as a worthy good-faith gesture. No gold, no silver, no diamond."

"How about that purple gold bowl in your bag?" I suggested.

Master gave me a dirty look.

"That's a gift from Emperor Xuanzong. I've never used, too precious."

"Perhaps Emperor Xuanzong had the foresight so you could regift it in exchange—"

It was with much reluctance that Master handed the purple

gold bowl to Ānanda; the senior monk looked so ecstatic and grinned from ear to ear.

"Shame! Shame! Shame!" all the other monks, old and young, started a chant as Ānanda retreated with the treasure in both hands.

This time we double checked each page of the scriptures with none other than Mahākāśyapa to make sure it was not blank, wordless.

The return journey was uneventful, a teeny-weensy boring, if you ask me. It took us only eight days, without running into any demons, monsters, ghosts, whatever.

What happened? Those demons, monsters, ghosts we had to fight, to outpower and outsmart, were no more real than projections of ourselves, our hearts and minds, in some forms and shapes, our splintered selves fighting each other for dominance? We were simply being tested a thousand times over, for more than fourteen years, the test is now over, and we are at peace with ourselves, free at last? I have no way of knowing.

Imagine how thrilled we were when we were led into the capital of great Tang, the palace of Emperor Xuanzong, to be welcomed by His Majesty himself with his Queen, princes, princesses, and the who's who of his court, marshals, generals, you name it.

Mission accomplished.

They were taken aback by the sight of me, Pigsy, and Sandy, though.

"These foreigners, my sworn brother," asked Emperor Xuanzong. "They are your disciples?"

"Oh, I almost forgot," Master said, and began to introduce each of us:

First Disciple, Wukong, Monkey King, originally from Flower Fruit Mountain, a troublemaker in Heaven more than five hundred years ago, now a pious Buddhist, without him protecting me all the way this mission would not have been possible, I would not have made it home, blah-blah-blah.

Second Disciple, Pigsy, originally Canopy Marshal in Heaven, condemned to Earth for an affair with an altar girl, redeemed himself for carrying the heaviest loads the entire journey, blah-blah-blah.

Third Disciple, Sandy, originally Imperial Honor Guards Commander in Heaven, old steady, always dependable, never giving me any reason to doubt his honesty, blah-blah-blah.

We did not prostrate before Emperor Xuanzong after the introduction and His Majesty was displeased.

"You'll have to forgive them," Master said apologetically. "They haven't learned our great Tang's manners yet."

"No worries," Emperor Xuanzong said graciously. "We great Tang welcome all from all corners of the world like a vast sea welcoming tributaries from everywhere, big and small."

A magnificent celebration followed that lasted for a full day, nothing less than any such celebrations I had seen in Heaven, dance, music, feasts, what have you.

When it was all over, we went to Master's temple, where his disciples welcomed him like a hero, like their long-lost father finally back home.

"We did see the tree on that mountain gate turning east this morning," one of them said to Master. "And you're indeed back, as you said!"

It was a long day of excitement even for me. The moment I hit the pillow in the guest quarters of the temple, a simple bamboo pillow in a simple bamboo bed, I felt asleep.

We're back at Thunder Sound Temple, in the presence of Rulai, Father Buddha. It turns out to be a grand award ceremony.

Xuanzang, our master, is awarded Grand Salvation for securing the true scriptures of Buddhism for great Tang and

saving the souls of the millions of its people. That's like a gold medal, the highest honor, and it's a well-earned, well-deserved prize, of course.

Me, Wukong, is awarded Grand Salvation for having distinguished himself in protecting Xuanzang during the entirety of this mission and hence redeemed himself for the trouble he made in Heaven. Me, the same Grand Salvation as Master? A gold medalist, too? Who knows.

Pigsy, Wuneng, is awarded Altar Attendant for having shouldered much of the heavy loads on the journey to the West.

"How come they are awarded the grandest of prizes and me this lowly Altar Attendant title?" protests Pigsy.

"For one," says Rulai in his deep voice, "that greedy, lecherous heart of yours has never died, and is not dead even now. You have the same big appetite, big belly, and big intestines. See that mountain of leftovers of delicacies pilgrims have put on the altar? We have no way to eat them all, so help yourself."

Pigsy mumbles something like he doesn't eat all that much anymore and zips his lips. This brother of mine may have earned what has been awarded him, but I somehow feel bad for him.

Sandy, Wujing, is awarded Grand Salvation too and sent to join the ranks of shiny armored *Luohan*. He is so pleased. This makes Pigsy feel the sting even more, but what can he do or say? This is Rulai, Buddha of Buddhas, almighty and omniscient.

The white horse is awarded Salvation, only a notch below Grand Salvation, like a silver medal, joining the ranks of Holy Dragon Horses. He is not much of a talker but has proved as loyal and indispensable.

You know there is one thing that's been on my mind, okay, on my head, that has bothered me like hell.

"Now that I'm also a buddha of sorts, like you," I say to Master, "there is no need to pray that spell of yours anymore, right? So, can you please remove this thing from my head, burn it, dump it into the sea, whatever, so it can never hurt me or anyone else?"

"Of course, that goes without saying!" says Master, beaming. "Why don't you feel your head and see if it is still there?"

I do as told.

That damned headband is gone!

I'm finally free. No one can ever control me and punish me anymore!

I woke up.

We've said goodbye to each other a thousand times, teary-eyed, Xuanzang, Pigsy, Sandy, the white horse, and me.

Fourteen years together, bonded by the same grand mission, through thick and thin, breaking bread together and sharing the same bed between Heaven and Earth, coming to each other's rescue in the nick of time, playing practical jokes on each other that sometimes go a teeny-weensy too far, being each other's best pal and worst enemy, you name it, but we did it. We have been the thickest band of brothers, okay, Master and disciples—most of the time, that is. We may not see each other again, but those memories are etched in stone—forever.

Soon afterwards Xuanzang organized the greatest translation project undertaken ever anywhere in the world, so I've heard, and I can only imagine what it takes to translate those hundreds of volumes of Buddhist scriptures into the language people of great Tang can understand. Another twenty years of hard work, day and night—who else if not my master, the right man at the right time for the job of utmost historical significance. One day, not long after the project was completed, Xuanzang tripped, fell into a ditch, and died. I know this is probably my master shedding his earthly body one last time 'cause his mission on earth has finally been accomplished. The real, true Xuanzang is now with Rulai, Father Buddha, in Thunder Sound Temple, in the land of nirvana.

I sometimes wonder, though, whether you can really find salvation in deciphering and memorizing those volumes of scriptures. You can be the most erudite in the big, wide world, but does that automatically make you a good human being? True salvation, if you ask me, is in how you live your life:

Be kind to yourself and to others.

But what do I know? I'm just a monkey, right? Okay, Monkey King.

I don't know where Pigsy went. I wouldn't be surprised if he returned to Gao Village to be their son-in-law again. He was a good worker and loving husband after all. Besides, as he said, he doesn't eat that much anymore.

Sandy and the white horse must be happy where they are, basking in the merciful glory of Rulai. Can't beat that.

TWENTY TWO

Home Free

They say you cannot go home again, but I've been back home, Flower Fruit Mount, for hundreds of years by now. A teeny-weensy sadder, wiser, and free, albeit not completely carefree.

Even where I am, paradise on earth, the air is less pristine, large patches of debris from humans, plastic bags, bottles, tires, computer screens, clothes, syringes, toy guns, old paints, you name it, drift ashore every two or three days, like scheduled delivery. Disgusting. It kills me to see on our beaches birds and seals covered from head to tail in thick dark oil half dead and turtles entangled in some synthetic mess struggling to free themselves.

I do go out and take a look now and then, can't help it, and I'm amazed by the kind of new gadgets humans keep conjuring up, gadgets that carry mountains of goods from sea to sea or go several times faster than sound, I should race them one of these days; people thousands of *li* apart now can see and talk to each other like they are in the same room breaking bread; I guess pretty soon people can 3-D print themselves to just about anywhere in the world, no need for airplanes or spacecrafts, you just press a few buttons and viola, you're there. I was so dazzled, my Fire Gold Eyes all but blinded for days afterwards, by mushrooms blasting over cities, charred bodies of tens of thousands sprawling everywhere for miles and miles. Need I mention famines, pandemics, genocides, and ignorant armies clashing day and night armed to teeth not with yesteryear's knives, swords, spears, but with weapons of ten thousand times more massive destruction? You humans are your own worst enemies, if you ask me, being too clever for your own good. Why so much hatred, so full of sound and fury? For what? Some God you believe or profess, pretend to believe? Gold? How much more gold do you really want? And glory? Glory wrapped in gory? One day you humans are going to blow up Earth, the only home you have in the cosmos, and when that happens where do you think you can go? Heaven? You think Jade Emperor will let you in and stay? Did I hear someone say Mars? Is your name Jeff Bezos, Richard Branson, Elon Musk?

Oh, yes, I'm guilty as charged, having done more than my share of killing in the name of fighting evil, so full of righteousness when, if I have to be honest, more than a teeny-weensy of vanity, okay, megalomania, is at work too, underneath it all. Regrets? Some, perhaps, but I don't know how I would choose if I face those impossible moral dilemmas again, and I'm not much of a believer in what ifs in life.

"Why don't you help us," you may be thinking, "if you care so much?"

Well, unhappy is the land that needs heroes, who said this, you remember? I am no hero, let alone a superhero, is what I've learned if I've learned anything. That Gold-Banded Cudgel of mine? It's stayed in my ear for hundreds of years by now, a tiny needle, a reminder, a souvenir, and nothing more. Only you humans can save yourselves, save yourselves from the demons and monsters in you, save yourselves from yourselves.

It feels good to have outgrown the kind of hero complex that enthralled me for hundreds of years and be the simple, free me again. No, I don't mean I don't care about anything anymore. Otherwise, I wouldn't have even bothered to tell my story as I've done.

Exactly how old am I now? I don't really know. I was born a stone monkey so long ago, like the beginning of time, yet sometimes it feels like only yesterday. I'm still a baby if you consider the age of the universe, or universes, billions upon billions of years pre-Pan'gu and Nüwa, one created Heaven and Earth with his axe, the other repaired the collapsed Heaven with colored stones, one of the stones slipped from her hand, remember?

Oh, by the way, have you listened to how the Black Hole sounds? Amazing. Scary. Mindboggling. I don't want to be sucked into that boundless, bottomless hole anytime soon, although who knows, I may be floating in it now, as I speak, like a dream in someone's dream in someone else's dream in someone else's else's dream, endless, infinite, see what I mean? That may be what immortality really means?

Sometimes, though, I still like to think that I am more than a mere accident in the universe, cosmos, *yuzhou*, a teeny-weensy dust. I'm here for a purpose, whatever that is. I'm still becoming, on a journey, going somewhere although I don't know where, and I know you're becoming, on a journey of yours, too. To where? Do you know?

Epilogue

The *Yuzhou* Gazer passenger plane begins to cruise comfortably thousands of feet above the clouds at Mach 4, four times the speed of sound.

OMG excitement still sparkles in the eyes of Emmett, 12 and Evelyn, 8, on their first trip solo, on their own, to the land of their parents and grandparents; they are glued to the view outside the window, virtual view choreographed for passengers by *Yuzhou* Gazer. They have seen 5D movies of outer space explorations, but this feels so much more real: they are not sitting in a cinema watching a movie of outer space; they are moving in outer space at mindboggling speed. Okay, they are sitting in a passenger plane that is moving at four times the speed of sound. It's as outer space travel as anyone can get short of being chosen for the first human mission to Mars.

Outside the window gazillions of stars and galaxies glitter and shimmer like a sea of grains of salt, an ocean of crystals and diamonds, a universe of universes of mesmerizing dreams, destinies, eternities, boundless, unfathomable, eye-popping and mind-blowing.

"What's that?!"

Brother and sister exclaim at the same time.

They are looking at a pair of eyes outside the plane looking at them through the windowpane.

Shiny, fiery eyes, glistening with wit and mischief.

A monkey.

Beautiful. Majestic. Like none other they have seen.

Going at the same speed as the *Yuzhou* Gazer passenger plane.

The monkey winks at them mirthfully a couple of times, turns from the window, and with a kick of legs catapults himself forward into infinity.

"Amazing!"

"Astounding!"

A jaw-dropping encounter not in the itinerary for the young brother and sister. A pleasant surprise planted by *Yuzhou* Gazer, perhaps?

"*Gege* (Elder brother)," asks Evelyn, finally turning her eyes away from the window. "How's *Yeye*'s Monkey King novel coming along?"

Yeye (Paternal grandpa) told them two summers ago that Monkey King wandered into one of his dreams and asked the retired professor of literature to write down his story, to tell his untold story. *Yeye* has been working on this nonstop since, as if possessed.

"Well," says Emmett, "I asked *Yeye* before boarding today and he says he's finished the novel and just needs to read it through one more time before sending it out for publication."

"So typical!"

"I know!"

They chuckle. How many times has *Yeye* enthused over stories they write, "I like this part…," "Oh, I really love how you…," and then come the much dreaded "but…"?

"Can't wait to read it!" declares Evelyn.

"Me neither."

EPILOGUE

They turn their gaze to the view outside the window again, the landmass of Asia, mountains, rivers, cities of lights, becoming closer, larger, more magnificent, more real than virtual, every thousandth of a second, the land of their parents, grandparents, of legends, myths, mythologies, and stories of ordinary people, amongst them *tainainai* (Grandpa's mother), waiting at the space center, from time immemorial to this very moment to the endless future.

Acknowledgements

This novel is inspired by the classic Chinese novel *Journey to the West*《西游记》by Wu Cheng'en 吴承恩 (c. 1500–1582), especially his portrayal of

Monkey King 猴王, aka Sun Wukong 孙悟空, Great Sage Heaven's Equal 齐天大圣

Xuanzang 玄奘, aka Tang Monk 唐僧, based on the historical figure Xuanzang 玄奘 (602–664), a 7th-century Chinese Buddhist monk who undertook an epic journey to India in 629–645, brought back over 657 Buddhist texts written in Sanskrit, and led the massive translation project.

Pigsy 八戒, aka Zhu Bajie 猪八戒, Zhu Wuneng 猪悟能

Sandy 沙僧, aka Monk Sandy 沙和尚, Sha Wujing 沙悟净